Best Bi Short Stories

Bisexual Fiction

edited by Sheela Lambert

Gressive Press

An Imprint of Circlet Press, Inc.
Cambridge, MA

Best Bi Short Stories: Bisexual Fiction edited by Sheela Lambert

Published by Gressive Press, an imprint of Circlet Press, Inc.
39 Hurlbut Street
Cambridge, MA 02138

The electronic version was produced in-house at Circlet Press. The PDF mimics the design of the printed book.

Please report any problems you find with the ebook to us by visiting the Bug Report section of our web site (www.circlet.com).

Print ISBN: 978-1-61390-088-8
Electronic ISBN: 978-1-61390-089-5

"Alex the Dragon" by Jan Steckel appeared online in *Lodestar Quarterly* in 2005.

"Angels Dance" by James Williams was an original story when submitted, but before *Best Bi Short Stories* went to press was published in his ebook short story collection, *Liberation: And Other Tales of Sex and Sensibility*, from Renaissance, 2012.

"Challenger Deep" by Kathleen Bradean was previously printed in the anthology *Cream: The Best of the Erotica Readers and Writers Association*, published by Running Press, 2006.

"Coyote Takes a Trip" by Deborah Miranda was originally published in the anthology, *Sovereign Erotics: A Collection of Two-Spirit Literature* from University of Arizona Press, 2011.

"Dragon's Daughter" by Cecilia Tan was originally a two-part story published in the anthologies, *To Be Continued...and To Be Continued: Take Two* from Firebrand Books 1998 and 1999.

"Inland Passage" by Jane Rule was previously published in her short story collection of the same name.

"Pride/Prejudice" is a novel excerpt by Ann Herendeen from her slash fiction novel *Pride/Prejudice: A Novel of Mr. Darcy, Elizabeth Bennet and Their Forbidden Lovers* published by Harper Collins, 2010. At the time I accepted it, it was an original story, as she had just begun writing the novel, but Harper Collins also recognized how good it was and the novel got snapped up and published before Best Bi Short Stories.

"Xessex" by Katherine Forrest was previously published in her short story collection *Dreams And Swords*, first by Naid Press in 1987, and reissued by Bywater Books in 2008.

Dedication

Best Bi Short Stories is dedicated to my mother, who, as it turns out, was bi and would have enjoyed every story.

Contents

INTRODUCTION

Bisexuality in fiction is more often hinted at than fully explored. Oblique references, tantalizing clues, a line here, a detail there, but we are often left reading between the lines. The stories in this book don't hold back: the bisexuality of their characters is on the page. *Best Bi Short Stories* represents a first in literature: a collection of short stories where the same-sex attractions of its characters don't negate the opposite sex ones and vice versa. But this is not the typical bisexuality seen in literature: this book brooks no stereotypes.

Bisexual stories make fascinating fodder for fiction. The creativity of our writers have taken this to the next level by sifting it through their imaginations and coming up with exciting, mysterious, inventive ideas that weave bisexuality through the tapestry of their subconscious into a captivating piece of fiction. This anthology offers a smorgasbord of genres that each show bi characters through their own unique prism: mystery/noir, vampire, sci-fi, historical fiction, experimental, micro-fiction, magical realism, slash fiction, as well as contemporary bi fiction. The world created by each author is extraordinary and specific, drawing the reader in.

Best Bi Short Stories has a variety of new bisexual characters we haven't seen in literature before, characters that leap off the page and into the reader's imagination. In "Alone, As Always" an abused wife falls for a mysterious woman; "Pennies in the Well" is a love letter written by a civil war soldier to a soldier on another battlefield; "The Idiom of Orchids" features a mysterious woman who seduces with exotic flowers; "Angel's Dance" involves a bisexual vampire contacting his long lost lover about a sticky issue; in "Dual Citizenship" a wisecracking detective debates whether to team up with a new partner; "Companions" is about a tavern barmaid who falls for a shy soldier with a secret in Medieval England; "Mother

Knows Best" is a piece about a man dying of AIDS whose ultra-religious relatives are driving him crazy; an elderly woman in a nursing home remembers her glory days as an activist marching in Pride Parades in "Memory Lane," two high school boys are confused by their mutual attraction in "Naked in the World;" "Alex the Dragon" features a bi dyke who appears to be acquiring dragon-like characteristics; "Challenger Deep" is about a daughter who travels to an exotic island to fulfill a father's last request and experiences a transformation; "Friends and Neighbors" shows an old codger making friends with the boi next door; a man is obsessed by a woman and her ambiguous painting in "Mr. Greene," and more. Transgender characters captured the imagination of a good half dozen of our writers, illustrating that transgender people are very much a part of the bi community.

There are also a few handpicked, previously published stories by notable authors, that you may have missed which feature wonderful bisexual characters. Jane Rule, whose bisexual novel, *Desert of the Heart*, was made into the classic les/bi film *Desert Hearts*, contributed "Inland Passage," a story about two widows who meet and fall for each other on a cruise ship. Although this story contains some 'politically incorrect' elements, I thought it should be included because of its historical value. Pillar of lesbian literature Katherine Forrest, whose Kate Delafield Mystery Series fills the shelves of queer women everywhere, dreamed up a beautiful alien who ignites unexpected passion in a disfigured space station captain in the sci-fi tale "Xessex." Circlet Press founder Cecilia Tan, known for her Magic University Series, imagines a Chinese-American college student who falls for an elusive, immortal goddess in "The Dragon's Daughter." Star of Two Spirit Literature, Deborah Miranda, created a homeless, but cocky, Native American graffiti artist who recovers his mojo after an unexpected bus incident in "Coyote Takes a Trip." And the author of *Phyllida and the Brotherhood of Phillander*, Ann Herendeen, reveals the hidden bisexuality of Mr. Darcy and 'best friend' Charles Bingley from Jane Austen's *Pride and Prejudice*, in a humorous and sexy chapter from her Lammy Award finalist slash fiction novel, *Pride/Prejudice: A Novel of Mr. Darcy, Elizabeth Bennet and their Forbidden Lovers.*

This book tries to avoid stereotypical bisexual characters and plotlines that have already been done to death. Is there anyone who has not read a story with a bisexual character who is two-timing their lover, is painted as shallow by engaging in a threesome, is a deceptive and manipulative liar or a sexy bimbo? As editor, I steered clear of stories that relied too heavily on infidelity or the surprise reveal of a same-sex attraction for their only source of drama. BBSS forges new territory with characters we haven't seen before and plotlines with a twist. Yet this book is far from the fictional counterpart to a politically correct bisexual essay. The characters in this book are unpredictable, multifaceted and run the gamut of ages, personalities, situations and time periods.

This is the first book of bisexual short stories ever published. Anthologies of gay, lesbian, straight or mixed short stories abound. There are even a handful of anthologies of bisexual erotica or personal biographical stories; but none of bi literary fiction, before now. Until recently, bi-inspired literary creations were few and far between and took a lot of detective work and good "bidar" to ferret out from the sea of literature. In fact, many lesbian, gay or even general short story collections contain stories with bi characters, but one must wade through to find them. Unfortunately, once found, the bisexual characters and storylines in literature are not as varied as gay, lesbian or straight ones and often fall into predictable bisexual stereotypes.

Best Bi Short Stories breaks that mold. We have showcased a rich variety of fascinating bisexual characters, storylines and themes, written in multiple genres and writing styles, all in one book. A buffet of bisexual literature, it's full of lively, unique characters, human emotions, discoveries, mystery, vulnerability, unexpected twists, courage and creativity.

Bisexual people have long been deprived of literary role models, characters that mirror their lives or explore new and previously unimagined directions. This book helps to fill that gap while entertaining anyone who enjoys good stories.

We also hope this book will inspire writers and publishers to create and publish more complex bi characters and storylines that avoid overused stereotypes and break new, more interesting ground.

Dual Citizenship

Storm Grant

"I have another meeting to go to, Detective Connor. I'm going to leave you alone for about fifteen minutes." Captain Grandy stands and I glance up at him. What kind of job interview is this? Sure, I want to be the American half of the Integrated Border Enforcement Team, but still...

Grandy holds up the thin manila folder. "I'm going to leave this confidential file on my desk. If you should choose to read it, I can't be held responsible, now can I?"

Okay. He's trying to tell me something. "Is there something I should—?"

"Just read the file, Connor. Fifteen minutes. I'll be back."

So I read the file. It's about the guy I'd be replacing, Detective Washington, plus some stuff about his Mountie partner. The file is pretty vague, but I manage to read between the lines. I'm sort of inclined that way.

Good to his word, Grandy comes back in fifteen minutes, asks me if I have any questions. I'm not sure where to start so I go with silence, just looking at him. The silence stretches. Finally Grandy says, "The Mountie and Washington. They were pretty close. Spent a lot of time together, both on the job and off. Now that you've looked at the file, do you think you can work with this Mountie?"

I tap the file against my thigh, playing for time. I look just to the right of Grandy's shoulder, not making complete eye contact, "So. The Mountie. Something queer about him?" I say finally, careful of my wording. It's hard to ask when the rule is "don't." As in "Don't ask. Don't tell."

Grandy harrumphs. Won't meet my eyes directly either. He's probably wondering about the two holes in my left earlobe. "Well, I think I can say for pretty sure that he's..." Grandy pauses, searches for the right word, then does meet my eyes, "...Canadian.

You don't have a problem with... Canadians, do you?"

"No sir. Got a cousin who's... Canadian. Not a problem." I fail to mention I've...been to Canada a few times myself since splitting with the ex-wife. Thinking about this, it occurs to me to ask, "Was Detective Washington... Canadian, too?"

Grandy looks uncomfortable, then runs a finger inside his shirt collar even though the top button is undone and his tie loosened. "That's not an easy question, Connor. Washington may have had, er, dual citizenship, but if so, he kept it pretty quiet. To outward appearances, he was more your all-American boy."

And that precludes what, exactly, I think. But out loud I say, "No problem, Lieutenant. I've worked with... persons of alternative nationality before."

"Even if he were to, say, invite you to visit Canada with him?" Unbelievable. Grandy is actually blushing a little. Again with the finger in his collar.

Now I've seen pictures of this Mountie—there were a couple in the file—and heard the gossip 'round the station, and my unspoken response to that is, I should be so lucky. I almost start to tell Grandy again that it would be no problem for me at all, but realize that might give away the game, so instead I consider a while. I think the moment has come to lighten the mood a little, so I ask, half-joking, "Just to be clear, sir. You're not asking me to... immigrate, are you?" Or should that be "emigrate"? Don't know. Doesn't matter. I look at Grandy and he's gone the color of really good merlot.

Then he starts fiddling with his stapler behind him, loses his balance and nearly falls, knocking over his almost-empty coffee cup as he regains his footing. "No. Oh, no, Detective." He mops up the spilled coffee with a wad of mismatched napkins; probably several years' worth of meals eaten at his desk. "The Detroit Police Department would never make such an unethical demand of one of its officers..." He trails off realizing he'd been plain speaking for a minute there. "We would never ask anyone to... apply for dual citizenship. I just want to make sure you can work with a... Canadian."

Grandy is really struggling now and the evil part of me is kind of enjoying this, but that's not a good way to land this job, so I try to put him at ease. "As an officer of the law, he's got to have the whole 'no means no' thing down pat, right? And I hear Canadians are very polite."

Grandy looks relieved. "All right then. You've reassured me that you've got what it takes to do this job. Welcome aboard, Detective."

He holds out his hand and we shake. I like him already and think I'll enjoy working here. I hand back the file, feeling only a little bit guilty for having "borrowed" a really good picture of the Mountie and stuffing it in my jacket pocket when Grandy was out of the room. I tell myself I need it so I can identify my new partner when I see him, but it's really so I can take it home and enjoy it while I... take a little solo trip to Canada.

ALONE, AS ALWAYS
JENNY CORVETTE

Friday AM, the day of...

He sleeps beside me, his arm draped over me like a cover on a book. I feel the hair on his arm grazing the bare skin of my stomach, which rises with each labored breath I take. A hundred times this has happened exactly this way. I've woken up before him, feeling his hot breath billowing against the back of my neck. He is so close to me, so physically close. Yet, I feel we are miles apart.

The feel of isolation does strange things to my mind and though I know this, I am no less a victim to my own madness. Danny, especially at strange times in the mornings, doesn't seem to exist. And if he does, he's a mere ghost of his former self, a holographic sliver of the man I fell in love with.

Always, a hundred times at least, I lay in bed, beneath the weight of Danny's possessing arm. I lay in bed and think such betraying thoughts, as if to validate my grim reality and justify my future behavior.

But this morning something's different. I can feel the other body in the room. She's a forceful presence, as forceful as I wish I could be. Gazing at me, she knows I'm not asleep, though my eyes are tightly shut. When I open them she is closer, standing near me, staring at me with that way she has of tilting her head back and sizing me up. As if to give me a stronger sort of relevance. As if her seeing me is the proof I need to know I exist.

She bends down to whisper something in my ear.

She's oblivious to my nudity. The backs of her fingernails brush my chin. And I'm strangely aroused.

"We need to do it now," is what she whispers.

Her breath is warm like her faint touch. Her words are tiny breezes on the arm draped over me. Can he feel her too? Before the sentence is punctuated in my head, she's gone.

Danny shifts beside me. "Honey," he says, rubbing his eyes. "What time is it?"

"It's dawn," I tell him but I can't be sure myself.

"Shit," he says, because he has to get up, and rolling off his side of the bed he stretches his arms and yawns. I continue lying there, staring hard at the empty doorway like she were still there. "You getting up?" he asks, running his fingers through his hair. Danny doesn't wait for me to answer. He walks around to my side of the bed and leans down to kiss me on the cheek. Pausing slightly, with a look of pity in his eyes, he adds, "Make me breakfast, baby." And with a slap of my thigh he heads for the shower.

Sunday AM, five days before...

I was in the garden when she drove up in a white convertible, wearing dark shades to match her hair.

"Excuse me," she called but I knew she was the type who never needed excusing. "Is this Hickory Street?"

I shook the dirt from my hands. "No," there was a slight quiver in my voice, like a child in front of the classroom called on by the teacher to answer a question. "This is Maple Lane. You want the next street over." I pointed with a dirty finger.

"Next street?"

"Yes," I said but was really saying Please don't go.

She didn't listen. Within moments, she was gone.

Like she was never there at all.

Monday PM, four days before...

It was a cold autumn night and I was curled under a blanket in my favorite chair with a book when I heard the doorbell ring. Instantly my heart dropped. The doorbell wouldn't normally evoke such a feeling of unease but I was alone this night, as Danny was in Minnesota on business. I crept to the door and spied out the peep hole.

"Who is it?" I asked but didn't need to. I recognized her instantly.

Her voice rang out. I recognized that as well. "We met yesterday. You gave me directions. Remember?"

How could I forget? I opened the door, but only a little. "I remember," I said, my words peeking out of me as shy as I peeked out from behind the door. "Are you lost again?" Such a stupid thing to say, I thought only moments after saying it.

"Always." She smiled at me and laughed a little. "Actually I just wanted to thank you. I was late yesterday and rudely sped off without thanking you."

"It's easy to get lost around here. I'm just happy I could help. I'm Vicki, by the way." I reached out, almost hungrily and she held out her hand to me.

"Stella." Our fingers fumbled in the partially open door and then pulled away much too soon. "Well, I should be going. Have to be in Chicago by morning."

Such a mystery, she was. What or who was waiting for her on Hickory Street yesterday and Chicago tomorrow morning?

"Are you sure? Why don't you come in and have some coffee? You'll need the caffeine. You'll be driving all night." I opened the door to her but really I was opening a lot more.

She then officially stepped into my life.

"You have a beautiful place," she said, like a burglar casing the joint. I pointed to the couch and headed for the kitchen. When I came back out, armed with two cups of coffee, she was sitting comfortably, legs separated just enough for me to notice. "I interrupted your reading," she said when she saw my blanket and book near the fireplace.

"Oh no. I kept reading the same page over and over anyway." When I handed her the coffee, our hands briefly touched, the cold of our skin contrasting with the warm mugs of coffee. "Cream or sugar, Stella?" It was the first time I'd said her name and I saw her smile when it rolled off my tongue. She shook her head and I took a seat next to her.

"Do you live alone, Vicki?" She said my name as if to repay the favor.

"No. My husband Danny, he's in Minnesota on business."

I was slightly aroused with the danger of not only allowing a stranger into my home but also telling her I was alone. Strangely I did not fear her, but she did make me uncomfortable. She touched the hand that held my coffee. "You don't wear a ring," She gazed deep into me, not in distrust, but in curiosity. Her dark eyes seemed to penetrate my soul and I worried that she could see into my thoughts and read everything I was thinking of letting her do to me.

"I don't wear it at night," I told her, which was true. My wedding ring was currently on the table near my bed, in my empty bedroom. "I started taking it off at night when Danny wanted to pretend to be with another woman."

She rolled her eyes. "Does he wear his?"

I tried to think of Danny. Where was he now? Really on business? Or in a hotel wearing nothing but his wedding ring, beside a woman wearing not even that much?

My silence was answer enough. An awkward pause followed, in which we both fondled our coffee cups a bit much.

"May I use your bathroom?" she finally said.

"Of course. End of the hall."

She stood and languidly walked out of my sight, my eyes fastened to her every move.

I have to be crazy, I told myself, for thinking what I was about her. I have to be severely out of my mind.

But I went on thinking it anyway.

Several moments passed and she didn't return. I was beginning to doubt her existence. Did I dream her up? I waited until I couldn't wait with a clear conscience any longer and finally I went down the hallway looking after her. On my way to the bathroom I passed my open bedroom door. I always kept it closed but Danny must've left it open before leaving for Minnesota. Leaning in and reaching for the doorknob, I noticed Stella standing near my bed, gazing at a photograph on my night table.

I cleared my throat to announce my presence.

Something fell from her hands and made a clang to the floor.

Embarrassed, she struggled with an apology as I walked in behind her. "I'm sorry. Your door was open and I... I was being nosy."

I didn't respond, not quite sure if I felt violated or seductively probed.

"Is this uh..." she looked to the framed picture by the bed.

"Danny, yes."

Her fingertips traced the image of his face. "He's handsome," she said, and turned her attention to me. "And lucky."

Both flattered and uneasy by her compliment, I looked to the floor for something to break our gaze. The shine of my wedding ring sparkled up at me from beneath the night stand. I bent down to pick it up, but couldn't quite reach far enough under the table.

"Here, let me," Stella said, lowering to her knees as her slender fingers danced over the dusty floor. When she handed me the ring, our fingers touched, but longer this time.

"Thank you," I said, looking directly at her. She didn't let go of the ring right away, so as to prolong our closeness near the floor.

"You're welcome." And with her words, and the gaze of her dark brown eyes, I was locked to her.

Locked willingly with her.

Our lips had nowhere else to go.

They leaned in together.

Tuesday AM, three days before...

He slept beside me, his arm draped over me. The hair on his arm tickled my naked stomach as it rose with each labored breath I took. But it was different this time. His arm seemed lighter. Softer.

As my eyes began to adjust to the morning sun shining through the window, they caught the glimmer of something gold on my night table. Slowly I recognized it as my wedding ring.

The body beside me rolled over, awake enough to ask me, "What time is it?"

"Dawn," I said but couldn't be sure.

"And this isn't Chicago," she mumbled back. And she wasn't Danny.

She crawled out from beneath my sheets, completely naked and asked to use my shower.

At first I thought I was dreaming. It had to be one of those dreams you have about waking up when you're still fast asleep in bed. So I tried waking up all over again, this time for real, to the sound of water running in the bathroom.

Danny wasn't home and when I investigated I found a naked woman in my shower. A naked woman who, last I remembered, was picking up my ring off the bedroom floor.

Memories are funny things. I remember some things very well, like yesterday's grocery bill, 43.38. As if that has some special meaning to my life. And yet I couldn't remember spending the night with the woman now in my shower. I couldn't remember how we got from the floor to my bed.

The water turned off and if I listened hard enough I could hear her dressing. The smooth fabric of garments brushing her sleek skin. The clip of her bra. Slowly and vaguely I remembered helping her out of those clothing restraints the night before. But I couldn't be sure that I wasn't making it all up. And that's all there was, vague clips of memories, almost segments of a dream that comes to you periodically throughout the day. They seemed neither real nor logical.

"I don't mean to run," she said, quickly stepping back into the room, "But I have to go." Her white blouse was unbuttoned, seductively exposing the tan bra that covered her small breasts. She moved across the room, grabbing shoes and a purse as if it were her room and she knew by instinct where everything was. "I left my number on your night table." But before I could look, she kissed me quickly on the lips and sped out the door.

As quickly as she'd come, she was gone.

All she'd left was her taste on my lips.

Friday PM, the night of...

How long ago that seems. How innocent it all now seems.

Three desperate days later and everything has changed.

After I cooked Danny breakfast this morning, bacon and eggs and three strong cups of black coffee, I sat quietly and watched him eat. I shouldn't have been watching him eat but I couldn't bear to do much else. I was supposed to be getting the gun out of the bathroom but I couldn't. So I didn't. I just watched him off to work and then was alone. Alone, again, with my thoughts. Not that I can remember any of them.

Hours passed. The whole day, almost. Before I know it, he's coming home.

His car pulls into the driveway shortly after six. Suddenly, as if this is my last chance, I hurry into the bathroom and lean against the sink. There, I catch a glimpse of myself in the mirror and am shocked at how awful I look. I barely recognize myself. There's something familiar about the wounds I see, but they seem worse now. My lip had ballooned up. My eye had almost swollen shut. The monster staring back at me reminds me of my mission. I lean down and pull open the drawer. There, inside, is the metal shine of a gun. I don't know whose gun it is but don't care. Picking it up, it feels like it fits my hand, and that's more than enough reason to go on holding it. My actions seem somewhere familiar, as if I've practiced them many times, although I don't remember doing so. Also familiar is the urge I feel inside of me. It's knocking on my brain something awful, daring me. I want to put my finger on the trigger.

The woman in the mirror is watching me. She also has a gun, a shiny one like my own. She puts her finger on the trigger, so I do too. And when I do, we both smile.

What is it about holding a loaded gun that makes you feel so powerful?

Loaded? I check and it is. Of course it is. You certainly can't kill someone with an unloaded gun, now can you?

The front door opens and closes. "Vicki," Danny's voice rings out. "You home?"

Silent, I count his steps to the bedroom. I know his entire routine without even seeing him. I know he's thrown his briefcase on the bed, and is loosening his tie. He's taking off his watch when he steps in the bathroom.

My finger is still on the trigger.

Tuesday, three days before...

The game was on. He wanted another beer and sent me to get one. When my head was stuck in the refrigerator, the phone rang.

"It's me," she said as soon as she heard my voice. "I wanna come over."

"Not tonight," I whispered even though I desperately wanted to see her again.

"Tomorrow night then. Will he be home?"

"He'll be gone."

"Where's he now?"

"Watching the Steelers."

"I want to be with you tonight," she said, louder now.

"I already said-"

"Touch yourself for me."

I was both shocked and turned on by her forwardness. "Stella-"

"Please. Pretend it's me."

I slid up on the counter, and spread my legs.

"Are you?"

"Yes," I answered, a bit flustered and embarrassed. The fingers of my free hand found the insides of my upper thigh. They began a circular motion, first outside of my panties and then beneath them.

"I need to see you."

"Tomorrow night. Late," I said, between hurried breaths.

"Faster," she whispered and I obliged, moving my hand back and forth in almost a chaotic fashion.

"Baby, what the hell are you doing?"

I dropped the phone at the sound of Danny's voice. He'd walked into the darkened kitchen, a sly smile on his face because he'd caught me doing something dirty. When he saw the phone, the smile fell from his face.

"What the hell?" Angrily he picked up the receiver and stuffed it to his ear. "Hello? Hello, is anybody there?" He slammed it down. Turned to me. "Who was that?"

I didn't answer him. I couldn't.

"Who was on the goddam phone, Vicki?"

I can only remember the moment before his hand met my face.

Wednesday, two days before...

I didn't see Danny off the next day. He left, for Wisconsin this time, around mid-afternoon and I busied myself with gardening and housework. Before I knew it, the sun had set and night had fallen. I routinely looked at the clock, not because I couldn't wait for Stella, but because with each passing minute I was relieved she hadn't yet arrived. It wasn't as if I didn't want to see her, but rather I didn't want her to see me.

The bedroom was almost completely dark, and silent except for the ticking of the clock beside the bed. The sheets were pulled up to my chin and beneath them I was fully clothed. I knew I was sending mixed messages but I didn't care.

A car pulled into the driveway. I could hear the beautiful hum of her engine. Then the shutting of the car door and quiet footsteps coming up the hall. They stopped and although I could barely see her, I knew she was standing in the doorway. She reached to turn on the light.

"Leave it off," I said urgently.

She obliged, walked in, and sat on my side of the bed.

"What's wrong?" she said, and I pulled the bed sheets a little closer to my chin. "You seem mad." She touched my cheek the way a mother might. "Or scared."

"Confused. About what happened between us."

She seemed short when she answered. "What's confusing about it?"

"I don't know. I just... I can't remember any of it."

This was only partly true. Since she arrived I remembered, little by little, making love to her, but my memories seemed fabricated. And while alone, I remembered nothing.

"You can't remember or you won't remember?"

I couldn't explain it to her. I could barely explain it to myself. I seemed to exist on two separate planes of reality. When Stella wasn't there, I doubted everything. When she was there, I doubted nothing. But it was as if my mind could not accept what my body knew to be real.

"I'm sorry," is all I could say. She seemed rejected, with a far-away look in her eyes, eyes I now remembered kissing as her fingers floated down my naked body the night before last. "It's like you're not real. It's like I'm dreaming," I said, but I knew I wasn't.

She pulled the covers down to my waist and saw that I was dressed.

"I'm real," she said, starting to unbutton my shirt. "I'm more than real."

I remembered more this time. The feel of her clothes, the touch of her skin seemed briefly familiar underneath my hands. She kissed more with her lips than she did with her tongue and they were soft and wet. She whispered little commands in my ear, as if it was my first time with her. "Lay back. Relax. Open your legs. Don't be scared." All the while, I was scared. I was scared I was dreaming. I was scared I was crazy. I did what she asked me, completely trusting her and totally seduced. I was like a ragdoll in her arms and beneath her probing hands. The light touch of her fingers were especially pleasing, teasing the insides of my thighs before they plunged between my legs.

Thursday AM, the day before...

When I awoke she was facing me in bed, eyes wide open and staring. I smiled and leaned in to kiss her but she pulled away.

"When were you going to tell me?" she asked coldly.

"Tell you what?"

She paused and looked away. "What he did." I didn't understand and my confused look must've shown it. "What he did to your face," she said, now with a hint of sympathy leaking out.

I suddenly realized what Stella was talking about. I'd completely forgotten that Danny had hit me and why I didn't want the lights on the night before. "It really isn't that bad," I told her as she reached out and touched my cheek. "I'm surprised you even noticed."

Something in my words riled her up, because she immediately rose from the bed and pulled me up with her. After dragging me into the bathroom, she pushed me hard into the bathroom sink. There I stood, in front of the mirror.

The first thing I noticed was that we were both naked, but that wasn't what Stella intended me to see. She put her hand underneath my chin and with a rough lift, made me look at myself.

My jaw was swollen, my lip was fat and my left eye was a seductive shade of purple. Had I not known better I would have thought I put on too much dark eye shadow and had gotten stung by a bee on the cheek. I did remember that Danny had hit me, yes, but I didn't remember the damaged he'd caused. It was like I was looking at someone else in the mirror. Someone weak and broken. Instinctively I reached up to touch my wounds, almost surprised at the tenderness of my own skin. Yes, it was me. I winced more than once.

"I'm gonna kill the fucker," said Stella, but I was hardly aware of her presence. I was too busy trying to remember how it happened, how my husband had beaten my face to a bruised pulp without my remembering it.

Barely aware of her hands on my shoulders, moving down around my stomach, my own hands moved around my face, traveling my wounds as if they were a roadmap to my memories. Stella was peering down in the mirror at my reflection. At what was she looking, my injuries, my body? I couldn't tell. From behind she held me, the bangs of her dark hair stabbing the eyes that peered at me so. This time she whispered it. "We're gonna kill the fucker."

Friday PM, the day of...

"Whoa, Vic. What are you doing with that?"

He doesn't seem to take it too seriously, my holding this gun. So I point it at him, and fear falls into his eyes. He takes a slow step backwards. "Put that down, baby. It could go off."

"That's what I'm counting on," I saw in a voice I barely recognize as my own. I step towards him and he steps back, like we're dancing.

"What are you doing?"

My voice is calm and cool. "I'm gonna kill you for what you did." I rub the trigger of the gun under my fingertip, lightly as I could, as if to tease it.

"What'd I do?"

"Are you blind, Danny, or just stupid?" I start waving the gun now, like it's a wand and I'm a magician who's about to make her husband disappear.

"You mean your face? You think I did that?" Danny's really nervous now. I've backed him all the way onto the bed and he's nearly sitting on his briefcase. "Vicki," he says, almost stuttering. It's amazing how a loaded weapon makes him choke on his words. "Vicki, you fell in the bathroom two nights ago. Don't you remember? You hit your head on the sink."

"Don't lie to me, Danny."

"Baby, I got home from Minnesota and you were unconscious on the floor. The sink was all bloody. Don't you remember?"

The gun is shaking in my hand. "Stop it, Danny. I didn't fall. You did this, after you caught me on the phone with her."

"Who?"

"Stella."

"Who's Stella?"

"The woman who's gonna bury you," and again I didn't recognize my own voice.

"Vicki, you're talking out of your head, baby. I don't know anyone named Stella."

I scream at him. "She was on the phone, Danny! The other night in the kitchen. She's... I've been sleeping with her."

He laughs but stops when I inch the gun closer to his head. "Vicki, honey, are you trying to leave me for another woman?" I can hear the meanness in his tone. The way he says woman sets my blood boiling.

"No darling, I'm killing you for another woman."

He has nowhere to go. He can only swallow hard, trying to speak as he realizes I'm serious. I'm dead serious.

"Wait Vic. Listen to me. There is no other woman. There was no one on the phone the other night. You haven't been having an affair with anyone. You hit your head on the sink and now you don't know what you're saying. You need to see a doctor."

"You need to see an undertaker," is my witty comeback. But what he said troubles me. His words are circling my mind, buzzing against my brain in the most annoying way. I know they aren't true. In a desperate attempt to save his life, Danny's doing what anyone would. He's sitting there feeding me lies.

"Why would I lie to you, Vicki? Because you're holding a gun? Put the gun down and I'll tell you the exact same thing. I'm not lying to you."

"Bullshit, Danny. Bullshit. Bullshit. Bullshit," I say because it's the only word in my head that makes sense. And with each time I say it, my finger tickles the trigger like a lover. He reaches out his hand.

"Baby, don't you know that I love you?"

I pull the trigger and a bullet rips through his chest. I fire again and his body flings backwards against the wall. There is no sound. No bang from the gun, no scream from his mouth. I fire a third time and watch the light leave his eyes and his torso thumps against the wall with a dry muffled thud. I don't remember how many additional times I fire. I just remember that the gun eventually runs out of bullets.

Blood is everywhere. Mostly on the bed and against the wall, but a good amount of it's on me too. I've managed to splatter myself quite well, in fact. I'm a walking wardrobe of bloody murder.

In the bathroom, the full stream of cold water wakes my ears to the sounds of the outside world. No longer are my own thoughts so piercing. I run my hands and forearms under the water and wash my husband's dead blood from my skin. From out of the mirror, I study myself. My swelling has gone down and my eye seems to look closer to its normal self. I almost recognize myself again.

"It's over," I say aloud in the room, to no one in particular.

Moments later, she's cleaning up at the sink, washing the arms that buried him in the garden, drying the fingers that moved his trash bag body into the freshly dug hole and covered it with fertilized soil.

"Fill out a missing person's report in three or four days," she tells me while splashing cold water on her face and wiping away smudges of dirt. "When they ask why you didn't report it sooner, tell them he's done this before. They'll think he's found another woman and probably won't even bother to investigate." She grabs the bloody towel from beside the sink as I stand behind her with my arms around her waist.

"You know what he told me... before I shot him? He said you weren't real."

She shuffles the towel from one hand to the other, furiously rubbing away the evidence from her body. "Did you believe him?"

"I didn't know what to believe. For all I know, I made him up."

"Now you're thinking. He never truly existed, except when you thought he did."

I look down at my arms and notice a patch of black dirt. "Stell, did I help you bury him?" I ask because I honestly can't remember.

"You said you couldn't." I rub at my dirty arm but the color won't come off. Seeing me doing this, she takes my arms in her hands and shows me it isn't dirt I'm trying to rub away, but bruises. Dark and patchy bruises extending up my forearms that I haven't noticed before. They're positioned where gripping fingers once grabbed me. She doesn't have to say anything. I know I've been held like this before and not by her. I knew the guilty fingers were now planted in my garden.

Overwhelmed with the confusion of reality, I kiss her, as if to confirm my own relevance to her. My body presses hers against the sink. I feel her still dirty fingernails scratch against the back of my neck as she pulls my mouth further into hers. Without really knowing it, my hands work their way beneath her shirt and spider around her flesh like the insects inside of Danny's mouth by now.

She eases me onto the floor, just beneath the sink and works her way down my body. Pushing aside my shirt still stained with Danny's blood, she rolls her hands up and down the length of my neck while licking a trail to my stomach, the ends of her dark hair tickling my skin.

My back arches. I moan. Almost instinctively my body lifts itself up and down off the bathroom floor and each time I feel her enter me deeper and deeper until her whole body is almost within me, as if we're one person in the same. The rush of orgasm flutters through my body and she holds me there until it's gone, until I fall back on the tile floor, exhausted and breathing heavy. My eyes close.

It's the light I notice first, the bright light on the bathroom ceiling. I'm lying on my back on the cold hard floor, the sink almost directly above me. On it I see a dark line, possibly dried blood that had dripped down the sink and out of sight. I reach up to touch it but I don't have to. I already know it's mine. Not fresh. But still mine.

Pulling myself off the coldness of the floor and into the brightness of the room, I notice a glimpse of myself in the mirror. It's me, all right. Nothing's changed about me. The sex doesn't show. The betrayal doesn't show. Not even the murder shows.

Murder? It feels like a dream, pulling that trigger. Danny's blood had splashed just like it does in the movies.

The bedroom is dark and quiet, but not vacant. Even in its stillness I can vaguely make out the shape of the body in the bed. It's a body I know well, with shapes my own body has memorized. If I don't breathe, I can almost hear the faint airy whispers of her breath as it passes her immobile lips. Stella is very much asleep.

I stand near the bed and let my clothes drop to the floor. Then I slide under the covers, hugging the sheets around me and as my eyes close my mind immediately starts to drift. Barely aware of the arm across my waist, caught in between the waking world and sleep I begin to dream. In this dream, someone's standing in the doorway, mouthing words to me. At first I think it's Danny, saying, "We have to do it now," with furtive glances to the female arm across my stomach. I blink awake and he's gone. Stella stands there instead, half dressed and sexy. Somehow I know she's leaving. She leans down to me in bed and whispers in my ear. Then she kisses the side of my mouth as my eyes close again. When they open, she is gone. Like she was never there at all.

My fingers touch my mouth, where I can still feel her soft lips.

"Now you're free," were her whispered words, echoing inside my mind in the empty room.

I barely recognize my own voice when I say, "Now I'm alone."

As always.

Companions
Kate Durré

Mikkel grinned as the grimy man across from him slammed his empty mug down. Of course he himself was no less grimy, and no less drunk. Him and all the rest of the men in the dark tavern; scratching themselves, scraping chairs across the floor, snapping cards down on tables and fingers for the girls. His smile broadened. This, he thought, is heaven.

Bar girls bustled from table to table, swaying their hips, leaning low to hand men their beer, pouting and playing and batting their eyelashes. His two companions sat weary and wet and covered in mud but warmed by the fire and ale. An old man in the far corner, hat tipped to his nose, snored loudly. Five young nobles' sons tried not to stand out as they drank gin at the bar. The huge barkeeper, wiping glasses with a cloth that was only slightly less grimy than the rest of him, smiled at his wife each time she came out with a tray of food.

Mikkel arched his back and stretched enough that his popping joints were louder than the scrapings of his hard, crusty leather armor. As he stretched each region of his body he realized just how sore it was. "I've gotta turn in soon," he said, yawning widely.

"Naw!" shouted the man in front of him, gesturing towards a pretty bar girl for more beer. "We don' have t' ride out till the day after tomorrow!" He belched, which set them both to embarrassingly boyish giggles. "C'mon, Kel, don't be a fucking woman."

Mikkel growled. "Did you just call me a woman, Lagton?"

Lagton cocked his head and squinted up out of one eye. "So what if I did, you want ter fight?"

"Don't start that, Lagton," came a lazy drawl from the man to Mikkel's left. "Don't embarrass the boy. Fighting you would only prove it."

Mikkel stood, puffed out his chest, and put his hand on his

sword in a sloppy and playful manner. "Rawler, you just don't want to clean up the mess."

"Of your arse ground into the floorboards," Lagton finished.

That set all three to boyish giggles again. The bar maid returned and Rawler, the only one of them old enough to have grey in his mustache, grabbed a new cup of ale from her hand. He downed the ambrosia, trying to mask his laughter, but instead snorted into the froth and sprayed it all over his whiskers.

The bar maid's sweet laughter joined their own. "Will that be all for you boys?"

"Naw," Lagton growled with a gleam in his eye that Mikkel instantly recognized. Lagton was a good man to have at your back and one you could always count on to be there—but he could be a randy drunk.

Mikkel snaked an arm around the girl's waist as she stepped near to hand him his mug. He hesitated and then he sat down, and pulled her into his lap. Lagton growled again, this time in a possessive way, and the girl squealed. She tried to squirm out of Mikkel's grasp but only slightly, and he was glad for the dirt that would hide his blush.

He pulled the girl closer to him. "I think Lagton here had his eye on you, but I got you first," he said. He was shocked to find his voice unexpectedly change from bold bravado to a high pitched squeak and clamped his mouth shut.

Lagton roared with laughter and said, "The kid's got it wrong, what I want is for you ter settle something for us."

Mikkel's cheeks flushed even pinker.

"Yeah, Lagton thinks Kel is lacking in manhood," said Rawler. "What do you think?"

She cocked her head and looked down at him. "I don't think I've got enough evidence to say." She winked across the table at Lagton.

"Well luv, we gotta know," he returned her wink. "And the boy says he's tired, so why don't you tuck him in and tell us in the mornin'?"

She looked down at Mikkel again. He bit his lip but otherwise hid his hesitation—her smile faltered. Being so close, she caught the brief expression that he always managed to hide from his companions, on the rare occasion that he found himself in this situation.

"I think I will do just that," the girl said, standing up. "If you boys will settle his tab, I'll just go sing him a lullaby."

Something in her smile, softer this time, lead Mikkel to stand and follow her. He smiled cheekily back at his friends, and swaggered his hips just a bit for Lagton's benefit.

She led him up the stairs, past the room he and his companions rented for the night and to one at the end of the hall. She pushed open the well-worn door, and he stood just inside it as she fumbled for a candle.

Light brought color to the room and Mikkel looked about. A small bed and a vanity were the room's only furnishings, but the linens were clean, the drapes bright, and the few trinkets on the vanity's top were clearly beloved.

"I'll get everything dirty," he said in a lost little voice.

She crossed to a window and pulled the pane shut against fall's damp chill, then turned to give him a puzzled look. "I've got you up here in my room and you're worried about getting the sheets dirty?"

He bit his lip, realizing how foolish that was, realizing that he was beginning to give himself away.

"Don't worry on it, honey, I'll tell those boys you're no woman even if you just curl up in bed like a babe. Then you can boast all you want of your manhood." She laughed gently and stepped forward, and placed a hand on his arm.

He stumbled backwards at her touch.

Her hands went to her hips. "Well aren't you going to say nothin?" She looked around the room, him standing between her and the bed, she between him and the door. Her eyes went to the corner of the room, and she smiled, again pinning him with a playful stare.

"So you're worried about getting my bed dirty, are you darlin'?" She darted to the corner, pulled out a tub, and hollered out the door for some hot water before Mikkel could think to protest.

He made no motion to move. She let a boy in and he filled the tub, water sloshing over onto his feet so that he left muddy footprints on his way out. Then they were alone again. Still they stared.

"You are a strange one, then," the girl shrugged. "But I've yet to meet a man who'll turn down a good scrubbing and massage. What do you say?"

She began to unlace her bodice and the motions of her slender fingers made him forget how to move his legs—he was unable to move even if he wanted to.

"Don't —" he said, a blush rising brilliant to his cheeks.

"What?" she asked, and paused with her bodice open, the thin white material of her shift falling in tantalizing folds. Her hands moved to the laces of her overskirt.

She soon stood before him in only her shift, the material thin from being washed clean so many times. He couldn't keep his eyes from straying, lingering, devouring her form.

"Well at least you find me attractive!" she exclaimed. "I was beginning to wonder if you even fancied women."

"I do," Mikkel snapped, surprising both of them.

She stepped around the tub towards him. "Well then," she slid her hands up to his shoulders, "would you like me to give you a bath and tuck you in?"

Her hands were at the back of his neck now, her body close but still far, her face at a height with his own and only inches from it. She cocked her head, and he bit his lip, suddenly very aware of the dimple at the corner of her mouth.

"Don't bite your lip," she growled.

"Wh—" he began a startled inquiry but she cut him off by capturing his lips with her own. The kiss was quick and darting and ended with a nip at his lower lip.

She pulled back, now catching his eyes, and her voice was

husky. "I'll do that for you."

She began to undo the laces that bound his armor together and he was only able to raise the weakest mewl in protest. If she was this determined, then, he might as well let her have her way. Until she changes her mind.

Dirt crumbled from the seams between layers as she lifted the cracked and muddy armor away. Her fingers skimmed over the fabric of his tunic which, too, was so imbedded with dirt as to be almost completely smooth. He could think of nothing but her touch. "Let me know if it tickles," she whispered.

Her hand slipped under his tunic, skimmed across his waistline. He shivered. "It's not that kind of tickling," he said.

He was still absorbed in her touch and so realized belatedly that he wasn't wearing the tunic anymore. He stood before her in only his breeches and the strips off cloth wrapped tightly around his torso.

"Oh!" she exclaimed. "Are you injured? Is that why you didn't want me?" She swatted his arm not too playfully. "And here I was afraid I was losing my charms. Let me take a look."

She reached for the wrappings but he caught her hand. "Wait." He pulled her closer to him, trapping their joined hands between them. "Let me do this again," he begged, and she closed her eyes.

He kissed her, savoring the taste of her and letting his fingers caress her soft skin. He pulled away too soon and she stood with her eyes still closed for a moment.

Her bright eyes met his and she smiled. "Now let me see to getting you clean," she scolded.

He sighed, shook his head, but made no move to stop her. She would find out anyway, this determined little minx.

She unwrapped his bindings slowly, gently, afraid of what wound they might hide. They were wrapped so tight that the pale skin beneath was clean—the only part of his entire body that was free of dirt.

What she found, she could not have expected.

She stepped back, almost stumbling over the pail in her

surprise. He closed his eyes, turned to the side. "See?" he asked. "You just had to see."

"Oh," her hand went to her mouth, shocked at the pain that was evident in his face. "Stupid, silly girl," she scolded herself.

"No!" he said. "Not—please don't call me—"

"Well you are, aren't you?" she shot back. "So what, you think to trick women into your bed? Is that it?" She scowled at the strips of cloth still in her hand, and tossed them to the floor at his feet.

"No, it's not...It's not that," he said, and crossed his arms over his chest. "It's just...how I am. And it usually means that I pass my nights alone."

"That doesn't make any sense," she fired back.

"What doesn't make sense?"

"That I—" her anger crumpled, she could no longer meet his eyes and looked away. "That I still want you."

Silence.

"I've never brought someone up here that I didn't want. And you, standing right there, even like that," she gestured at his naked torso. "Even like that, I want to come back over there and—"

She rushed to him, threw her arms around him. "Stupid," she cried into his neck, and kissed it softly before hugging him tight.

He hesitated, sighed with relief, and tucked her tightly into his arms.

The bath was forgotten.

Pennies in the Well
Robert L. Barton

Virginia,
July 10, 1863

My Dearest Friend Jonathan,

It is the prayer of my heart that this letter finds you well. I find myself at times, standing in a world where the smoke of gun powder has obscured the field around me. Were it not for the smell of war I would think that I was adrift in a cloud hearing distant thunder rather than cannon. Then a thought of you will cross my mind and send me back to days of our boyhood in Charleston, with fond memories lacking care or concern. That is until a worry after your own well being brings me back to the horror of these fields. I often wonder what battle rages where you find yourself and though I know not where you serve at any given moment I have a certainty that you will conduct yourself with courage and honor. Some nights ago I stepped out for a word of prayer and I realized that I was speaking not to God but that like some ancient Pagan of Athens I was speaking to the Moon. I was asking her to look over you wherever you may be at this time. Is the sin of praying to a false god offset by the love for a friend which motivates the prayer, I wonder. Or perhaps, as I am told, that love is itself a sin though I cannot understand love of any kind being of a sinful nature. Not for me to answer such questions, though. After all, I am merely an army surgeon and by no means, a theologian.

Let me apologize for the tenor of my letter and the uncertainty of my hand which shakes with a pervasive tiredness. I have been awake for days and find that tired as I may be sleep does not come. Morpheus has deserted me of late, or perhaps I have deserted him though I think that I should gladly accept his gentle touch were it offered. These several days have been to me a misery, a misery so profound that I have come to question God. If there be any place on this earth that is forsaken of His touch it is a town called Gettysburg. I know not if you have yet heard the details of this storm of horror which has broken upon us, but I should think that there is neither paper enough in the world nor sufficient words to convey what has been done to those beautiful young men in that place. Echoes of pain and horror will be heard in those hills and hollows for generations to come. I do not believe any man will ever be able to cross those fields and complete his journey with a light heart; even should he have no prior knowledge of what has transpired. Though the mind of history may someday forget, as history is wont to do; I think that no heart shall ever be able to be in that place and not feel the pain that the ground there holds; the memory of man is short but stones and hills forget slowly and they shall recall these scarlet colored days forever.

Life is precious, or so I have been told, as this has been the nature of the teaching that I have received throughout my entire life, as a child, in church, in school and in medical school. I just cannot understand this world now and my soul rails against a callous fate which spends so many lives as though they are merely pennies for candy. I do not know how often word from home finds you, in the event that you have yet to hear of my sad news it pains me to tell you that Charles has been one of those pennies so carelessly tossed into this well. His face comes often before the eyes of my heart for he was dear to me and surely the kind of older brother that every young man should wish for himself. I certainly must count myself fortunate to have had Charles to emulate these twenty seven years that I have walked this world. God has certainly granted a blessing in allowing me to be the brother to such a fine man as was he. I have no awareness of Charles ever speaking unfairly to any man or in such a way as to bring pain or harm to another; in these many years of your friendship with myself Charles never had a word of you that was not kind. That first night in Boston was the only time that I have ever heard Charles speak sharply to any man, and I must admit that his words for you and I were the wages that we had fairly earned. To my knowledge that night was the only time that my brother ever perjured himself and that was only in order to protect you and I from a most grievous fate arranged for us through our own youthful foolishness and exuberance.

I must say that after nearly ten years I do find a certain humor in the events of that time, a humor that was lacking at that moment, perhaps due to our extreme fear. You will recall that it was our first night upon arriving in Boston concerning my inquiries into medical school, you having joined Charles and me on that journey. I was myself shocked in the extreme to see how flawlessly my brother, known for his honesty and truthfulness, created such a likely fiction in response to the tale told him by the police officer who delivered us to our hotel. How easily Charles was able to dismiss the accusations against us no matter the probable truth of them. I still hear his words to that officer as though they were being spoken here in the tent where I sit writing this to you.

"Officer as you can see my brother and his young friend have been drinking and for this I apologize. We have only today arrived in Boston where it is our hope that my young brother Richard here will attend medical school and realize his dream of becoming a surgeon. I must assume the responsibility for their offenses since they are in my care and it was my own mistake that has led to this. You see, earlier this evening I gave in to the pleading of my younger brother and allowed he and young Jonathan to have more license than is their custom and certainly more than was prudent. They wished to discover the charms of a certain type of lady and being so far from home I thought that no harm could come of it. The result of this decision found us in the parlor of a particular house where these ladies may be found and I trusted that these two young men would remain sober enough to find their way back to the hotel and so I returned earlier upon the completion of my own business. It would seem that my trust in my two young compatriots was misplaced and they have had more than their share of wine. I neither know of this area of town wherein you apprehended these young men nor of the debaucheries that transpire there. I daresay that they also lack knowledge of it and that simple blind fate rather than intention guided them there. I would imagine that this neighborhood of which you speak must stand somewhere between here and the house where I left these gentlemen and they managed to wander into this unseemly section of town while trying to find their way to this, our temporary home. Looking at them, I see that each is wearing the jacket of the other—it would appear that revelry has, in this instance, led to some confusion I can assure you officer that I shall keep them firmly in hand for the remainder of our stay in your fair city. I am also sure that there are fines concerning their behavior and I would be perfectly willing to pay those now if you can be so kind as to deliver payment to the proper authorities and perhaps save their mothers some embarrassment and myself the shame of explaining to my father how I could be so careless in my duties."

And then he paid our "fines" to the officer and dismissed him into the night with no harm done to us. His words for us when that door closed were certainly deserved if painful. It was the harshest look that I have ever seen in his eyes, and the only time that I saw anger for me in them. I recall those words delivered as they were by the edge of a sharpened but just tongue.

"Gentlemen! I am appalled by your lack of discretion! I am gentleman enough to generally not speak of things which are not my concern but your actions tonight have made it my business for this moment. I love you Richard, both in as much as you are my brother and in as much as you are a kind and gentle young man. I also have a fondness for Jonathan, neither as great nor of the same nature as your own close friendship. In my effort to be a good brother I find that I have been too permissive on this journey. As the ancient and wise king recommended I have been blind among secrets. You risk your own reputations and the reputations of families who adore you. Look at yourselves! It is not your jackets that are misplaced, it is your pants. You will do in your lives as you must, I hope that you would see to it that the honor of your families and yourselves remains intact. Now, for the duration of our trip there will be no blindness and there will be no secrets. Now to bed with you and each will keep to his own room. Goodnight!"

A dark time indeed was that night to my heart, nearly as dark as these recent nights through which I sit alone save for the memories of horrible days, days into which the suffering of years have been poured. I had, in my hubris, always prided myself on the possession of a great skill at the practice of secrecy and discretion. I was, by those unfortunate events, brought about by my own carelessness, forced to the realization that our secrets are not always kept by us and that many times we are allowed the keeping by those who are too kind to tear them from us. I tell you, these nights have been also dark to me in as much as sleep so rarely visits and when it does come it brings with it dreams. Dreams that I believe could only be borne in the arms of some cruel angel, himself fallen into misery. When sleep last did come to me I awakened from a fitful and disquieting vision in which I found myself in surgery over some over some poor wounded boy. Even in my sleep I can not find respite from this apocalypse. A movement, my own, brought me to wakefulness and my eyes opened to be greeted by the sight of my hands waving about in the air before me as though they held my instruments and struggled to dam up this flood. Many hours yet remained in the night but repose did not return to me. Tears certainly can purge a heavy heart but I find that they are an inadequate substitution for restful sleep.

The battle is now several days gone and we have removed ourselves from the fields of Pennsylvania. The train of wagons to carry the wounded away from those fields was, I am certain, a dozen or more miles in length. I remember the horses though, they were everywhere dead, those beautiful creatures. So marvelous in life they are pitiable in their demise especially when they are thusly wasted and left scattered about as though they are refuse. As the last wagon left with the wounded I was aboard it tending to my charges and after a short remove from the fields I glanced back and saw the carnage of these beasts and I wondered if we had destroyed more horses in these few days than Alexander himself had in the years during which he conquered the world. Will there be someone who counts the sacrifice of dumb brutes, I wonder. Strange the thoughts that enter the mind of man at these times when we seem to have laid before us the Revelations of John. Bless those beasts who do not even know why they die, serving us with complete trust as we march them away to join us in our slaughter. I was riding in the last of the wagons of the wounded, my intention being to continually work my way forward from wagon to wagon and then to return in opposite fashion, and we chanced to pass the body of a small puppy. A mongrel really, certainly not an animal of great account just a single lifeless body among thousands. He seemed to have been struck by some ball that had gone astray, as was he himself. Foolishness overtook me and I broke down and cried. Over a puppy! I had held dying young men in my arms for days and I had no tears left for them but the sight of a simple pup reduced me to a school girl lamenting some lost butterfly. I thought that I may be mad until the realization came to me that the men around me were likewise grieving for this animal. A sad sight we must have been, a wagon borne requiem for an unknown dog. Perhaps our grief and compassion for man has spent itself.

Or perhaps we simply should return to our homes and renew our capacity for compassion in the arms of our ladies. My Charlotte is such an example of compassion, I learn so much about caring from her. I remember the night that I first came to make her acquaintance, her family newly domiciled in our home town. It was a social event hosted by my own family, but you would remember that you were, after all, present. My mother Mme. Baker felt a strong kinship with the young Mlle. Devereaux. Perhaps it was that my mother had also been transplanted to Charleston from Louisiana at a similar age. I remember when we were introduced and I looked into those eyes, it was as if they were already familiar to me. Even more, it was as if they were already well known to me. It was as though we had known one another prior to this world. It was a familiarity that I had only ever felt with you yourself. I must have been perceptibly taken with the young lady for I overheard my mother and father speaking of it in an approving fashion when they thought that they were beyond the ability of my eavesdropping. My mother said. "Maintenant il y a une jeune dame qui peut-être faire reprendre ses sens à un jeune homme." And M. Baker uncharacteristically responded in this clumsier tongue. "Or perhaps rob him of them." Mother looked at him showing her disapproval and asked. "Est cela que je vous ai fait, M. Baker?" Father at once served charm and wisdom in his reply, delivered in a tongue more appropriate to the company of a lady. "Je ne pouvais pas le compter le vol quand je leur ai si librement donné avec si peu de défense

The true affection and friendship that my parents have for one another has forever been an inspiration to me. I will all of my life seek to show as much affection and companionship to my own dear wife. And to you my friend I hope that I am always as thoughtful and considerate as my mother and father are to one another. You have certainly been a good and faithful friend to me. I remember my studies in Boston and those intractable periods of time away from my loved ones punctuated as they were, with fleeting occasional visits home. My constant letters to you must have been burdensome; however you bore it without complaint. You so dutifully answered each one, understanding my need for assurances from familiar lips and a touch from home. Funny, the things that we remember at these times; I would open your letters when they arrived and I would for a moment be able to smell the presence of our native soil.

The second day of the battle was the longest of my life. It was as if the sun hung still in the sky and would not complete the journey to the western horizon. At times I had to turn away from dying children who had wounds so grievous that, though they yet lived, I could do nothing for them and my energies were better spent tending to those who may survive than easing the pain of the dying. It is the rational decision, I know, but still when their weak and pitiful voices call to my back as I turn and step away my heart is torn from me as they beg for my help. There was that day a young man, he couldn't have been more that fifteen, brought to me with a simple wound easy enough to treat, a ball in the flesh of his leg. I looked into his blue eyes and assured him that he would be fine as this was something that I could easily manage. Just then a wayward cannon ball tore him from beneath my hands. The weapon did not explode it was as if it were meant only for this child alone. In a moment he was looking at me with trust in my assurances and in the next moment he was gone from this world. I told him that he would be fine. I wonder, will he stand to identify me a liar on the Day of Judgment?

Clearly I can recall the blue of your own eyes; why I remember the day that I first realized that your eyes were so colored. How can you imagine that we had been friends from the cradle and it was not until we were nearly thirteen years old that I ever noticed your eyes. It was that late afternoon at the fishing hole frequented by the boys of our age. It has left my memory, the event that so prompted all of our friends to remain in town, but I do remember that you and I decided to seize the opportunity to have all of the fish to ourselves that day. And so by the by we ended up at the fishing hole alone, with the exception of good old Cyrus, my constant shadow or as my mother thought, her constant spy. But Cyrus was always loyal to me and remains at my side serving me even now here in this place where he gently snores on his pallet just outside of my tent. What was it that prompted me to send Cyrus away that day to watch the trail and warn us should anyone approach to share our fish? I do remember that it was July in Charleston that convinced us to put down our poles and strip off to swim. Even the water felt warm on our skin as the sun was sinking that day; it was so hot I remember wondering if perhaps I had a touch of a fever coming on suddenly. And I saw that your eyes were blue, as I realized so many new things in the heat of that afternoon and evening. My, were our mothers angry when finally we returned home supper having long past, our only excuse that we lost track of time. Poor Cyrus I thought that my mother was going to do that boy a harm.

As I am sure you will recall, we were living in Washington when it seemed that war might bear down upon us, and so my Charlotte returned to Charleston while I accepted a commission in this Army of Northern Virginia to serve with General Lee. At times the wish comes upon me that I should have rather returned to South Carolina and enlisted there in order to serve with you and our friends. These are good and brave men to serve with, to be sure, however it would feel better to stand beside those whom I have known all of my life. Like those ancient soldiers that we so fondly played as children, shields locked side by side, the warriors of Thebes standing against the onslaught of Persia. But this is no game, and no shield turns back these blows, our companions fall at our shoulders and our enemies fall at our hands and their blood mingles at our feet.

I correspond constantly with my Charlotte looking forward to the birth of our first child. I am concerned that the health of my wife has always been so delicate that we have been unable to, until now, become parents, and I do worry after her so. You have stood by us as our dearest friend for so long now, and I thank you for that. I am a lucky man to have at one time a friend as dear as you and a friend as dear as my deeply understanding Charlotte. If the child is a boy we shall name him Charles, after my father and brother. There is still some good natured contention concerning possible names should it be a girl child. But I cannot seriously contend with the younger Mme. Baker, and she shall have her way in the name Isabella to honor her own departed mother should we be graced by providence with a girl. Though a son would be a source of great pride I shall thank God for any child safely born to a healthy mother.

Her own parents having departed this corporeal form, Charlotte is in the care of mine, who watch over her with great affection for she is the daughter that they wished for and did not have.

Their love for her is so complete as is my own—but you know all of this you who knows my mind better than anyone perhaps even better than I myself. I should rather say that my mother is watching over her since, after the passing of my brother Charles, my father resumed his commission and is now serving as an officer in the Army, as though he were a young man. While I respect the abilities of my father, and he has surely provided well for our family, he is not the young officer that he was so very many years ago and I am uncomfortable in the extreme with a man of his seniority going in harms way. I expressed my concerns to him, a mistake for which I was at some considerable length verbally rewarded and a mistake that I will be loath to ever repeat. Col. Baker told me that he was of no use at home due to our company ships being unable to pass the Northern blockade of our ports. The ships are running in Europe and generating some profit though they are managed currently by business agents of my father located in Paris.

Ah Paris, I was so excited to accompany my father on that journey to Europe I wish that you had been along with us. I pleaded with my father to allow you to join us on that business venture but Mme. Baker would not hear of it my mother having no appreciation of the importance of our friendship to me. I found Paris at first to be a dirty city but there were portions of that city which held a certain charm and which were exciting to me in my youthfulness. It was then that I felt so fortunate that my dear mother had insisted in the use of French among the family which provided each of us with an easy fluency of tongue allowing me to better move through Parisian social circles. I made many friends in that time and I should like to visit there again someday. There was a marvelous cuisine to be had and the society of constant events with balls, music, and theater and dancing, I shall never forget the dancing.

Do you remember, I wonder, that night of dancing when you escorted that young lady Missy and I escorted Charlotte? I must say that your choice of young lady caused some consternation in polite society that evening, it was quite nearly scandalous. Luckily the chaperones were beyond question or reproach or we would have continued to hear whispers of judgment concerning that choice for weeks. Our carriage being covered against the moist night also afforded some protection from prying eyes and wagging tongues. Cyrus drove we two around in that carriage for so long that rainy night after the ladies were safely home affording us a very private conversation. It was a rainy evening with an unpleasant wind and yet it is such a dear memory to me that I imagine I shall treasure it forever.

There was harshness in that second day I tell you, a harshness that I cannot erase from my memory. That I survived is a mystery to me and I wonder if it shall take me yet. through the agency of terrible echoes that I cannot escape. I confess that I have more than once here alone these nights considered raising my hand against myself. I saw that day, a man will himself to die, I believe. He was brought to my surgery with wounds from which he should have recovered for he was strong and one of our more senior soldiers in age. His treatment went well and he looked as if he would recover. And then there was a young man brought in with wounds that were beyond the gifts that God has given me and he could not be saved in body, I prayed that he was saved in soul for he would need that salvation soon. I did not know that the younger man was son to the elder and that father watched his own son expire and his will to live drained away from him like a tide ebbing from the shore. He called to death and it came to him as he bid it and this strong man with mild wounds passed before my eyes simply because he wished it so. I have never seen a man desire his own end so much that he could will it to be and I have never thought that a similar desire could so threaten to move my own hand.

My courage in this matter has been so very close to failure, I have not told any man until yourself how afraid I have been in this war. When I find myself wanting for bravery I recall that thirteen year old boy that you once were and how you stood against that horrid tutor that so terrorized the children of our station in

Charleston. He seemed to have a wrath in him that rivaled the Old Testament. So many of the families of our society employed his services and he was such a menace to the hearts of children with never a kind word. I wonder was it just my own perceptions or did he truly bear a significantly greater dislike for you and myself than he harbored for children in general. Unpleasant sort of man that he was yelling at us as he did that we were naught but confused little boys and that we should sort ourselves out. I remember the momentary look of fear on his face when you told him that we were his charges to be educated and not heads upon which to vent a wrath born of his own frustrations. I cannot escape the feeling that there was somehow in your words a deep subtlety which I have never been able to comprehend, and I imagine that I shall never understand unless you should decide to explain this to me. I thought that you would be struck for speaking to him in that fashion for he looked so enraged, but he just returned, after a moment to compose himself, to our academics. Whatever depths there were to your words you became the hero to every child of us for standing against that tyrant. As I recall he soon had a falling out with his landlord, he was the only boarder in the house of that old bachelor Mr. Zale, and left Charleston. I'm sure that he found another town in which to torment children. He certainly must have been a difficult man to live with for bachelor Zale never took in another boarder.

As we left the field after the battle I was moving along among the wagons of wounded. I am sorry my friend, I have written of this earlier in this letter, my mind is so hard to govern as I am sure these pages reflect. I spring in a moment from thoughts born of the depths of horror to the heights of my fondest memories. Know that your face comes before my eyes of memory only when I recall the heights of my life, for you like my Charlotte inhabit the finest moments that I have ever known. Please remember that always. Should anything unfortunate befall me, do not harbor hate or anger for any hand of man or God that should rise against me for perhaps it would be doing me a mercy.

In my studies I have learned that among the Hindoo of India it is believed that life is repeated and that one may walk this world not once but many times. It may be a blasphemy but perhaps they are right and I have known Charlotte and yourself before and it is this that engenders the familiarity and attachment that I have always held for you both. Or maybe as we were taught we pass away to another land of reward or punishment according to what we have earned in this single life. There are those who believe that we may after physical death remain behind, to haunt as a spirit the places that we so fondly frequented in this life. Were I allowed the choosing, that is perhaps the choice that I would make. I remember when we buried my grandfather in the family plot just across the way from that of your own family, I looked there at the graves of your ancestors and the thought came to me that someday we shall both of us be buried here across from one another, our eternities shaded by the same trees. If after death we should remain as phantoms, we can perhaps haunt together those places that we have so loved to visit in our living.

You should know that this battle was an accident, not even planned for. I cannot imagine any general mad enough to have planned this carnage which has visited itself upon all sides in this affair. Small groups of foraging soldiers from the two factions in this contest stumbled upon one another in the town and they exchanged some small violence. Wisdom should have left it at that but prudence fled and the armies came together inexorably in this place that afforded no real advantages to anyone. There was no reason involved in this, it just swept along like a storm that could not be avoided, one event unfolding after another. And then one fateful morning came and a scythe was called forth and it fell again and again and so the harvest began.

It is said that the Unionists on the far side of that field fell at their breakfast in that first terrible moment when our cannons opened up. I came to be sure that some of those men on the other side of that field from us were acquaintances of mine from my time in Boston and in Washington. I saw the body of a young doctor dressed in his northern blue and I recognized his face as a young man with whom I attended medical school. His name was beyond my recall, I prayed for him there in that field but I wish that I could remember his name, I am sure that God knows of whom I spoke. My God Jonathan! We are killing men with whom we have sat at table; we are making widows of women that we know. I wonder if there is enough grace in God to forgive the sins that are pouring forth from mankind at this time. It makes a man wish that he were a beast of the forest without cognizance of himself or others. But were I a beast, I would lack the treasured acquaintance of my Charlotte and of you. Perhaps it is in our capacity to feel tortured that we find our ability to perceive joy. I cannot say if there can be one without the other.

I do not mean to repeat myself but I know such excitement that I am finally to be a father, my lovely Mme. Baker is expecting our first child on whom we have waited patiently these several years. I receive correspondence from Charlotte often and it does so brighten my day. I try to answer her when I can; I should have responded to her tonight but I lack the feeling of eloquence due the French language and I have never written to my wife in any language other than that of our proper society. So my letter to her must wait until I am not so tired and can find the literary inspiration to manage words properly as is fitting for correspondence with a lady. And so I do in my clumsiness of word tonight write to you. I hope that you do not mind my shaking hand or confused words and will forgive whatever moments of foolishness have spilled out onto the page.

Oh my friend, when I sat down last evening the intention was to prepare a short missive in order to send to you a few bits of news. While the sky is still clothed in a diamond scattered mourning dress of black I feel a chill in the air that forewarns that Apollo approaches and will take the heights above us bringing dawn on his chariot; and still I sit here rambling in my aimless manner. I apologize that I have for so many pages scattered my thoughts with so little organization. Tonight it seems that my soul bleeds ink and

I have soaked it up with paper and I know that you in your kindness will read every word, even those that are not within my ability to write and which inhabit only the empty spaces and margins of these pages. Looking back through this letter I have perhaps said too much or perhaps not enough as I have repeated myself and leaped from one thing to another. I am certain that there must have been a particular matter which was for me the impetus to write this letter to you; whatever it was I hope that it somehow made its way into these pages. I will trust in your wisdom and ability to perceive and understand me so well and rest knowing that whatever that message was you will find it buried here in my night's madness.

May the hand of God rest upon your shoulder and shield you from all harm.

Richard

The Decision
Ammy Achenbach

The rhythmic drumming of the rain on the pavement outside rushed over her in waves as she nestled her head in the crook of her elbow. She listened as the gentle hum washed over her, engulfing her in the sounds of its vertical currents. In her right hand, she played with a diamond ring, catching the light in it with every turn. Her eyes followed each facet like a child watching the light dance around a carousel at a summer festival.

What should I do? she thought, a tear running down her cheek. He loves me. I know he loves me. She sighed, tilting her head so she could look out the window from her reclined position on her bed and watched the water pool like quicksilver, smooth and shiny as it slithered across the blacktop in the lamplight. And I love him. But is it enough? She released her neck, letting her head fall back onto her arm. The ring fell gently around her index finger as she ran the tip of her nail over her bottom lip.

Her straight friends didn't know. They saw her with Kyle and just assumed she was straight. The conversation never came up, and she never pushed it, not wanting to embarrass him. The heavy drops pounded the pavement harder, surging through her ears until it rang through her body. She let her hand fall gently on her shoulder and watched the pools overflow into rivers streaming down the sides of the slight bulge in the middle of the street.

But that caused problems with her gay friends, who often considered it convenient for her to be gay whenever she wanted to be instead of being completely out. With a sigh, she rolled over onto her back, her dark curls falling away from the delicate features of her face so they created a soft frame. She was stuck living a half-life, existing between the two worlds that had rejected her. Her gaze fell with the droplets of water as they hit the slick rise in the road before dividing their paths to join the rushing streams, creating a thin stripe of silvery tar that loomed between the diminutive rivers.

Can I live with only being half of who I am? She sighed, and her gaze fell on the gold mesh bracelet that encircled her left wrist, a birthday present from her last girlfriend. She played with the catch, her brow furrowed, as her thoughts churned in her mind, sloshing like liquid that had not yet turned into butter. She wasn't as concerned with not feeling the gentle touch of a woman again. She could live with the slightly rough touch of Kyle instead of the knowing caress of more slender fingers. But knowing that from now on, people would assume that she was straight, uncomplicated and conventional? Those assumptions rankled her. The rain became less rhythmic as it broke into a downpour, striking the thin panel of glass.

Will he be okay knowing he can only have a part of me? She already knew the answer to that. He was nothing but understanding. He knew her, and she loved that. A smile played on her lips as she pulled herself up and leaned her back against the window. The cold glass penetrated through her shirt until she thought the rain was soaking through the glass, uniting with her moist skin. She held up her right hand, letting the diamond glisten in the dim lamplight that filtered through her window. She slid it off her finger and held it in the palm of her hand.

I love him, and he loves me for me, even my sexuality. Her mouth curled slightly up again as her tears subsided, the last one mimicking the droplets on the window behind her. The rain lost intensity as the storm exhausted itself, becoming once again a gentle wave against the pavement. Cassandra lifted the ring from her palm and held it up in the streetlight again. The clear diamond sparkled as the moon peeked out from behind the parting clouds. She gently slid the ring on her left hand and watched it settle into place on her finger. She turned her head, lightly pressing her fingertips against the glass, and gazed outside as the tail end of a cloud glided across the sky, revealing the sliver of a moon in the dark sky.

Coyote Takes a Trip
Deborah A. Miranda

"I have substantial evidence that those Indian men who, both here [Santa Barbara] and farther inland, are observed in the dress, clothing, and character of women—there being two or three such in each village—pass as sodomites by profession (it being confirmed that all these Indians are much addicted to this abominable vice) and permit the heathen to practice the execrable, unnatural abuse of their bodies. They are called joyas *[jewels], and are held in great esteem."*

(Pedro Fages, soldier, 1775)

Standing in the cold, sand-swept Venice Beach parking lot watching his clothing scatter in the four directions, Coyote decided to head for New Mexico, catch up with his brother, and leave his broken heart behind.

He'd been living on Venice Beach for a long time; he liked the ocean with its tall jade winter waves and generous people who camped in the parking lot. Something about their vehicles—old school buses, pick-up trucks with handmade campers, station wagons from the 1970s equipped with curtains and propane stoves—felt like home. Coyote was always welcome to add a paw print or play with bright paints, contribute his own unique touch to the vivid vehicle decor. And no one objected to his new favorite signature, a bumper sticker of two naked women kissing, emblazoned FUCK CENSORSHIP.

On Venice Beach, even in the winter Coyote could get cheap pizza by the slice at a kiosk that also sold Pall Malls and condoms, find regular guys always up for a good game of go or checkers, or soak up an afternoon's entertainment from a wandering minstrel with a sexy 3-string guitar and cheerfully resigned dog. Not to mention the sweet crazy woman with sleeping bags in the back of her van just waiting for Coyote to heat them—and her—up.

But this one winter, the rain just didn't let up. The sand never dried out, the paint bled off his best graffiti, and the sleeping bags felt damp and gritty. Heavy squalls blew in off the Pacific day after day, the checker players hunched grouchily under the few covered shelters arguing about whose turn it was to score some hot coffee, and even the cement walkway between Venice Beach and the Santa Monica Pier seemed sodden. Must be friggin' global warming, Coyote muttered to himself, wringing out the only pair of socks he owned (who needed more than one pair of socks in Southern California?)—world's goin' ta hell these days.

Yeah, Coyote figured maybe he'd take a road trip to see his brother in the drier climes of New Mexico, where it might be colder, but at least a guy could stand outside for a smoke without wearing a plastic garbage bag. Seemed like his sweet crazy woman wasn't so sweet anymore. Maybe more crazy than sweet, eh? Why else would she move her van while he was out cruising—er, walking, the beach? He'd come back from a little hot chocolate sipping under the pier to find his rickety suitcase teetering, lonely and frayed, in an empty parking space.

"Gah!" Coyote surveyed his wardrobe of obscene T-shirts and gangsta pants scattered amongst the scraggly pigeons and seagulls, grabbed a few handfuls (time was, he wouldn't be caught dead with baggage, but the economy wasn't what it used to be). He tucked the soggy mess into the rickety rolling suitcase that served as pack mule and safety deposit box, shook the sand out of his fur, hitched up his low-riding green canvas pants and slouched up the hill to catch a #1 Santa Monica Big Blue Bus to Westwood. From there he could catch a shuttle to LAX, where he had relatives who worked in baggage.

Maybe one of them could box him up and put him on a nonstop to ABQ. Anything would be better than this soggy gray sponge of a beach!

Trudging past the bright but mostly empty tattoo shops, massage parlors and taquerias in Venice, Coyote wondered how his life had taken such a tragic turn.

He'd lost his mojo, that's what it was—lost his touch, lost his way, lost his magic. It must be these SoCal women he'd been hanging with. They just sucked the life right out of a guy, and not in a good way. Made him feel every one of his immemorial years old. Geez, they wanted you to bring home groceries!

As if that's what Coyote does.

Groceries? Gah. What woman in her right mind would waste her Coyote on groceries?

Yeah, he'd never had any trouble getting fed or otherwise taken care of—until this winter. But something—maybe the endless rain—was diluting his powers.

My prowess! thought Coyote, bumping his old green suitcase up and over curbs and around puddles. Dude, where's my prowess? I can't even hold my tail up anymore, let alone my pecker.

The shoulders of his jean jacket slumped, excess inches of pants sloshing in the rain; Coyote stood at the bus stop with water dripping off his snout and didn't even have the heart to flick his ears.

Oh well. At least the bus was pulling up, he had 75 cents for the ride, and there was his brother's wife's cooking in the near future. Just thinking about a big round bowl of Macaria's smoldering beans topped with diced peppers and some hunks of goat cheese cheered Coyote up a little bit. And oh, Macaria's homemade corn tortillas!

He perked up enough to let three old ladies get on the bus ahead of him.

Of course that meant the three old ladies took the last three seats on the bus, the row right up front under the sign that said in English and Spanish, "please give up these seats for elderly and handicapped patrons." On the opposite wall of the bus, behind the driver, were more seats, but they'd been folded up earlier for a wheelchair and never restored.

Coyote lurched awkwardly trying to pull the seats down without losing his balance on the already-moving bus, but he couldn't find just the right button or switch. Story of my life, he growled. Finally he just threw his suitcase down on the floor and plopped right on it. He smiled up innocently at the three old ladies—one Black, one Indian, one Korean—as he perched at their feet.

Buncha dried up old viejas. What's so funny?

Crouching on his suitcase at eye-level with three old women's knobby knees, his cold feet throbbing and wet pants clinging to his cold calves, Coyote made a strange discovery. It was something he'd never noticed before: all three of these broads had perfectly dry pant hems. Of course that meant that when they sat down their high-waters rose practically to their knees, but he had to admit, it also meant they didn't suffer from water wicking up the fabric and freezing them to death, either.

Interesting, Coyote thought, but distinctly un-cool.

And in the gap between the saggy tops of their white tube socks and the bottom of their nylon stretch-waist pants, strips of even less attractive bare, hairy skin gaped.

Ay!

Well, hairy on four of the six legs—at least the indigenous woman, the one in the middle, seemed relatively smooth-skinned ...

Coyote sniffed.

She used lotion, too, or maybe just a nice laundry detergent. Fresh. Lilacs, maybe, or could it be lavender? Gee, it'd been so long since he'd been with a woman who actually did her laundry with something besides public restroom pump soap.

Coyote tilted his head so he could get a look at that middle woman's hands grasping the curved dark top of her wooden cane. He didn't want to seem obvious.

Ah, yes. A modest but tasteful home-manicure. Nails not long enough to do a guy damage, but grown out a bit, filed, polished with clear stuff, and clean. No wedding band, he noticed, but a nice silver signet ring on the left pinky, turquoise stone, probably a high school sweetheart's old token. Cinnamon-colored skin, weather-worn but not too wrinkly, hard-working hands, sturdy hands with calluses and a few old scars across the back, a scattering of well-deserved age spots.

She would never have been a beauty, Coyote admitted, but with those hands, she surely could have made a man happy.

She even had a cloth shopping bag sticking out of her coat pocket;

obviously, off to the grocery store. Senior Tuesday at Von's, he remembered. Important day for those beach-dwellers on a budget.

He risked a quick glance up at her face as she shifted to let someone squeeze toward the exit. She knew how to use make-up, that was certain; a little foundation, some blue eye-shadow but not too much, and a discreet but feminine coral pink lipstick. A bit heavy on the rouge, perhaps, but then again, maybe that extra tinge was from the effort of hoofing it up to the bus stop in the rain. Firm chin, a good nose with some arch to it; not ashamed of her strength, he decided. Her hair, mostly silver with black streaks, pulled back into a tight braid, protected from the elements by one of those plastic baggie-things old women always carry in their purses.

Suave, in a sweet way.

She'd tied a silky blue scarf, just the right color to set off her eye-shadow, at her throat. Coyote would've liked a better look at her neck, but as it was, he was surprised to find that one old woman could hold his attention this long.

Shi-i-i-t. What was he thinking? He was on his way outta here, not the best time to be oogling a woman. Disgruntled and hungry, he looked out the wide front windows at the rain and resisted the awful thought that he was inside a mobile aquarium. Okay, he thought: I'm on the road, heading toward a whole plate of Macaria's enchiladas...

The longer he sat on his rickety old suitcase on the floor of the bus, the better Coyote felt about his decision. It was time to clear out of L.A. Venice Beach in the winter was no place for an unappreciated Coyote like him! He needed to be where stories were told, hot food dished up, and a woman was only wet when he made her that way himself. Yeah. Albuquerque

"*When the missionaries first arrived in this region [San Diego], they found men dressed as women and performing women's duties, who were kept for unnatural purposes. From their youth up they were treated, instructed, and used as females, and were even frequently publicly married to the chiefs or great men... Being more robust than the women, were better able to perform the arduous duties required of the wife, and for this reason, they were often selected by the chiefs and others, and on the day of the wedding a grand feast was given.*" (Fr. Geronimo Boscana, 1846) for sure, hit some bars with his brother, a few excursions to the Pueblos. Didn't he have an old girlfriend at Zuni?

Lost in his dreams of glory, culinary and otherwise, Coyote damn near missed his stop. Wait! he yelped, leaping up to snag the yellow pull-cord and bending down just as rapidly to grab the worn handle of his rickety suitcase. Wait for me!

Scrabbling, Coyote had an odd, hobbled sensation, like a horse, unable to move more than a few increments in any direction no matter how hard he tried. And what was that cold breeze at his back—or rather, his backside?

Just as he straightened fully, suitcase firmly grasped in his left hand, Coyote's very baggy pants, held up by a dirty-white piece of rope, suddenly became a lot baggier.

Oops.

Not only was his butt hanging out for all the world to see, but so was his pride and joy, and wouldn't you know it, right at eye-level with the old Indita who'd been ignoring him the whole ride.

There was something about her expression that he couldn't quite figure out, but reminded him of his brother's face when they'd hit the jackpot in Vegas one time.

An involuntary guffaw escaped Coyote's mouth as he grabbed the front of his pants and yanked up, clung desperately to the handle of his suitcase, and tried to spontaneously sprout another hand as the bus driver went from 30 mph to nothing, screeching to a halt. Barreling forward, Coyote blew right past the driver, bounced off the dashboard down the steps, landed breathless and barely clothed at the foot of a gently dripping palm tree.

He looked up at the bus windows to see three pairs of eyes staring back.

The Black woman's face was mapped with new laugh lines Coyote knew he had just personally inscribed.

The Korean grandma's eyes glittered with outrage, her lips moving with words he was glad he could only imagine.

But the old Indian lady—could it be—was he just imagining

it, or—well, was she giving him the eye?

Admiring his prowess? Almost applauding what she'd witnessed for one brief sweet second?

Coyote felt it then: his mojo.

Like an illegal firecracker smuggled off the rez, like a long drink out of a fresh bottle of tequila, it was coming back to him, streaming into him, filling him with a terrible joy: that was no little old lady. The qualities that had so intrigued Coyote, that mix of strength and serene femininity... that old lady was a glammed up—and impressed—old man.

The bus squealed outta there, the driver blasting into traffic, and Coyote found himself with a suitcase in one hand, his family jewels in the other, and a confused but very happy mojo.

He stared after the bus, unconsciously licking his chops.

Not exactly a man. What was that old word?

Joto?

No, older than that, and sweeter.

Joya? Jewel of the People?

Nope, still Spanish, and just thinking it conjured up vile images of humiliation before loved ones, being stripped naked, mastiffs set loose, flesh and souls mutilated. No, we had our own words before the padres and soldados de cuero, Coyote thought; it was coming back to him now, how many beautiful words, each tribe creating a title as unique as the being it described.

Standing on the sidewalk, Coyote rolled his slippery pink tongue around in his mouth as if he could rattle the lost names out from between his teeth somewhere. One word in particular, something he'd learned long ago on a warm beach, whispered by a Ventureño with sparkling eyes and a ticklish belly... a word that meant honor, medicine, truth... then his mouth remembered, and Coyote cried the Chumash word aloud:

'aqi!

He looked down the street toward the airport shuttle stop.

Then back down Westwood toward Santa Monica Boulevard, and Venice Beach.

S/he must live down there. He was sure he'd seen hir around. Yeah, s/he sat off to the side during checkers matches and read books, sometimes brought a bag of cookies from the Hostess discount bakery to share. Always had a warm chuckle when Coyote threw up his arms in triumph, or a soft, "Awww..." and a click of tongue in sympathy when Coyote slumped in defeat.

What name did the 'aqi go by? Dolores? Estéfana?

Juanita.

It was really cold in ABQ this time of year, Coyote remembered. Ice, even.

Slowly Coyote pulled up his baggies and re-knotted the ratty rope around his waist. He replayed that swift glance of pleasure from Juanita, his thrilling moment of chaotic revelation, his tail waving and erect.

Then, without waiting for the light to change, he pulled out the extended handle of his rickety rolling suitcase and hauled it across the street, where the Big Blue Bus #1 headed down to Venice for a mere 75 cents.

A cheap trip, Coyote smiled amidst a chorus of honks from a Prius, a Mercedes and a shiny yellow Hummer, accented by well-honed expletives from their drivers. He didn't mind. Now he knew where his mojo had gone, and he was gonna be there waiting when it came back this afternoon.

Hell, he might even help carry the groceries.

"The priests [at Mission Santa Clara] were advised that two pagans had gone into one of the houses of the neophytes, one in his natural raiment, the other dressed as a woman. Such a person [was] called a joya. Immediately the missionary, with the corporal and a soldier, went to the house to see what they were looking for, and there they found the two in an unspeakably sinful act. They punished them, although not so much as deserved. The priest tried to present to them the enormity of their deed. The pagan replied that that joya was his wife." (Fr. Francisco Palou, 1777)

The Lottery

Florence Ivy

I win the lottery and bring my husband to pick up a long awaited prize. She is a beautiful chestnut filly, full and Arabian in the cheek. Her seller offers me a ride before I pay and I accept, leaving my husband behind. We walk through the woods, slowly, my thigh close to her side, and then build up speed, first cantering and then flying at a full gallop through wet trees, past streams and stones. Suddenly my steed takes a misstep and falls to the ground, taking me with her. She writhes in agony and I can see that one of her hooves has become twisted. I place a hand on her warm chest, it is heaving and wet. I feel her heart racing under the skin when she begins to change. Her color runs, until she is pale as milk, and her hooves change to hands, and feet. Her tail disappears, and her muzzle shortens to the nose and face of a beautiful woman. Her eyes, still deep and equine, plead with me, she is naked and afraid, and we are alone. We lay on the ground for a moment and she paws at her newly formed ankle, making strange grunts, and whinnies. I take off my coat, wrap it around her and help her to unsteady feet. As I lead her by the reins, we begin the long walk back. I wonder what my husband will say when we take her home; I have waited for her my whole life.

Angels Dance

James Williams

Dear Roque,

How nice to hear from you after all these years. I'd begun to fear they'd come for you at last and that my next view of you would be unpleasant; but your letter reassures me.

I especially liked the business about the stake in the heart. Along with garlic and sunlight I have always found that one most amusing—though I have to say that when I am abroad in the broad daylight, enjoying the pungent smells of people cooking, I prefer to place my stake elsewhere. Is that what you meant by your remark about my taste in men?

I was also glad to hear from you because I find myself confronting a pair of puzzles in which I am about to involve you. One emerged recently, unexpected; the other is related to a question of long standing that has to do with our immortality—spelled, please, with a "t."

My long-standing question is, now that you have it, do you think you'll always want it?

What will you do when there are no longer any people to suck off? What will you eat? How will you maintain yourself? I know you will not die, but that is the point: just how hungry do you want to be, and for how long? When even the gods go pale and no one is left but us, what are we going to do to pass the time that does not ever pass? Toss molten rocks into an iron sea? You see, these are no longer idle questions. Think about that 20th century cartoon crazy man in robes with his sign that says "The End is Coming." You know his end is coming, and he may even know that the end is coming, but what about your end, my concupiscent friend?

Ah, what about your luscious end.... But really I do mean what

I ask. Though I expect it may still be new to you, I have thought about this question for many, many, many years by now. It was brought home to me with renewed gusto the other evening when—speaking of ends both the and yours—I had congress with a woman. Yes, it's true; and though it was not the first time, yet you can't imagine how unexpected it was.

Women taste different, as I know you know. The flesh of women is either soft because of that fatty layer that lies, no matter how lean the animal, just under their skin, or else ironic from overstimulation. And as you also know, women were my preference until I turned you out. Although it has never dampened the pleasure I have taken in the women who have come my way, that singular event, sinking my teeth into your yielding yet resilient pulp, aroused the pleasure I have taken ever since in meaty boys like you. I like the way the tissue hardens and gives way: it whets my appetite. Your masculine meat and its appetizing aromas arouse me, yet allow me to hold in check my desire to go for the jugular, so when I finally do slake my thirst on your most special bodily fluids I am o! so well prepared.

Males like to imagine they're in hot pursuit, just as females often—I know, I know: not always, but often—prefer to pretend they are pursued. And so I have also, as I know you know, learned to take pleasure in the act of plunder when young men, just on the brink of the adventure they expect their adult lives to become, believe they have seduced me and then suddenly start to squirm in their delightfully horrified, dawning realization of just what sort of predator I am; when they find themselves hoist by their own petards, pinned on the horns of their own dilemmas, caught between a genuine devil and their last, receding glimpse of the genuine deep blue sea.

You remember that instant, don't you, when you knew that you were the conquered and not the conqueror? When, no matter how hot we were, you saw that there was danger? And still you wanted nothing so much as to come with me, whatever the awful cost might turn out to be, and yet you knew it was a bad choice, one you would live—and live and live and live—to regret. Except, of course, as you could not quite have known, you would no longer actually be the person who would have regretted what you chose, and so you would never actually live to regret your decision, as you necessarily would have done if you had really had a decision available to make. That might even have been worse: then you would have wondered for the rest of your brief eternity what my kiss and this subsequent after-life would have been like. How impossible! Such exquisite torture! Such unspeakable throes!

Now you know that much, at least. And while I like to watch young men wrestle with such questions, I knew your choice had been made already: I never regret my decisions.

So you came to me and so we lived, you and I, after our surprisingly loving fashion. Yes, that was the surprise you brought to me. How would I have dared to imagine that a boy of your young years, hardly able to hold your own in a tavern, would be sage enough to love? Yet love you did, and love you brought me, and love we have shared down the corridors of time. And if in love ours was the furtive existence of fugitive aliens secretly skulking from the light, described in century after weary century by purple novelists; or of errant cavaliers plumbing the wealth of our decadent, twilit, subterranean worlds, yet for lovers such as we are there was ample time for even the most brilliantly sunlit lust to grow torpid. Still, there you are, my boy, freed, stolen, by the need to live your own life unencumbered by the one who brought you out: thousands of miles and hundreds of years away, and bound to me forever nonetheless—forever: bound to me forever—as if you were a precious tumor on my very flesh.

You were so pretty when I bit your neck: naked and nearly hairless except for that curly black shock on your head, flat on your back with your long legs high in the air and your arms thrown wide to receive me, your charming little eager snake jumping up and down like a kitten getting ready to pounce, your hungry portal clamoring for my entry. I showed you a whip and you just moaned. I showed you manacles and you moaned louder. I threw you over onto your face and beat you with a rod and strap and just when your skin was getting ready to break you burst out in the rudest Plainsongs I had ever heard, singing loudly, shouting in your glee, Deo Grazias! Deo Grazias! Master! Master! Master Me!

And so I did, my child; so I did. So I do. So I shall. You are mine forever. That is precisely why these questions, as they apply to you, matter to me.

I don't expect you to have answers yet, but I want you to begin considering what eternity might really mean. "The Rockies may tumble, Gibraltar may crumble, they're only made of clay," as you were also, once, but as you are no more[1].

No more, my pretty. Now you are the stuff that dreams are made on.

Anyway, that was my question. Here is the unexpected, but as you will see related, puzzle.

I was in France. I was at a party: a Parisian daytime party of the debauched epoch, filled with witty Sufis and displaced eunuchs and the odd Nubian standing around with his hands under his shirt as if waiting for a promising ride home. I had gone with a sense of acidée because I was hungry and the home in which the party was held lay so near the religious students' quarters I thought I might chance upon a fresh-faced lad or lassie with which—with which, I say, and not with whom: you know you are absolutely sovereign, safe in my embrace—to indulge my other carnalities as well.

And I did, I did: I spied a long-haired Asiatic boy in a purple-black tunic that lit his parchment skin with moonly hues, whose rounded lips were dark as venous blood, whose simple presence made his every utterance an invitation, whose wide sloe eyes never seemed to blink. He already had been taking my account while I was reading the temper of the room, so when I reached him with

[1] "Our Love is Here to Stay," from Goldwyn Follies, 1938, music by George Gershwin, lyrics by Ira Gershwin.

my gaze his own gaze undressed me as if he already stood there naked. His stare was wholly undefiled, hid nothing, offered everything. Do you know what I am? I wondered, as nearly shocked as I have ever been; but before I even knew that I had had that thought he bowed his face without moving his head or eyes and turned aside to speak to the woman next to him, deliberately showing me the perfect tender skin of his throat and its softly pulsing artery.

My! Word! He reminded me of the time you and I joined a sect of nomads in the desert—remember?—and were frightening the camels night after night with that colorful boy who was so proud of his ability to interpret dreams. But him we left alone except for the usual requisite means of mammalian congress, changing places as the spirit moved us without disquieting his spirit as we might have done. We were not hungry, as I recall, because—well, who ever had to go hungry there, with so many fervent idolaters chanting in the sands anticipating miracles? We could feed when we needed, sport when we wanted, and sleep our peculiar form of sleep in peace, though I will tell you now that even then I had been wondering about our future.

I did not want to let the boy in Paris go with such impunity, yet every time I thought to make a move toward him he had moved himself already, and stood or sat in some other place, talking with some other person or otherwise hovering out of my range. It happened so often and with such regularity I knew it could not be by accident, but when I sought to outflank him he seemed to vanish altogether, even though I could still see him standing exactly where he had been when he ceased to be there. Do I make sense? I had never in all my years encountered such a lithe magician, and his dance just made me want him more. I could have waited by the gate, I suppose, or forced myself on his attentions, but I enjoy a deft game too. I have never yet been beaten, but that is not because I do not play: I play, I played, and I had found a match at last. He knew the stakes as well as the moves, and seemed to be enjoying his part nonetheless.

By very late in the afternoon we had clearly entered into some sort of endgame. Numerous guests had drifted off already, some with prizes and some with nothing to show for their frittered hours but degeneration. I let a gorgeous harlot pass despite the way she changed my blood's direction, and I permitted conversation with a self-important prelate who was glad to keep his back to the room as long as he could have my face to talk to, so I led him in motion like a sight by which I kept my eye on my prey.

That prey, meanwhile, offered no resistance, made no effort to evade my eyes, and showed himself as unconcerned as if I were just another ordinary guest. At last, in fact, it was he who interrupted and asked my prelate to fetch some favor for him: an unseemly request that should have seemed impertinent, but to which the prelate acceded with such alacrity I could have imagined the Asiatic boy knew something of his fetishes.

Then, when we stood alone, the boy held up one finger and before I caught myself I had followed its direction to his riveting, liquid eyes. "There is one condition," he said as if he spoke my language. And when I did not reply because, in truth, I was speechless before his presumption, he lowered the finger until it pointed toward the woman he had turned to when I first set eyes on him. "This is my sister, whom I vowed to protect when our parents were turned by someone like you. She wants to find them so we must go together. In exchange for me, therefore, you will also have to take her."

Presumption? Audacity! I will not be dictated to, especially by some upstart pipsqueak! I took him in my arms right then, gripped his hair, threw back his head, and sank my teeth as deeply as I have ever done. I meant to feed, I meant to rape, I meant to conquer, I meant to destroy. I did not bite in love but in revenge, in pride, in wrath, in gluttony. My satisfaction was to be his gasping death, my pleasure his ravishment, destruction, eternal servitude. I wanted nothing less than everything from him, and everything is what I meant to take.

When I had fed I flung the body away from me, but Roque, it

just kept flying through the air, exactly on the right trajectory for something of its weight that had been hurled with such force, but never starting what should have been its inevitable descent. Instead, it slowly spun and turned and wafted across the room as if it chose its careful pirouettes, touching nothing and passing every person just as the person turned away, so no one saw its flight but me; and as the body passed beyond the narrow doorway, it had to arch around in order to avoid colliding with the walls.

I felt a deliberate hand grip my elbow. I spun to it still frenzied, frothing in my rage, blood dripping from my face and smeared all over my shirt and hands—and there was the woman the boy had pointed out. I could see she was his sister in the skin and lips and eyes; there was even a similar feline grace. But as sometimes happens between or among siblings, her proportions were just slightly off: texture, color, angle, and curve, everything that was beautiful in him turned horrifying and wrong in her. Surprisingly fast and surprisingly strong, she threw herself on me and actually tried to kiss me, and I could not fend her off. Frantic, in desperation, all but weeping to be rid of her, I locked my teeth around her vein and bit. She stopped as if I'd nailed her brain.

Despite all my long history of love and pleasure with women as well as with men, with the living and the dead, with royalty and commoners, her blood intoxicated me as no blood ever had: I did not like it, not at all. I did not like the way it gushed, I did not like its eager over-ripeness, I did not like the light-headedness that came over me with its infusion, but her grip relaxed and for that I was glad. I pushed her off me and she staggered back, an unhurried smile coming slowly to her face.

Her eye glittered in the orange sunset glow the way I imagine a fly's eye might in my simple human eye were the fly's blown up to the size of mine or to the size of the fly itself, and she started to speak but actually bit the tip of her pale pink tongue instead, to stop herself, I suppose. Then, taking back her lingua franca, she exhaled in a rush as her shoulders sagged forward and her head fell down so that the life-long loosening of skin behind her chin was pressed against the swollen, uplifted, underwired flesh of her lace-draped breasts. She did not stop there, however, but continued to collapse until she sank toward the floor like a burst dirigible folding slowly at its tail and starting a wavering, accelerating descent toward the ground, its thin skin shriveling on its skeleton like the buoyant armor of a fragile knight pierced by an angry god's hot thunderbolt in some jerky black-and-white newsreel of a dozen centuries ago. Flame engulfed the failing craft but nothing and no one moved to break her fall; and as the last bright arc of sun was covered over for us by the turning Earth, as the shimmering clouds' high pastels shifted like bright bruises on the face of heaven, she crumpled altogether to the floor with the distant rippling sound of a well-insulated house of bones coming down.

I do not know how long I stood there, watching as if waiting for her corpse to decompose. I had taken her as I had taken thousands over my course of time, but unlike all the others she did not reawaken. Her eyelids did not flutter, she did not inspire with that reverse rattle I have come to revere: she only lay where she had fallen, dead not only to the world but dead, as well, to me.

Except she was not. By this time the party had well and truly ended. As a last guest under the impatient eyes of mine hostess, I did the only thing that made sense to me at the time. As if she were dead drunk instead of just sort of dead, I heaved the woman over my shoulder and made off with her like booty. Now I skulked; now I ran like a furtive fugitive, sidling down back alleys with the feral cats while I hauled around my not-so-solid sack of flesh. What had she been thinking? What had I been thinking?

When I got her home I laid her body down in the sarcophagus I generally use to curdle people's blood and contemplated what my lust for the boy had wrought. I did not even want this package I was encumbered with: far from it. Instead I was saddled with her. She slumbered not nor slept; but, on the other hand, neither did she decompose. She had escaped the curse of living without encountering the curse of dying.

I felt as if I were dealing with a riddle from the sphinx—what goes on four legs in the morning, what is the sound of one hand, how many angels dance. Like you and me, Roque, she was neither living nor dead, neither one thing nor the other, yet I could not reach her. Though I could not say whether she was aware of her state or not, she had, like us, entered a condition of suspended inanimation. But while I did not really comprehend her sort, I came to think that in her incomplete transition lay the answer to my longer-standing riddle about eternity: where is she? And where then, my fine and succulent immortal, are we?

Finally, I kissed her again, this time on the lips. And then, my fine young immortal friend, I recognized something about her at last. It was in the promise of a smile that seemed to hover just behind her facial mask, some attitude of knowing that blended with contempt.

Do you remember our last night together, Roque, when we flew in tandem over all the capitals on Earth, seeing the world through every dawn? Of course you do. So you remember also that we grew hungry over Hungary and sped on through the night toward Southeast Asia where you found an estimable couple, newly sprung from some wretched serfdom of the times, and plunged down on them far too fast to recognize my alarm that they had babies and were to be considered safe from our predations. You fed and you were drunk with blood, and howled so loudly like some crazed banshee that I thought you'd bring the village's enforcers on the run, so I dragged you away to where we could have a full and proper good-bye.

But before we left I had a look at the sleeping, then bestirring, pair you'd abandoned like leftovers from a too-sumptuous feast, and the lazy look of malevolent curiosity that passed across the woman's mouth was just the look I saw today on the face of the eager sister. The boy and girl I turned today were long-descendants of the couple you enjoyed, I feel certain. My surmise will explain to you what remains of my message.

I told you I kissed the woman but really it was a kiss in form only. I bent down over her immobile form, pinched her nostrils shut, and exhaled into her rubbery mouth. Having realized the nature of the siblings' game I felt disgusted with my own behavior, as if I were going down on one of the old-fashioned erotic shop blow-up dolls, but she responded: her chest expanded as her lungs filled with my breath, as my mouth had filled with her blood, and I thought I felt a murmur in her heart. A souffle au coeur. A heart soufflé. I did it again and I did it again and I did it again until I felt so dizzy the room was spinning in my head, and when I looked up to clear my vision the Asiatic boy was sitting in my big old carved walnut throne with the lions' feet and the serpents' heads for arms, smoking a cigar from my locked humidor. Apparently the exchange was complete.

Now, Roque: since you are intrinsically involved in this dilemma, I am going to involve you in its question, as I said I would. In fact, I am going to turn it over to you.

Instead of leaping on the boy's figgy pudding I bit the woman's throat again and drank again of her distasteful blood, and thereby sent her newly reacquired breath back to from where it came, and consequently, inadvertently, sent him reeling from my home in a cloud of must. He even left his cigar behind, an unkind reminder of what I do not know. Now I am going to send this empty woman's body on to you, quick yet breathless once again, and with it the key to the disappearance and re-appearance, dead or alive or both or neither, of my quaint late acquaintance, the Asiatic boy. A crimson coffin will arrive at your door in the next few weeks on the back of a wagon drawn by a pair of black horses. I know it's old-fashioned and melodramatic, but you know how well that suits my style.

But also, perhaps, I send to you the key to our—perhaps—not inevitably nonexistent future. Can your young heart begin to contemplate the ramifications of the task with which I present you? I set eternity before you. Again.

When you have come to whatever conclusion satisfies your mind, return her to me and I will give you in my turn what may be my last assignment on this Earth: to take from me what once I took from you.

Meanwhile, take your time, my boy, for that is the commodity we have in—almost—boundless plenty.

Your devoted maker,

Guy

The Idiom of Orchids
Camille Thomas

In the marsh pink orchid's faces
With their coy and dainty graces
Lure us to their hiding places—
Laugh, O murmuring Spring!

—Sarah Foster Davis, Summer Song

If Dilys hadn't thrown such a tantrum at the news office this afternoon, tearing into our newbie columnist with the fury of Echidna, the winged she viper, I wouldn't be sitting here at Grace's right now ogling the raven-haired beauty, the woman sitting next to the window with a dainty dimple on her chin and a Sphinx-like smile on her face. After orchestrating peace talks between my two co-workers, I had been determined to pamper myself, so, on the way home, I slipped into Grace's, my third space, to sneak a vanilla-pumpkin spice latte and savour a brief interlude of sanity.

There's nobody waiting up for me tonight. I am a free agent. This morning, I had driven my husband Rob from our stone duplex, tucked away just beyond the Animal Welfare Station on Waller Mill Road in Williamsburg, to the airport in Richmond, a one-hour drive away. He is spending a few days in New York on a business trip. "Cutting corporate fat at headquarters" was all he'd mumbled when I'd asked him about his mission. Dutifully, I had kissed him goodbye and driven straight to work, getting there fourteen minutes late.

Lifting the pricey latte to my lips, I have a moment worthy of Proust: I inhale the spices—nutmeg, ginger and cinnamon—and am enveloped in a lost age of innocence where the sole object of my desire was an extra slice of pumpkin pie at Thanksgiving. I sigh in contentment and discreetly angle my chair, so that I can drink in the features of the woman I have started to covet.

She sits two tables away, absent-mindedly clinking a teaspoon in her Chai tea latte. She's gazing at an oil painting of the so-called slipper orchid—Paphiopedilum. Asian—possibly Chinese—she is to me a veritable cornucopia of delight: her ebony hair is scraped back from her face and tied in a cheeky pony-tail; her skin, creamy and translucent, shimmers as the fall sunshine bathes her face in autumnal light. She sports ridiculously long, spidery eyelashes whose ends curl up coyly. I sip my latte and try to catch her eye. When she turns and looks over at me, her chestnut eyes flicker—twin fireflies concealing themselves deep within the confines of a mysterious, unexplored garden. I start to fantasize. How would she react if I walked up to her right now, laid my hand on her shoulder, asking, "Will you come home with me?" She returns my gaze, her eyes hooded. This is ridiculous, I chide myself. Is she really thinking what I'm thinking?

Unsettled, I shift my weight around on the mock-Chippendale chair. Has she parsed the fine signals of my face? Is my desire etched, for all to see, on the surface of my skin? Has she perhaps rejected me already? I avoid her gaze and redirect my attention to the oil painting of the speckled Venus slipper, which hangs opposite the seamless, metal counter where a sweaty barista froths up a frappuccino. The hum of the appliance reverberates through the room. Paphiopedilum combines the word Paphos, an island in Greece that houses a temple devoted to Aphrodite—a goddess the Romans renamed Venus - with the word pedilon meaning "little shoe." I remember Cate telling me the story of how this orchid came to be named. Carl von Linné, the 18th century Swedish botanist baptized it. Its slipper-like shape made him think of an old Roman legend concerning Venus. One day, the goddess of love and beauty was out hunting with Adonis when they were caught in a thunderstorm. They took shelter and made love until the storm had passed, but in the course of their love-making, Venus lost her slipper. A mortal stumbled upon it, but before he could pick it up, it was transformed into a flower. The central slipper-like petal, the labellum or lip, of Paphiopedilum is golden, just like the legendary footwear mislaid by the goddess. I feel as if I have mislaid something precious too. My thoughts inevitably course back to Cate. "Orchids are like people, Helen. They need to be touched and talked to."

Oh, Cate, why did you leave me? To name something is to control it. I wish I could name the feelings Cate conjured up. Spectral glimmers, as if from some deserted campfire deep within me ignite, stirring yet more memories to life. I stir my latte, synching my movements with the rhythms of the Asian woman. The vanilla aroma wafts up and stirs yet more memories. The time Cate and I had hand-pollinated dozens of orchids in an evening. We had whispered sweet nothings into the racemose inflorencenses of every single one of her blooms. I watch the steam from my latte swirl up. The Chai drinker looks at me curiously. Racemose inflorencenses—orchid blossoms—the word has a sultry quality to it, one that promises hours spent basking in tropical sunlight followed by nights lightly brushing up against shimmering filaments of caladenia, calanthe and cheirostylis - once the code has been cracked, the Greek-and-Latin orchid words translate into labyrinthine English equivalents that have meanings both explicit and erotic. There is talk of Adam and Eve, Babes-in-a-Cradle, Black-Tongued orchids ... Do orchids have a gender? I had once asked Cate this question. She had laughed "Don't talk gender, talk sex. Orchid comes from the Greek word, 'orchis', meaning testicle. But orchids are as spiritual as they are corporeal. And have you ever seen a flower more feminine-looking? Orchids are just as ambivalent about their sexuality as us."

The Asian woman bends down briefly to retrieve a cell phone from her purse. "Nihao—ni zài gan shén ma?" Who is it that she's talking to? A boyfriend? A girlfriend? It's none of my business, I know. I watch her hold the cell phone delicately to her ear, hypnotized by the intricate counterpoint of her intonation. Is she talking Mandarin or Cantonese? I have read somewhere that there are twelve varieties of spoken Chinese. Would we ever find a common tongue? I experience a flutter of doubt. I sigh and consider Paphiopedilum once again—its curves are delicate. Just like Cate's... I scoop up a teaspoon of froth and remember my initiation into the idiom of orchids.

Despite my lack of knowledge of all things antiquarian, I got a job, last year, working half-days at "Bookosphere," a second hand bookshop near the Waller Inn Mill in Williamburg's college district. My task was to help Bill, a friend of Rob's, run his store. I was due to start work at the newspaper in the fall, but, before then, two long months stretched ahead of me. Bill's offer of a part-time job was like an answer to a prayer. We got on well and by the end of August, I had learned some of the niceties of the second-hand book business. "Yuh d'vlop an instinct furrit." Bill was apt to say, not bothering to rein in his slurred enunciation for me, his humble assistant. His pitch to wannabe customers, on the other hand, was delivered in pristine vowels and well-formed consonants. No matter how much he had drunk, he was always mentally prepared for that one day when someone might wander in looking for his Holy Grail—a rare edition of Ben Franklin's almanac which he kept together with a bottle of whiskey under lock and key in a secure glass cabinet in the back chamber. But what he said was true - I had learned how to differentiate those customers prepared to buy something from those who just wished to browse. The latter entered the shop merely to run their hands over the dusty spines of the leather-bound books housed on our creaking shelves, or to inhale the musty clouds of erudition that circulated languidly in the micro-climate of the six-roomed basement. It was my last day at the Bookosphere before starting up at the newspaper. Bill's latest bargain from the thrift shop—an antediluvian air-conditioner—spun the air around in melancholy eddies. Dressed in just a thin T-shirt and cotton slacks, I was shivering with cold. Misreading my body language, Bill assumed I felt sad about leaving. "Chill out! Yuh gotta learn to relax, gal." He opened a bottle of champagne with a flourish. "Here, have a drop of the good stuff!" He filled a glass flute and handed it to me, then disappeared into the back chamber to brood on his Holy Grail and drain yet another bottle of whiskey.

Up until then, I had resisted all of Bill's inducements to make me into a co-dependent, but now I succumbed. After all, it was my last day. What harm could it do? After downing the first, I drank a second, feeling deliciously warmed-up and woozy. And that's when it came to pass—my metamorphosis.

I hadn't noticed her enter. A waft of dusky perfume heralded her presence. Before even catching sight of her, her scent filled my nostrils. I replaced the champagne flute onto the desk with a drunkard's exaggerated care, and turned around sharply... only to stumble straight into the arms of a slender woman with silky dark brown hair and sparkling, chestnut eyes. "Whoah—easy there" she cried, grasping hold of my shoulders. Her fingers were now pressed against my bare arms, and her touch made tiny hairs all over my body tremble into life. "Sorry, I didn't mean to scare you. But do you happen to know anything at all about orchids? I'm Cate, by the way." She released her grip and I swallowed nervously. "Hi, Cate. I'm Helen." I can't remember exactly what she said next. Her words cascaded around me and I felt as if I had been plucked into a fourth dimension. Maybe she said something like" I'm interested in ornamental orchids. cattleya aclandiae, for instance. Maybe you know the one—it has a bilaterally symmetrical purple and white flowers—like royal robes. It's zygomorphic—it has three petal-like sepals and two normal petals dangling deliciously around the labellum." OK—maybe she hadn't actually said—dangling deliciously. But she had nudged closer to me as I took down the orchid volumes from the shelves in our horticultural section, a remote area of the shop that was hidden away in a secluded recess, and laid them on a small table for her inspection. Bill's store was a veritable Pandora's box of arcane lore, and we had a surprisingly large number of orchid books—The Orchid Thief, Ghost Orchid and Other Tales from the Swamp, Orchidelerium... I sat down at the table and began to leaf my way through the pile, hoping to find something that would pique her interest. I read aloud from the introduction of a volume entitled Orchids—Myths and Mysteries: "Orchids serve no medicinal or nutritional purpose. They are treasured purely for their beauty, and as Keats said, 'Beauty is Truth, and Truth, Beauty -that is all ye know on earth, and all ye need to know.'" Cate gazed at me, her chestnut eyes, luminous in the gloom and I couldn't help blinking. My soul, naked and fragile as a snowflake, still hovered in the frigid air of winter, but sensed that the sun's rays were turning vernal.

"Orchids do strange things to you" she said with a Mona-Lisa smile. She stretched out her hand to stroke the glossy image of a vanilla orchid and as she did so, her hand brushed lightly against my bare arm. I shivered involuntarily.

"Vanilla is thought to be an aphrodisiac, you know."

I swallowed and tore my eyes away from her damask lips, trying to concentrate on the brittle pages of the volume heavy between my hands.

Enthusiastically, Cate pounced on yet another illustration, pointing out stigmas and anthers, raving about exotic sub-species and eulogizing something called Paphiopedilum. When she pronounced this word,—paff-eeo-peddy-lum—her lips fluttered like a butterfly. I listened entranced. "They are also called Venus slippers—their lower two sepals are fused—you know, the lips have become as one." I found myself suddenly hypnotised by her black V-necked T-shirt—she always wore black, I found out later. Drawn to the murky cleft between her candid breasts I felt like a deer caught in the headlights of a sleek convertible that was doing 100 in a 30 mile zone. I breathed in her fragrance and fantasized that she was about to kiss me. How would I feel if she pressed her breasts tightly up against mine?

"O.K., I'll take Myths and Mysteries. Fifteen dollars? Here you are."

Was she talking to me? She peeled a few bills out of her wallet and thrust them toward me. Wordlessly, I plucked them out of her hand.

"Would you like a coffee? After work? Do you know Grace's?"

"Sure," I murmured, as if in a trance.

"What time?"

"Six is good. Or six ish. I get off at six," I mumbled.

"Six ish. See you then."

I finished my latte and glanced down at my watch...again. It was a quarter to seven. I glanced out the plate glass window, hoping to catch her running down the street or coming out of a cab. Storm clouds were gathering outside and the first drops were coming down. Humiliated and convinced that I had deluded myself into believing in an apparition, I was just about to get up and leave when I smelled a whiff of something dusky that seemed borderline familiar. I looked up ... she was there, looking down at me, soft tendrils of burnished chestnut hair framing her dark, sparkling eyes, a mischievous grin playing around her slightly parted lips, painted a seductive shade of pale magenta.

"Hi there. Sorry I'm late.

"Cate?, I had just about given up on you."

"Uhm, sorry about that.... Can I get you a latte to make up?" She glanced up at the board but already seemed to know the menu.

"Mmm... the Hot Aztec Chilli Chocolate sounds good. Ideal in weather like this. Would you like one too?"

I started to demur and make my exit, but she was already up and ordering for two.

Cate returned with two steaming mugs. With an air of ceremony, she placed the twin vessels carefully on the table, but then she plopped down casually onto the chair opposite mine. This combination of gravitas and levity was her hallmark, as I was later to discover.

"I've been reading the new Orchid book and there's some beautiful color plates in here."

She drew out the oversized book from her bag, brushed off the table with some napkins and placed the book carefully down on the table, opening it from the center. Let me show you one of my favorites. An endangered species native to North America. Sabatia stellaris—or the humble Marsh Pink. Grows in the salt marshes of New England. Where you come from, judging from your accent." She flipped a page and pointed out a delicate pink bloom. "Looks as if it's blushing, doesn't it? Modest, unassuming, yet utterly charming." She gazed at me thoughtfully, twisting a tendril of hair that had fallen at an angle across her face, intricately between her fingers. You know what? This flower reminds me of you."

Blushing, I quickly turned over the page. We spent the following hour, sipping hot chocolate, leafing through the book and basking in the magical mysteries of orchids, while outside the storm clouds that had been gathering, were slowly dispelling. By the time the rain had finally stopped, my soul had melted too. Cate touched my wrist .

"So, Helen, would you like to see a Marsh Pink in the flesh, so to say? I have a few specimens at home if you're curious...

I nodded dumbly, feeling a delicious rush of blood invade the deep layers of my skin.

"Let's go." Cate said. I followed her into a cab.

It was still light when we arrived at her place. She drew down all the blinds and we were plunged into darkness, I was dimly aware of ghostly forms leaning over into the room from shelves, counters and table tops. A thick, intoxicating perfume hung in the air.

"It's a bit overwhelming at first but you get used to it."

Cate flung her purse and her keys onto a side-table and grasping my hands, drew me into her bedroom. She threw a switch, and an array of orchids appeared to be glowing pink on a table near her bed, although the rest of the room was still dark.

"Those are the ones, are they?" I asked, following Cate to the side of her bed to take a closer look.

"Yes, they're Marsh Pinks. See, they each grow on a single stalk"

Cate bent over one of the flowers, probing the five soft pink petals with her finger. In the center of flower, a bright, yellow star streaked in red and outlined in white shone forth.

"Would you like to touch?" Cate was enthusiastic... "You'll

never believe how soft they feel. Like a butterfly kiss."

I reached out my hand and stroked one of the petals. It was like fairy velvet. Cate was waiting for my reaction. I hesitated, knowing that I once I crossed this Rubicon of desire, there would be no gong back.

"So what do you think, Helen?"

I turned my head away from her for a moment. The bedroom was dark and full of mystery. Illuminated by the spotlight, the orchids shimmered gem-like below my hand, I looked back at Cate, stroking the orchid once more with my index finger.

"Hard to say, Cate." I smiled. "You see, I have no basis for comparison. I've never been kissed by a butterfly."

Cate bent towards me, her butterfly-lips brushing up against mine.

"I'll light a few candles just for atmosphere," she joked as she stripped off her jeans and T-shirt. Dressed just in her bra and panties she slid a lighter out of her discarded jeans and lit three candles in a Kokopelli candleholder. I noticed she had a small scar on her abdomen, a mark that heightened the beauty of her body like a bindi. Then she approached me, and taking my hands once again in hers, drew me down onto the bed and began to disrobe me.

"Has any man ever told you how beautiful you are?" she murmured, sniffing the scent of my skin and tracing petroglyphs on my body with her long, slender fingers. The whole night long, we enjoyed the exotic, yet familiar geography of each other's bodies, reveling in our sticky lusciousness. I had come home.

Days, no it must have been weeks later, her daughter was at a sleepover, and her husband was away for the weekend. Mine was too. We had a don't ask don't tell policy when it came to weekends apart. Cate and her husband did too.

We wriggled beneath swirling silken sheets on her bed; I asked her how she had known.

"Known what?" Cate propped herself up beside me on the bed, an amused look on her face, tendrils of corkscrew curls bouncing like tiny springs in front of her naked pink breasts.

"You know. How did you know I would come home with you?

Cate looked at me wryly. "Come on now, Helen. Every woman wants to come home." As she bent her head, her curls grazed the tender skin on my breasts.

Her mysterious answer didn't satisfy me. Like a dog with a bone, I wasn't going to let it go. Although my whole body tingled with anticipation, I was determined to know her secret. I sat up.

"But I was straight till I met you. I had never even so much as looked at a woman like that before, let alone touched one. And you...You've made me question everything. How did you know?"

"I didn't know," she said, raising an eyebrow.

"But, weren't you scared of... rejection?"

Cate picked up her iPod, lay back again on her pillow and flicked through some albums.

The surfaces in her bedroom were full, laden with delicate pink, white, purple and orange Orchidaceae—in addition to learning about Sappho's concept of ecstasy, with Cate as my guide, I had also learned a lot of botanical nomenclature.

Cate, apparently having found what she was looking for, depressed the central button on her ipod. Strains of a melody seeped into the bedroom through the loudspeakers. The rich vocals were being sung by a woman with a brooding, romantic voice.

"Are you breathing, What I'm breathing, Are your wishes the same as mine.... My hands tremble... if I'm alone in this I don't think I can face the consequences...."

I sank back into the pillows, soaking up the poetry like a sponge. "Who is this?" I wondered.

Cate smiled, "k. d. lang... from an album called Invincible Summer." Kate turned toward me.

" Everyone's afraid of rejection, Helen. There is no secret. But if you don't try, you're dead anyway."

She was right, I guess. But, somehow, I'm sure she had known.

I certainly, however, didn't feel the urge to unweave her spell and analyse the language she had used to seduce me, any more than I would have wished to deconstruct a fragment of Sappho's poetry.

"Orchids make you see the world differently. They help you draw exotic nutrients out the soil." Cate had employed the language of orchids—a weapon of splendid yet deceptive stillness—gently as an instrument of seduction, a tool of enticement. Nothing is as static as an orchid, or as ecstatic. I steal a look at Madame Butterfly, but it is Cate's name that echoes in my heart. Cate—how I miss you. Our time together was a mere three months span. Three chrysalis months in which I completed my metamorphosis. You awakened a lode of longing within me. You nourished me with music, poetry... and orchids. You made me feel beautiful in a new way. You are my soul mate. You always will be. Eight months ago, you left, moving to California with your husband and daughter, taking your orchids with you. One day I know we will meet again and it will be like coming home. But you left me two things. The first, "Invincible Summer," the k.d. lang album. A farewell gift. "Au milieu d'hiver, j'ai découvert en moi un invincible été.—In the midst of winter, I discovered within myself an invincible summer. "I listened to the songs from the album that bore the Camus quote every day for at least six months after you left. They helped me come to terms with the new entity I had become. Now I relish feeling the way I do. The woman sitting two tables away from me smiles at me, her face glowing. She is like an orchid unfolding its petals in the sun. My heart thumps wildly against my ribcage. I haven't felt this alive for months. "Are you thinking what I'm thinking? Does your pulse quicken like mine?" The melody and lyrics of the song Cate played for me over and over again fast-forward through my mind. But Madame Butterfly has turned away from me, the glass containing her Chai latte almost empty. Am I alone in this? I hope not. But even if I am, there is an invincible summer within me now. What do I have to lose? The second thing you gave me, Cate, is a new language, the idiom of orchids.

I pick up my half-finished pumpkin latte and get up. I walk over to the Chinese woman, touch her shoulder lightly and sit down on a vacant chair next to her just as she is about to get up and leave. "Hi, I'm Helen," I say. "Please don't go yet. I couldn't help noticing you were looking at the picture of that Paphiopedilum over there." I point to the oil painting and enunciate each syllable of the orchid's divine name religiously—paff-eeo-peddy-lum, feeling my lips flutter in synch with my heart. One day I'll develop my own language, my own personal patois, but for now the idiom of orchids will do. I look into her chestnut eyes. Coy fireflies dart for cover behind her eyelashes. I screw up my courage and ask my question: "Would you like to know about orchids?"

Mother Knows Best

Charles Bright

"Pastor Transgressel says, 'turn or burn!'"

His mother was furious when he told her he would take his chances not being heterosexual. She said she didn't know the difference between homo-sexual or bi-sexual and to her and the rest of the family they were all the same and equally unacceptable. Standing alongside his hospital bed with his mother were his two older sisters and his older brother. His mother sneered at him each time she spoke.

"Who else have you told about this?"

"My doctor."

"What? Why? How can I face him again? Now I'll need to find a new doctor!"

His sisters and his brother chimed in,

"SO WILL WE!"

"Mom, he prescribes the treatment that controls my illness. And besides, the law says he can't tell anyone about my diagnosis."

His mother sneered again,

"Your lifestyle should be against the law."

His oldest sister interjected,

"It is."

Hives sprouted on his skin. It happened every time he spoke to his family.

"No, it isn't. Not in this state."

His oldest sister persisted,

"God's laws apply to ALL states. It is illegal under God's laws. Pastor Transgressel says so."

"Is that the same Pastor Transgressel you wanted me to go see so he could pray me straight?"

His oldest sister frowned and shook her head, but said nothing more. His mother continued.

"Well anyway, I forbid you from telling anyone else about your so-called illness."

"So called?"

"Yes, how do we know you aren't doing this for attention?"

"At my age? I don't do things for attention. And as for telling anyone, I can tell anyone I choose."

"And you'll ruin the family more than you already have, if that's possible. I cannot believe you told my doctor."

"He's my doctor too. And how else am I going to get my prescriptions?"

His mother quickly changed the subject.

"I just don't understand this liking boys thing."

"I like men, Mom. Not boys."

"It's not too late to change, dear, and start liking girls."

"Mom, I already like girls, but I also like guys. And anyway, I don't like girls, I like women."

"Well you obviously got sick because you chose to lead this sinful homosexual lifestyle in the first place. It's God's punishment. You'll see."

His strength flowed out of him. His heart sank. He looked into his mother's eyes, which were green like his.

"Mom, do you have any idea how much it hurts me to hear you say things like that? That isn't what I need from you right now."

"Well, I don't know what else you expect me to say. It's a sin against the Lord and if you had listened to me, you wouldn't have ended up like this. Haven't I always told you children that Mother knows best?"

Pastor Transgressel says it's just a phase anyway, this homosexual thing. You'll see. Remember when our cousin Tommy thought he was a tree for a while? He came around, eventually, with medications."

"I'm 45 years old. Trust me, it isn't a phase. And I'm bi, not homosexual. And I'm perfectly normal, not physically healthy, but psychologically normal. God made me this way. It wasn't my choice, it was his."

With a collective gasp, his mother, his two sisters, and his brother quickly clapped their hands over their ears. From his bed he stared at the four of them standing with their hands over their ears. He said nothing. He waited patiently for them to remove their hands from their ears. When his mother, his sisters, and his brother finally removed their hands from their ears the conversation continued between he, his mother, and his oldest sister. The two middles said nothing. As usual they stared at the ceiling looking angry and confused. His mother spoke.

"You said you had something to tell us."

His oldest sister cut in immediately.

"Yeah, what is it, hurry up. My husband and my kids are waiting for me to come home and make supper."

"My condition is far worse than I expected."

The two middles remained silent. The middle sister picked her nose.

His mother smirked,

"So?"

"So? I have three days to live."

No one spoke. Instead, his oldest sister took his mother's hand who took his middle sister's hand who removed her other hand from her nose and took his brother's hand. With all his own remaining energy he lifted his right hand from the bed and reached for his brother's hand, but his brother took hold of his oldest sister's hand, completing the circle without him. At once his oldest sister closed her eyes. She began to moan. She started shrieking wildly. She shrieked so wildly that people passing in the hall stopped to see what the excitement was in his room. His oldest sister replaced her shrieking with quieter chanting, "Oh sweet lord in heaven save my brother from his awful affliction! Send away his demon! Take away his tremendous agony! Make him whole, lord! Heal him from this horrible disease!" The rest of the family shouted, "Amen!" He was stunned to see his family praying for him to recover from his crippling lethal illness. He was overwhelmed by their sudden compassion and expression of deep meaningful love. He believed in God and believed that God moved in mysterious ways. His family's sudden devotion to his well-being was itself nothing short of a miracle. He felt strength return to his legs. His heart quickened. He felt hope. He laid his head back onto the soft pillow and closed his eyes, letting his family take him into their loving arms and hearts. For a moment all of his pain went away. He focused his attention on his oldest sister chanting and occasionally hooting over him. He decided that if this was what she had to do to help him get well, then more power to her. At this point, he had nothing else to lose. When he opened his eyes his oldest sister was hopping on one foot. Her head rolled back. Her eyes rolled up into her head and her tongue hung grotesquely over her lower lip. The room grew strangely cold, but she persisted in her rituals. Once again she began to shriek, but this time more wildly and loudly than ever,

"AND WITH THAT OH LORD, WE PRAY TO YOU TO HEAL MY BROTHER, HEAL HIM NOW, HEAL HIM FROM HIS HOMOSEXUALITY!"

The rest of the family shouted, "AMEN!"

He died alone three hours later.

"... Leave a Light On For Ya"

Gretchen Turner

Between the onslaught of snow and my gas tank that had been squeaking by on E for the past 39 miles, I knew it was time to pack it in for the night. My little skyblue Rabbit, with recent smirks of rust making cameo appearances along tire rims, had passed a friendly big, blue Service Area sign only one or two miles back (what luck!), but the highway sign had included the not-so-friendly information that the next pitstop/place-to-park-for-the-night lay another 48 miles ahead along the dark, snow-obscured, oil-slicked asphalt (hmm, must've missed that part in my opportunistic, selfinterest-motivated memory). The nearer service area itself was still visible from where my car tooled along. Only it wasn't welcomely situated in front of me, to the immediate east, inviting my right-blinker-activated automobile onto its ramp. It was now receding like a squirrel into the distance after having just stolen its nutmeal for the evening and needing to tear off to perch itself way up in a tree out of reach of other hungry, needy rodents. Guess I was a rodent availing myself too late the Area's Services. The last nut had already fallen from its limbs and been nabbed by more alert, paying-attention squirrels. I maintained my Volkswagen motor's 56 mile-per-hour hum and asked the gods of nature to smile amiably on me until I had clocked another 48 miles on my odometer. ("Please don't let this snow squall mar my vision to the sorry point where a rabbit and a girl go careening into a six foot ravine.") I also sent some prayerful back up to the gods of human blunder. ("Please don't draw a bright line under my automotive negligence by actually letting me run right out of gas here in the middle of nowhere! [well, somewhere but all the road signs had been coated with enough new white-out to effectively render every town an anonymous location on the map]. Amen.")

My attention was certainly not being paid to necessities-of-the-moment or I certainly wouldn't have missed my last-chance-in-48-miles to refuel and pitch tent...or park hood as the case may be. My attention was a bur on the fresh cotton sock of fantasy! I was guilty-as-charged! (down goes gavel in mind, innerjudge decrees: "I accuse me of being totally, unrehabilitatably in love!") lost in the reverie of the woman I had met less than twenty four hours ago. Only I hadn't actually met her. Well, sort of I had. At least I had while I slept. And, whoa!, the sensations imprinted on my body after that full night of dream-drenched sleep were sending 'signals through me that my mouth and head were having a hard time trying to interpret today' (S. B.). I had met the woman of my dreams. Well of course I had if it was a woman with whom I shared company and my dream gave us life. But I mean she was the one I had always dreamed of meeting, knowing, loving. The one who would make me swear the rest of my life to...in sickness or health...in life or death. She was the one waiting for me, 'like words in a pen' (A. R.)

And I had just spent the night with her. In a deep way. Unfortunately, in a deep sleep sort of way.

But the memory of her was as fresh, as real as the urge to hurl it prompted in my knotted and terribly overwrought stomach. It's not that the thought of her makes me sick. Not even close. It was the thought that I'd never see her again, that she was confined within the deceptive barbed wire walls of my over-too-soon dream. I was now driving along, within a snowglobed, woodland-besandwitched interstate, semi-sick, lovesick over a woman whom I would never meet again (Right? Dreams can't possibly be premonitions??) yet would have vowed to meet tonight.

I'd had dreams before, conjuring idealized women, fusing features from faces of past lovers. And nostalgia for sandpaper kisses, from those gorgeous gentleman who turned one night stands into one night horizontals, multi-month romances or long-term relationships. But She was an entirely new creation. She was a goddess standing apart from any pantheon to which I'd ever thought I was paying homage. She was a whole new reason to believe. She was a promise: That a feeling this strong could exist, that it did exist and that I had already become acquainted with its source. Somehow she had always been alive in me and last night She finally made her appearance known. And now I couldn't erase the vision of her as she packed herself into my doggie-bag-waking-life to nourish me after-the-fact.

Yes, the image imprinted across my mind's-eyesight nourished me but moreso, it bothered and ate away into cockpit of my thoughts; I couldn't think of anything else. Just her. There we were last night, safe in the refuge of my dreamworld, in the skies spreading timelessly under closed eyes. Yet here I am, now, unable to shake myself from the craving to see and touch her again, to confirm her reality…and what can I do but gnash my teeth against a cardboard coffee cup rim whose fluids taste like milk to one expecting another succulent sip of freshly squeezed orange juice. She wrung out all other feelings in my chest like an Indian-burned towel twisted so tightly that not one more drop of wetness could be spared. I had nothing left to my feelings but the specter of what I wanted to feel for the rest of my life, yet I didn't even have a name to go with the womanfantasy whose post-facto hold over me had just made my little Rabbit-that-could whiz by the service station my gas tank sorely needed to visit. So I grievously placed the Mobilmart, (ridiculous-psychological-transference-receptacle) coffee cup back in the holder beneath the sound of Mr. Mister, who uncannily crooned "Broken Wings" from the radio within the cavity of my dashboard.

What tantalized me immensely was not even so much that I got to connect my body with this strawberry haired goddess and now longed to recreate such sensual perfection. Yes, our lips briefly met and her cocooning arms drew me in with a size of desire matching my own, but it was the recollection of the expression in those eyes that had me noticing nothing else now. (Yikes, just crossed the dotted road line and elicited a "beep beeeep" from car to immediate rear. Better at least try to notice fact of my driving just a little bit!)

It was the enamored and enamoring clutch of her life to mine, not just her body to mine, conveyed in the way her earthy deep eyes looked at me, that had me driving in a haze now, line between reality and fantasy so effectively blurred. And how strange to be able to recall now a scent exclusive to a dream (like a scratch-and-sniff: scratch against doors of memory and inhale intoxicating singular fragrance) or even to experience such a distinctly seductive fragrance within the mostly visual framework of nocturnal imaginings. But yes, did She ever come with an astonishingly amazing smell! For a nose to remember this exquisite eau-de-skin is for this suitor to never forget. To miss it in a way that only lovers separated in war can understand. A uniquely arousing hint of eternal gardens where only True Love sows Its aromatic beauty. Like every rose and cupcake and human sweetness joined hands and paraded their talent across the globe of my inbreaths, I now felt her through my pores and needed to eat of her cupcake, to prick my finger on thorns of the rose I was valorized to remember yet seemingly condemned to never pluck.

I could hardly see the darkness in front of me; everything was becoming pitched with the effect of frenzied snowflakes falling in furious sheaves. And my gas tank was beginning to pound fists in objection, or, rather, sputter a Rabbit's steady highway pace, due to my conscious ignorance of its drum-empty belly. I would have to pull over to the side of the road and hope miracles were on call tonight and they'd find my broken car. Could miracles fix a dream broken down the middle, too?

But what do you know?! Wouldn't a propitious Red Roof Inn have 'left a light on for me' just as I was deciding on where to best temporarily junk my automobile and me for the remainder of the blizzard swept, gasoline-challenged night. I've always had a quaint sort of love affair with roadside motels, but this one couldn't have been any more opportunely road sided, like a diamond ring in the rough of the night. I was ready to 'settle down and started a family with it' (S. B.)! This time my right-blinker was flipped on in time as I caught sight of Saving Grace Red Roof before it was too late to pull off at the next exit and enter its drive-up parking lot. I opted to forego a desultory search for a gas station within reasonable miles from the exit. The snow left no room for autonomous human will. Plus, I only wanted to lay my head down just like I had the previous night, on a different pillow but in the hope that I could elicit that same sensation of lifelong dedication I had found and come to believe in thanks to the appearance of my lightauburn-locked, softly-freckled, supple-bodied, eternal-eyed, heaven-scented Dreamwoman. I was ready, with all my heart, to create a monogamous commitment with my slumber. If this woman were not a prophetic outcome ofTrue-Love-longing, wishful thinking, and she existed only in my heart-governed dreams, then I would learn to fall in love with bedtime. Every night…or anytime I couldn't keep my car on the road or my coffee in hand because it was She I needed to fill me up and provide my life's direction.

I parked my struggling dusty Rabbit on the gravel fronting an array of red, numbered doors held together under one giant, Red tiled Roof. The check-in desk was flush right so I had to walk a good number of paces, catching snow in the mitt of my face like a Major League catcher who doesn't drop a single ball. The flakes threw strikes every time: eye,

lips, cheek, other eye…a flurry of perfect wind-ups and follow-throughs. I figured I'd cut the engine of my hobbling Rabbit then just deal with the gas situation in the morning. If the car didn't start, it was an infinitesimal price to pay if I could meet and Be With my Dreamwoman tonight. If I could walk down the aisle of the rest of my life in just another encounter with Her.

I fell into the warm lighting of the check-in room, a soft maroon, cottonball-fluffy carpeted interior with candleholders flickering their prizes on four walls under important-looking portraits of _____ (maybe forefounders of Red Roof Enterprises??). The woman behind the desk brightened her already affable demeanor and put Mystical Gems and Crystals down on the surface in front of her to resume reading once she had learned my name and given me a home for the night. I shuffled slushed boots up to greet her.

Typically loquacious, I honored my predilection and began explaining the unfortunate situation. I began with just the mundane haplessness of my fuel-neglected Volkswagen coupled with snow cancellation of onward automotive pursuits. But the understanding, almost motherly, trusting look glinting from her jade-mottled irises somehow reached right into the soothsaying voice of my heart. The next thing I knew she had gently reached over the counter with a "there, there honey" arm around my shoulder. And I couldn't be sure but the moment she touched me, it seemed every candle perked its glow and send a ripple of "We'll take care of you" thorough the pleasantly cozy room and through the snow-soaked sleeves of my jacket. Right into the place in me that needed to hear it—no, feel it most. I hadn't heard anything, but the presence of this saviorinthenight-like woman at Red Roof check in desk somehow had let me feel—no, hear in my soul, without overt words, that I was Meant To Be here right at this time. I couldn't possibly tuck my feelings into words, but the language that enflamed those candles, reinforced by the solacing arm of this stranger—no, instant friend I've known all my life in an inexpressible way—around my dejected, tired body, couldn't have spoken more clearly. I felt like I'd come Home and the lit fireplace under one of those impressive gold, fancyframed portraits, seemed to understand just how warm I felt inside.

The friendly, twinkly-eyed woman exchanged one last smile with me and placed in my hand a copper key attached to a forest green diamond shaped plastic key chain. I dunked my head to look at the room number etched into the plastic plate and to learn which direction I needed to turn after departing back through the front door I'd come though (rooms 1-25 up the stairs to the immediate left, rooms 25-50 on ground floor to the right). My heart did a little leap as "24" smiled up at me from my hand. Twenty four has always been my lucky number—but it is so much more than a lucky number. It is like a guardian angel in numeral form.

I clumped up the row of red carpeted (thrifty delight! astroturfed) stairs and made my way toward the second to last room on the right. (Hmmm, that's funny, a lamp's light already seemed to be coming from that window. Maybe, this quaint motel is extra-

hospitable and really drives home their slogan that promises to "leave a light on for ya." How sweet, I thought.) A few footfalls more and now a tremor of nerves, that really had

no right to be in my nervous system's domain, had been awakened in me: that was definitely movement coming from room 24, the second to last window on the right. Before I could put my key in the lock, the redpainted door opened slowly, and before my eyes could make out the sight standing calmingly in front of me, my nostrils had been greeted with the exquisite scent that I could never forget. Parading her sweetness across the globe of my disbelieving eyes, this strawberry haired, befreckled goddess, with a childlike, knowing smile, spoke and my tongue began to taste the salt from tears now falling like raindrops upon the roof of my top lip... "I sure hope you like roses and cupcakes."

Dragon's Daughter

Cecilia Tan

This is a story that began in ancient times, so it is hard to know where to begin the telling. Perhaps at the beginning of the end, although even the end is a beginning, just as the end of the night is the start of the day, and the end of the day the start of the night.

Let us start then with sunset, with summer heat shimmering on the streets poured with copper light, as the fire eye of sun burned away a late-day thundercloud. Jin Jin stood in the window staring into the street, one hand holding the other against her fine silk dress. I start the tale here because it was the first time I saw her, placid and still like a statue brought from some dynastic museum and installed there as decoration for the restaurant. Which, in a way, I suppose was true.

I was rushing up the stairs, all sneakers and blue jeans, while Skinny Dou cursed in Cantonese and English from the bottom of the steps to hurry myself up. Imagine me, a bundle of sweaty energy bursting into that room, where the window burned with gold and she stood in cool silhouette, like an empress. The new world and the old colliding, my questions piled one atop the other: who was she, would I find clothes up here, why would no one explain anything to me, ever. Maybe Uncle Charlie would change his mind about this job. My mind was so busy, but my body went suddenly still when faced with her image and one last question: why did she stare out the window so, and for what or whom did she look?

And then the moment broke and she came toward me, speaking accented but understandable Mandarin. I could understand her! She said hello, asked if I was lost. I said hello back, but then couldn't find any more words. This is the ignominy of the American educational system: that to speak the tongue of my ancestors I had to fight to be enrolled in a special college class and trudge to it every morning at 8:00 AM. I didn't think I knew the words to explain what I was doing there, anyway—how to explain the complicated relationship of favors and feelings and resentments that had led me to this, especially when I was only dimly aware of them myself.

My mother was thoroughly against my being here, embarrassed at the existence of the "restaurant" side of her family, as if somehow she was failing as an adoptive mother to keep me from falling back into the Mainland sordidness she thought she rescued me from. She and my father were both born in the States. My father's society brother, whose real brother was Skinny Dou, needed someone with good English and a Chinese face. Then there was my own insistence on providing for myself, a stubborn youthful rebellion in the only way I knew: I turned away the things my parents would give me in the same way I yearned to turn away their attitudes about all things Chinese. No, these things I could not articulate then. We exchanged names instead. Jin Jin Tsu, hers; Mary Yip, mine. But she could not say "Mary" and pronounced it "Mei" instead. So on that day, in that place, Mei is who I became.

Skinny Dou came into the room with his rapid-fire Cantonese, and Jin Jin herself was transformed from empress into seamstress in the instant she shooed him out and opened the wardrobe. As the sun dipped below the horizon, the glare turned to glow and I could see the room clearly. It was full of dark furniture, much of it lacquered wood upholstered with faded silk, chairs with carved feet and small tables at the edges of the room, a larger table in the center where four people could sit, and a surprisingly mundane-looking single bed pushed against the far corner wall, its white and yellow flowered bedspread looking like it could have been stolen from a cheap motel in Illinois. Maybe it was.

From the wardrobe Jin Jin pulled dress after dress, some large, some small, and held them up one by one, measuring them and me in a quick glance. She handed me a blue, high-collared chongsam and urged me with gestures and a few rapid words to try it. My eyes flicked to the doorway through which Skinny Dou could charge at any moment, but that was another thing I could not yet express in my textbook vocabulary. I could talk about baby things—pencil and car and tree and food, mother and father and brother and sister, house and shoe and cat and dog. But I had no words yet for worry or conflict or secret or dream. And so I changed my clothes, there in the middle of Jin Jin's room, while she hung up the unneeded dresses. No one came through the door. And once I was dressed, and the loose button at the shoulder mended, and my hair tamed and shaped into a compact bun held in place by two black lacquered sticks with tiny dragons on the ends, Skinny Dou came back. We easily heard his heavy footsteps on the stairs (for he was not at all skinny, no matter what his name) and his bellowing about how he would only pay me half for the night if I did not hurry. And then he opened the door and saw us, two little empresses, and he gave a nod and went back down.

Thus began my first evening working in the bar, trying to milk as much money as possible out of white men who had crossed the line from the financial district or downtown for cheap drinks and deep-fried dumplings. It was not, technically speaking, a hard job. My title was hostess—not really a waitress, not really a bartender, but something of both and more. What made it hard was my unfamiliarity with the workings of the restaurant, and the seeming unwillingness of any of the cooks or waiters to aid me in learning about it.

At the slow point of the evening, just before midnight when the dinner crowd was gone, but before the late night crowd came in, everyone ate dinner. Cooks and busboys in stained whites emerged from the kitchen and joined waiters in ill-fitting bowties at a round table in the back. Some sat while others ate standing up, sitting as soon as another would leave, all of them digging in hand-sized bowls of rice with chopsticks and chattering on about what I couldn't be sure. They were probably talking about me, from the looks and occasional words I could guess at. Too put off to vie for a seat, but not too timid to do something about it, I took a plate of greens and stir-fried fish and two bowls of rice and a pair of chopsticks in my hands, and before any of them could quite figure what comment to make, I marched upstairs to Jin Jin's room.

So, you see, that night was the beginning of many things, my first quiet meal with her, the first time she told me a story, the first time I earned money that my mother did not approve of, my first step into a world of Chinese Americans that was so unlike the one of violin lessons and tennis that I had known. I could not have guessed how far it would take me, at that time my mind on graduation a year away, with decisions to be made all too soon about careers and where to live and other things I did not yet know. Things that were easy enough to forget once I went up the stairs to Jin Jin's room, where she made me look proper, she said.

Every night I came upstairs to find her watching the sunset, even in winter when gray flakes clouded the sky. And we would sit at the mah jongg table (for that's what that little table was, of course), her East, me South, sharing siao bao and trading stories. I decided not to start taking the Mandarin class again in the fall, not when I was spending late nights in her room listening to fairy tales and rhymes meant for children's ears, only now I was the child again, learning anew. She insisted that I tell her stories, too, as she learned English a word at a time, urging me on like an empress to an ambassador from a strange and faraway place. I traded her "The Old Woman Who Lived In a Shoe" for the tale of seven brothers who all looked alike and fooled an evil emperor who thought that it was but one man coming back again and again.

But now it is me that comes back again, looking the same, but never the same again.

I should tell you of another first, the first night I knew there was more to fairy tales than whimsy. I had always assumed that some of the stories she told me were made up inventions, while others were based upon real people and events. I swapped "The Three Billy Goats Gruff" for the story of a fishseller to whom the Immortals gave a pill of life to keep his fish fresh. One day he swallowed it accidentally when hiding the pill from jealous rivals, and so became immortal himself. I told her the story of Cinderella when she told me of a pair of young lovers who cheated the gods. The gods banished the woman to the moon, and her sad face peers down forever at her lonely partner on the earth. And when it came to people who became legends, like Robin Hood and King Arthur, I heard the stories of a princess who became a warrior, of a scholar who saved the city from demons, of the emperor's concubine who became immortal. You cannot know what a treasure these stories were to me, whose mother had only told her Mother Goose and Hans Christian Andersen, and never the story of the seven lucky gods or of the dragon's daughter who could travel anywhere that the sky touched. But imagine me one evening, this maybe four months into my time at the restaurant, autumn air carrying the smell of hot oil over a crisp, cool breeze and night coming on early, climbing the steps above the dining room and finding the door to Jin Jin's room closed, locked. Through the door my ear detected a muffled, rhythmic sound.

I was naive, I suppose. Twenty-one years old, I was supposed to be a decadent American, raised on violent television and subliminal sexual advertising. But what did I really know? Some experimental fumbling with cute boys, a passing knowledge of "stag" videotapes. It had never occurred to me to think why Jin Jin was there at the restaurant, whether she was a relative of Skinny's (no, of course not, she would speak Cantonese then), or a boarder (where were her possessions? her pictures of home?), or what. Nor had I ever given a second thought to the Chinese men who often sat and drank tea with Skinny Dou at the back table, and sometimes went upstairs to play mah jongg. If I had tried to consider it at that moment, I might have explained it to myself by saying that she had a suitor and that she was a wealthy renter who had no work. But maybe some things I had heard said that had not made sense at the time finally filtered in, or maybe I wasn't as naive as all that, because as Skinny Dou came up the stairs like a determined elephant, I knew that Jin Jin was not entertaining a suitor, and that she was not renting that room. How can this be possible, I was asking myself, that a man can keep a whore above his restaurant like it was the 1850s, here in America at the dawn of the twenty first century? But no, I thought, as Skinny pushed me away from the door while hushing me with loud words, this is not America, this is not the same place and time. This is Chinatown.

I reeled back from Skinny, suddenly dizzy, as if I could not quite breathe. I clattered down the steps, not looking behind me, listening to the heavy clang of utensils against woks as I neared the kitchen, knowing that downstairs it would be as it had always been.

But it was not as it had always been. The room was bigger, a live fish tank bubbled in one corner, and familiar-looking yet unknown waiters stared at me as if I had just fallen out of the sky. Which, perhaps, I had. I must have come down the wrong set of stairs, I thought. Is this the place next door? I rushed out to the street to find the air warm, the breeze heavy with humidity, and the sun up in the sky. Not comprehending, not knowing, I sat down with my back against the warm concrete of an alley wall and hid my face in my sleeves, rocking back and forth like the released mental patients one sees in alleys in any city.

When I came to, I found myself looking into Jin Jin's eyes, stoic with Chinese concern. All was as before in the restaurant, as it had been every day I had worked there. That is, everything except Jin Jin's room, which I now saw in a different light. Jin Jin herself touched my cheek, but I could not, would not ask about what I now knew. We did not tell stories that night, I did not work at the bar, and I did not think I would return the next day.

But I did. In the morning I sat with my cornflakes, the TV on, in the kitchen I shared with three other students, and wondered once again what I was supposed to do with my life. Work in an office, make photocopies and type in a word processor? Build automobiles? My parents were both doctors, and I knew I did not want to be that. So what was left? Working as a hostess in a restaurant did not feel like a career, but it did feel better than not knowing. So many petty things are needed to make up a modern life:

ATM card, traffic reports, touch tone service. I could not eat the corn flakes. I felt terribly homesick suddenly, even though it was not my parents' home I thought of. I thought of the smell of frying dumplings and the clack of mah jongg tiles punctuated with laughter as if remembered from an early morning dream. I could not sit there and worry about my diploma and a resume, when yesterday I had gone down a stairway and emerged in a sun-filled city somewhere else in the world.

I went to the restaurant in the afternoon, when I knew Skinny Dou would be sipping tea with his cronies at the tea house down the street. Jin Jin was asleep, her black hair unbound from the dragon sticks and wrapped over one shoulder like a scarf. I found her clothed in simple cotton and lying atop the daisy bedspread. She sat up suddenly as I approached and rubbed her eyes, then smiled as she saw me. I had tried to guess her age so many times, but could not. She had the eternal youth of Asians, I thought, always like we could be twenty, until suddenly one day we go gray and stoop, or get fat like Skinny. I said her name but could not form the question I wanted to ask—I was not even sure what it was I would ask. I tried to conjure the Mandarin words to describe something I was sure was real and yet thought could not be. Eventually I stuttered out, "Where did I go?"

She smiled again, her lips closed. Her hand over mine she answered, "China."

I laughed at first, until I saw she was not making a joke.

"You know now," she said.

I thought she referred to the fact that she was a whore, and I nodded.

"You can take me with you," she added.

And I, yes, still naive, still confused, and still trying to follow my heart said, "Yes, yes of course."

So here is the danger of making promises when one does not know what one has promised. She was in motion then, braiding her hair into a queue, even as she crossed the room to the wardrobe. From the bottom drawer she brought out more clothes like the ones she wore now, unembroidered, of a sturdy blue cloth, with wide-legged pants and black slippers. I changed into what she gave me, not knowing why I was doing so, assuming that an explanation must be coming soon. Then, her hand pulling mine, we were tiptoeing down the stairs, and I began to think that perhaps I did not know where we were going after all, and that perhaps this was meant to be some sort of escape.

When Skinny Dou came in the front door and saw the two of us, and he shouted something that I could only guess was, "Stop where you are!" or, "Don't let them get away!" and Jin Jin pulled me at a run through the kitchen doors, then I knew it was an escape. Again I had that thought, this could not be happening, that a woman could be kept prisoner above a restaurant against her will, not today, not here... but mostly I was dodging the grabs of kitchen boys and then trying to see ahead of us in the narrow diagonal alley that ran between buildings. We weren't going to come out anywhere near my car, but maybe we would see a policeman, or we could run all the way into Downtown Crossing and take the train from there back to campus. In the alley there was the hiss of steam from other kitchens, the smell of rotten fish, and the sound of our slippers hitting the cobblestones and Jin Jin repeating in a low urgent voice "Take me back, take me back," even as we rushed away.

We emerged on the other side to a narrow, traffic-filled street, the sidewalk crowded with tourists. I pulled my hand from Jin Jin's and called for her to wait. I was out of breath, dizzy, and wanted a moment to think about details: car keys, visas, police. As the crowd moved around me, it felt like sometimes people suddenly changed directions and I was jostled. I pressed back against a wall and searched for her face.

Jin Jin was gone. People moved this way and that and cars crept slowly along. Across the way from me was a tea house I had never seen before, with a red-lettered sign I could read in Chinese and English: "Great Flower House of Tea." The street sign was in Chinese and English as well, though it was clearly no Boston Street:

Santiago. Not China either. Sweat trickled down my neck from fear and the air's heat. Inside the teahouse I found a newspaper that told me the answer: Manila, the Philippines. In a moment we had come halfway around the world, and in a moment of confusion, I had lost her.

They accept American money most places in Manila, and a dollar buys you all the tea you can drink. I sat down with a pot of jasmine and struggled to put my thoughts together. Why had I let go her hand? I had thought I was the one leading us but I was mistaken. In the tea my face looked round and brown and sad like the woman in the moon. I had somehow opened the gates between places but had stopped short of finishing the journey. Where was Jin Jin now? Had I left her behind in Boston, to be caught by the cooks and returned to her prison? And how was I to get back there?

I supposed I could have gone to the US embassy and told them who I was, but I could not bear the thought of my parents, of passports, airlines, and metal detectors. No. I had to be sure she was not here and merely lost in the crowd. And if she was gone, I had to find her though I knew not how.

I began to walk down to the main street, gaudy with red lanterns and the bright T-shirts of tourists, and up another alley. It ran alongside the back doors of laundries, bakeries, and butchers whose doorways offered glimpses of brown-faced people, the scent of soap and fish and frying oil, but no Jin Jin. On another corner I watched two boys steal a mango, one distracting the shopkeeper with a sudden cry, the other hurrying past. Then they were both gone. The shopkeeper looked at his neat stacks of roots and leafy cabbage and fruit and frowned. Further down the row from him, two old women argued with a pharmacist, sending him up and down rows of hundreds of tiny drawers in search of the cure for what ailed them.

This could be happening anywhere, I thought, on any street in any Chinatown anywhere in the world.

As I turned to take in the scene I felt a breeze blow that I sensed was not from this place. Once again reality shifted. Around me, infinite gates with curved horns wormed away into the distance like a never-ending parade dragon. I held my breath, afraid to move and find myself in New York, or San Francisco, or I knew not where. And yet I knew I must take a step.

"Jin Jin," I whispered, and stepped through.

It would take lifetimes for me to describe all the things that I saw on the journey, because lifetimes I did see—in cities across the world, in old Hong Kong and new Shanghai, in Chicago and Los Angeles, sometimes going back in years, sometimes going ahead—until I almost forgot that I was looking for Jin Jin. But never completely. I knew I had to continue my quest, because I finally knew the answer to that question I had asked so long ago: when she looked into the sunset, what did she hope to see? Jin Jin searched the fire eye of the sun for someone to take her back to an older day, to a time when she was more than just a menu item, to when she had been concubine to emperors. She looks into the lucky red sky for the dragon's daughter, and that is me.

She is out there, in the vast timespace that is China, somewhere within the maze of kitchens and secret parlors that define it, and I will find her...

Part Two: Hall of Mirrors

Memory is a hall of mirrors. When I was twenty years old, I discovered one of the great secrets of the Universe. I discovered the magic that ran in my blood and the truth of ancient stories. I knew, in one moment when all of time and space and history cracked open, what my destiny was.

But, as I found out, there was still much I did not know about myself. As I stood on the threshold of the vast timespace that was China, as my power flared to life and I stared into funhouse mirror images of rickshaw drivers and fish sellers and wise old sifus, I knew at last that I was the Dragon's Daughter. I had come to life from a Chinese fairy tale, but I felt like Alice gone through the looking glass, lost and alone. In one foolish moment I had lost Jin Jin and I knew it was my duty to find her again. What I did not know was why I felt so empty. And even as I searched for her in the wide world, anywhere the lucky red sky could touch, I searched the hall of mirrors of my own memories. I can see myself now, moon-faced girl at piano lessons, dragon girl in silk at the senior prom, stumbling bar hostess with glass dragons hanging from sticks in my hair, placed there so carefully by Jin Jin's hand.

* * * *

I'm on a street corner in Manila at sunset, the afternoon rain steaming off the hot pavement as the clouds clear the way for that red eye to sink into the bay. It is my second time here, and this time I am prepared. Tea shops that had closed their shutters for afternoon siesta are open now, back-bent people in blue cotton sweeping their stoops and raising their blinds to welcome dinnertime tourists. Neighborhood children spot what they think is a well-dressed man fumbling with his cigarette and begin to swarm around me, selling candies and mangoes, tin birds on sticks made from Coke cans, more cigarettes. They tug on my lapels and I push my way into a restaurant to get rid of them. The proprietor brandishes a broom and they move down the street to intercept others making their way up the hill from the new hotels.

"Can I help you?" he says in Fukienese. He has a Chairman Mao face, balding and basset-houndish. The restaurant is shabby inside, cafeteria-bright with round fluorescents, tiled in chipped white tiles. I doubt Jin Jin is here, but it is the first lead I have. Prostitution is frowned upon, after all, and cannot be asked about too openly. And I must start somewhere.

I clear my throat, tugging at my tie, and quietly inquire in my soft Mandarin about his "house specialty." My suit is impeccable, double-breasted to make my shoulders look broader. I am a milk-fed American girl (though they don't know that) and I tower over everyone in the place. The trick is not hard to pull off. He demurs, in heavily accented Mandarin. I pretend he has misunderstood me and repeat my request, this time putting a hundred dollar bill into his hand. He shakes my hand to hand it back, saying "I cannot help you, sir."

"Can you tell me where to go?" I let my shoulders slump. "I've come a long way."

He directs me to a tea house up the street and off the main drag. That, at least, is something.

* * * *

When I was fifteen years old, my parents told me I was adopted. It's funny. So many things I remember so clearly: our California living room, the fish tank humming in the silence between my mother's halting admissions, the hunch of my father's shoulders as he sat on the couch, elbows on knees, his slacks riding up his calf and showing his black socks. Like something from a made-for-TV movie. I remember my heart beginning to beat faster and faster under my skin as they talked, while my face stayed stoic, while my surface froze like the ice on a pond. I remember so much, but I don't remember why they chose that moment to tell me.

You came from the mainland, they told me, from the same province as our ancestors. Mom's medical difficulties had led them to the decision to adopt. Mom cried a little, while telling me this, and I'm not sure which of us she was crying for. They seemed to think they should have told me a long time before, but they had never been sure how. I remember feeling stunned, but it all making sense somehow. I had always felt there was something different about me but I had never known what. That day, I thought I knew—I was the ugly duckling in another bird's nest. But how little I knew, how little.

* * * *

I climb the cobblestone street, stepping onto the crowded sidewalk to let a side-banged Toyota creep past. Watching the crowd, I realize my suit looks too Hong Kong, too upscale, for Manila Chinatown. That's okay, I don't need to pass myself off as a resident. Rich Hong Kong tourist looking for action should be good enough. I pray that Jin Jin is somewhere like here, somewhere small and easy to search, and not Shanghai, or Beijing.

I have tested my power since my first accidental visit here. I can go anywhere that is somehow undeniably China. I have been to New York, to Los Angeles, to Guanzhou, just to look, just to see. I have walked to the past and flown across oceans, all in the blink of an eye. Manila was the first place, though, the first place I stepped through to, before I knew what was happening, before I knew not to let go of Jin Jin's hand. She must be here, I insist to myself, but the voice of doubt begins to chant in time with my uphill steps: it'll take forever to find her, what if you never find her? Never find her, never find her...

I put the thought out of my mind and swagger into the Red Dragon Tea House. My heart skips a beat at seeing the name—would Jin Jin choose a place with such a likely name? Would she think to tip me off like that, or would she settle down in the most comfortable place, figuring she might be in for a long wait? Wait for me, Jin Jin, I'm coming.

I take a table in the tea house and order some dumplings while I examine the place. It's dim, with a dark wood interior and landscape paintings on the wall, a much classier place than the previous. I hope I can afford their house specialty, and have my pick. Then again, this is cash-poor Manila and I have American money. I should be fine.

* * * *

I had picked up the money from an antique dealer in New York who paid in cash. I'd chosen his shop at random when looking for a place to unload some souvenirs of my experimental trips through the lucky red sky. I'd expected some brusque, suspicious old man and was happy to find Quan young, personable, even friendly.

"Here's four hundred," he had said, putting a pile of bills into my hand. "I'll have another two fifty for you later." Quan always spoke English with me, a slight hint of British accent betraying either Hong Kong roots or a British education. Whenever a customer would come into his store he would switch to coolie-pidgin, "You like? Fifty dollah." I assumed this increased business somehow, but I never pried. I think I hoped he wouldn't pry back, though of course he always did.

I counted the bills, some crisp, some limp. "How much later?"

"Two, three days. Why, going on a trip?" He leaned on the glass counter top and stuck a ball point pen between his ear and his New York Yankees baseball cap. Quan had one of those wrinkle-free, ageless Chinese faces. He could have passed for twenty, or forty. More like thirty, I guessed. I didn't say anything about where I was going.

"You do a lot of traveling," he pressed.

"Yes. How else do you think I get you all this stuff?" I'd just brought him some jade earrings over two hundred years old. Other than the baseball cap and his cash register, there was little in his shop that looked like it was from the twentieth century, or from this hemisphere.

"Mei, Mei," he said, as if to imply 'don't be testy' but he would never say any such thing. "When do you leave? I'll try to get the money by tomorrow. Meet me for dinner at the Hunan House and I'll have it for you."

Quan wasn't married. He'd told me his father had passed the antique business on to him when he died. I assumed his mother was also dead. He was overeducated for a shopkeeper and fancied himself a historian. Quan tried to get me to have dinner with him on a fairly regular basis.

"Two or three days is fine," I said. "I'll be back."

* * * *

It is early in the evening and it appears I have succeeded in being the first customer for the Red Dragon's specialty. After I have finished my dumplings and a pot of tea, a nicely dressed middle-aged hostess takes me upstairs where she seats me in a parlor. We haggle and I discreetly pass her some cash. Through the thin walls I can hear the sharp twang of women's voices as the whores ready themselves for the night's work. In my mind's eye, I imagine Jin Jin among them, helping them to get dressed, painting their faces. I imagine her leading the group out into the parlor like a madame herself, and catching my eye. I see myself, looking like a handsome young man, not like the smoky, drunk businessmen that they regularly see. Then, her breath caught in her throat, Jin Jin recognizes me. I choose her, of course, from among all the others, and to her back parlor we go...

My heart is pounding as the hostess pushes aside the curtain and the women come in. I try to look calm. Then I try not to look disappointed. Four women stand in front of me, and it does not matter if they are beautiful or bored, young or old, clean or slovenly. None of them is Jin Jin. I have two choices now, pick one in order to maintain the masquerade, or weasel my way out. I decide to disparage the women, claim they don't look good. The madame assures me these girls are 100% Chinese, no Filipino blood in them. The naked racism makes me angry, and my stomach churns with bile, but it is a useful lie. I claim not to believe her, I point to this one's nose, the color of this one's skin. I tell the madame to keep the money, I don't care, I'm not letting one of these ape-women touch me. I storm out of the restaurant.

Later, in an alley by myself, I cry.

* * * *

I had no date for my senior prom. My parents wrung their hands so much over this fact that I kept my mouth shut about what I thought of marriage. I had never planned to get married. Never planned to have children. Somehow I just knew it was not for me, just as I knew I was not going to become an endocrinologist or a surgeon like the two of them, and like they wanted me to. I had learned, though, not to protest too loudly, because if I did, they would moan and cry that if only they hadn't told me I was adopted, surely I would have gone along with their plans. There was no convincing them otherwise. So I would nod and smile and then do what I wanted for myself anyway. So it was when I applied to college in Boston. So it was when I had a relative in San Francisco Chinatown make me a dress. My mother was scandalized that I hadn't picked a more Western dress.

It was imported silk, embossed with tiny flowers, edged with satin pipe and closed with knotted cloth buttons. It was everything a ball gown should be, a Cinderella dress, but a Chinese Cinderella in flat silk slippers. I wore jeans and sneakers to school every day, but for this one night I wanted to be a princess. I think I knew the prom was no place for me, so the only way to do it was to become someone else. Chinese Cinderella danced with all the boys and made all the girls give her funny looks. I didn't find a Prince Charming. I was not surprised.

* * * *

With the help of a bellboy at my hotel, I uncover more brothels in Manila, and one by one I check them out. The pickings are slim, my insistence on Chinese girls narrowing the search, until I have been to almost every backroom bordello but one. This last one is a big one, above a nightclub. In the basement there is a gambling den. The music is loud, which is unfortunate because if I raise my voice too much it becomes womanish. I keep my sunglasses on and peer over the tops of them as I make my way to the bar. The bartender acknowledges me with a glance. I hold up the business card the bellboy gave me, the name of the place written on the back. The bartender nods and disappears through a mirrored door behind the bar. I take a seat.

People are dancing amid flashing lights and pulsing music. Single men line the bar, some in sharp suits, some holding cigarettes and whiskey in the same hand. None of them even glance at me. I see bar hostesses in short skirts carrying trays through the crowd.

Time passes. A hostess lays her tray down at the bar and leans next to me. Her thick, black hair falls in waves down her back and her lipstick is bright magenta under the bar's lights. She says something in a language I don't know, one of the Filipino languages, I am guessing. I shake my head and hold up my hands.

"You want upstairs?" she says in English then.

I nod. She tugs on my tie then like a dog leash, and I follow her. She skirts the edge of the club and goes up a set of dim back stairs.

On the second floor is a registration desk, as if this had once been a small hotel. A bored-looking Filipino man in a white button-down shirt sits at the desk. He and the hostess exchange a few words. I tuck my sunglasses into the breast pocket of my jacket and try to make it clear what I am looking for.

"Why only Chinee girl?" he asks, with a leer at the hostess.

I put money on the counter in front of him.

"She busy right now. You wait." He jerks his chin toward a vinyl-covered couch across from the desk and takes the money.

I sit. The hostess sits with me, one arm twined in mine. After a few moments, another Filipina comes from down the hall, and snuggles against my other side.

"How long?" I ask the man at the desk, but he ignores me.

The women are starting to breathe in my ears, tickling the small hairs on my neck where I've had it buzzed short. I shake my head as if to dislodge flies. They giggle and begin again.

"Special tonight," one says.

"Two price of one," says the other.

I'm trying to think of the best way to tell them to knock it off, that I want to wait for someone else, when one of them slips her hand onto my crotch. Her eyebrow goes up and I am sure the surprise shows on my own face. This is not a contingency I've planned for.

She says something in rapid-fire Filipino to the hostess, who rubs a hand on my cheek and stands up.

The desk clerk is standing up, too, now, shouting at me what I can only guess are the local equivalent of "dyke" or "pervert."

I'm trying to explain myself but there is no explanation for me. One of the girls slaps me across the face. I find myself running down the hallway, opening doors, yelling Jin Jin's name, the man from the desk and the two women close on my heels. But I am the dragon's daughter and no one can catch me.

* * * *

I had bought the double-breasted suit in San Francisco, where the tailor seemed unfazed that a woman wanted a man's suit tailored to her. I stood looking at myself in the mirror, resisting the urge to Napoleon my hand between the two wide buttons. I'd gotten my hair cut that morning and it seemed like a stranger, or maybe a long-lost brother, stared back at me from the glass. I had been in San Francisco for a week at that point, and was losing hope of finding Jin Jin there. I had been trying to make friends with the whores so I could ask around if anyone knew her. But it was difficult to make friends with these women who were, by and large, closely guarded by their men and who knew very little of the outside world. I could not become one of them and it took too long to gain their trust. I needed a faster way to go from house to house and it was overhearing the bragging of some Taiwanese businessmen about how many whores they could see in a night that gave me the idea to impersonate them. In the mirror, my twin smiled.

* * * *

Back in New York, memories of Manila fade like bad dreams. She was not there, not anywhere, and I must decide where to look next. I am in the little pensioners hotel a few blocks from Chinatown proper where I keep a small place. I am sitting in the kitchen, in the chair with one short leg that came with the apartment. I am waiting five minutes before I try to call Quan again. There is one phone at the end of the hall that we all share, a bathroom at the other end. I hear the squeals of children through my door and the thump of their feet as they chase one another through the hallway. Quan's phone has been busy all afternoon and with each try I feel more and more alone.

I should just go down there, I decide. Get dressed and go out. No one here notices me much in the hubbub of families and sweatshop workers. I wear the same overcoat whether I go out dressed as a man or as a woman, so they can never see. What I'll do when summer comes, I don't know. I suppose there's no real reason to be secretive, or is there? I put on my sneakers to leave for Quan's.

Out on the street it is New York noisy, crowded with people and cars and activity. I chose New York as my hub because it is always easy to find, so similar to the overcrowded beehives of China's cities, cities that have been buzzing for four thousand years. I turn the corner onto the twisted dragon back of Mott Street and then into an alley to Quan's door.

I see him through the window, the shop dark except for the lamp on the counter, casting a circle of light onto something he examines with a loupe to his eye. I open the door with a tinkle of bells and his head comes up.

"Mei, Mei! I was wondering when you'd be back. Where were you this time?"

"Manila," I answer, seeing no reason to lie. "It's only been a few weeks."

"Bring me anything good?"

I hold up my empty hands. "That's not what I went there for."

"You have family there?"

"No." I try to give him a look that says drop it.

He bundles up the scrolls he had been examining and makes

them disappear behind the counter. "It's late. Do you want to catch some dinner?"

"Quan..."

"Mei, please. I'd just like the company, is all." He shrugs.

I don't have any reason to be afraid of Quan. And I am, undeniably, lonely. "Okay. Let's eat."

* * * *

When I first met Jin Jin, I thought she was the most beautiful woman I'd ever seen. That is, she was the most beautiful woman I had ever seen, and I wasn't even conscious enough of the thought to know I had thought it. It was only later I began to realize what my thoughts were, as I as she occupied more and more space in my head. My poor overworked brain, all crammed with women's studies classes and contradictory politics and comparative literature. When I arrived at the restaurant to begin my evening's work I would forget it all.

Jin Jin's hands were soft as they brushed my hair and pinned it into place, as they buttoned my silk embroidered bar hostess dress. Each night she transformed me from an overworked college student into something more elegant. But she herself never changed.

* * * *

Quan steers me to a table at the restaurant, near the kitchen door. I want to protest, but it seems not worth the effort and he seems slightly nervous about something. I sincerely hope he is not going to ask me to marry him, a worry I only become conscious of as we sit across from each other. Quan pours tea for the two of us. We each sit sniffing the jasmine steam in silence. He sits with his back to the wall, a garish painting of some folk scene hanging above his head: it's a parade of villagers led by a man carrying two buckets of fish on a pole hung across his shoulders. I smile at the memory of Jin Jin telling me the story of the fishseller who became immortal by accident. If I ever see her again, what stories will I have to trade?

Quan sees me looking at the painting and says, "Do you know the story?"

"You mean about the Immortal Fishseller?"

"He wasn't immortal while he was a fishseller," Quan says. "He used the pill of immortality to keep his fish fresh. But when the other fishsellers tried to steal it from him—"

"I know, I know, he hid it in his mouth and swallowed it."

"Thus becoming immortal, but no longer being able to sell fresh fish."

"I wonder what he did after that?" I put down my tea. "I mean, are there other stories about him? Stories end, but they are never really finished, are they?"

Quan peers over the top of his cup at me. "He decided to travel and see the world. But he always found himself coming home again. If he spent too long away, he found his mortality slipping back, bit by bit. But whenever he came home, the seven lucky gods smiled on him."

I feel my eyes narrow as I look at Quan. "Cute." I am still imagining that he's either going to hit on me or propose, and am trying to anticipate where what he says is going to lead. So I am completely unprepared for what he does say.

He puts down his cup and says, "I know who you are."

"Like hell you do," I say, annoyed for some reason I cannot define.

"I know the stories, too," he says, and I can see his face reflected brown and round in his tea cup. Like the man in the moon.

"Mei, listen to me. I'm not the only immortal in China. I know another one when I see one. And you..."

"I'm not immortal." I want to tell him he's crazy, but it feels wrong. What would Chinese Cinderella say? "I was raised in the States. I had a childhood, a life."

He shrugs, matter of fact. "There are three kinds of immortals,

Mei. You, you can die and be reborn. Me, I've lived one long life." He closes his mouth as a waiter puts plates of bright vegetables down in front of us. A bowl of steaming rice clouds the air between us. "That doesn't change who you are or what you can do."

My heart hammers and I'm not sure why I have the urge to run from the room. I feel my face beginning to freeze and I blink my eyes rapidly. "What do you want from me?"

He makes a disgusted noise. "I don't want anything from you, Mei. I wanted you to know about me. I wanted you to know that we can help each other. I can introduce you to some others, if you want. Even Wong F—"

I grab his hand. "Do you know where I can find Jin Jin?"

He cocks his head; he does not know that name.

"The emperor's concubine."

His mouth opens in a silent oh and he nods. "I have not seen her for a long, long time."

"I'm looking for her," I say, not sure that I can explain why. "She, she's waiting for me."

"Mei—"

"How can you tell who the other immortals are? Is that why you helped me when I first came to you?" The food sits, uneaten, in dishes between us. "Can you help me find her?"

He starts scooping rice onto my plate, then his own. "One thing at a time. Yes, I knew you were someone right away, I just was not sure who. Once you began to bring me things, well, it could only be you. I'm not sure how to help you find her."

"But how do you recognize the others?"

He begins to eat, chopsticks clicking against the plate. "Center yourself and relax, and see how the world looks. Some things will seem thin and insubstantial, things that won't last. Others will seem vivid and solid. Buildings, people, roads. Some of them are part of us, some are not."

"I've never noticed that."

He shrugs. "What can I tell you, that's the way it is. Either you see it, or you don't. What have you been doing thus far to look for her?"

I describe my incognito investigations.

"Needle in a haystack," is what he says to that. He shakes his head, sadly. "And what will you do once you find her?"

"Take her back, I suppose. Wherever she wants. Whenever she wants."

"And then?"

I stare into my plate of rice and vegetables.

"Mei," he says, his chopsticks still for a moment, "you do know who she is, don't you?"

"What do you mean?"

"You know the story, she who was so loyal to him that the gods granted her immortality. She's looking for her emperor."

"Of course she is," I say, annoyed, but for some reason on the edge of tears. I start to eat, angrily grabbing at the food with my chopsticks, chewing hard.

Quan eats quietly for a while, politely looking away while I calm myself. Then he goes on. "I said there were three kinds of immortals."

"Yes. Like me, like you, and...?"

"And like Jin Jin. Mei, she's lived one long life, like me, but she is not like me. She is... like the embodiment of an ideal. Perfect loyalty. The woman behind the throne. The yin that yang power demands to balance it."

"That sounds like a warning."

"She's... she's not like you."

"What are you saying." I am ready to jump down his throat if he criticizes me or tries to tell me any more about myself that I don't already know. I am angry at him for forcing me to see what I already knew: she does not feel for me the way I feel for her. "Are you saying she couldn't love an empress too?"

Quan gave me a long-suffering look that said I was no empress. But his voice was kind. "She could have loved an empress too. But she's not a person, Mei. She's an archetype. She... she is perfect, and cannot change. That's why she wants to go back, because there's no place for her here, now."

We eat in silence a while as I digest everything he has said.

When he speaks again, it is with a soft, forgive-me voice. "Have you looked in New York yet?"

"No." I am calmer now, but still a bit taciturn.

"Perhaps I could make some inquiries by word of mouth." His desire to help seems genuine.

"Thank you." I feel I should apologize for being angry with him, but now is not the time nor place for that.

He goes on. "And have you considered that she might be in Boston?"

I stare at him.

"When you lost her, you were in Boston, isn't that what you said? And the next moment you were halfway around the world, in Manila. How do you know she went anywhere at all?"

I cannot chew because my heart is in my throat.

"You never went back to check?"

"I was afraid to." Skinny Dou and his army of cooks waiting for me. I'd tried to steal his golden goose. But, god, what if she had gone back? "Quan, you must help me."

He opens his mouth to speak but I overrun him with a sudden plea, my anger and reservedness gone. "Come back with me to Boston. They don't know you there. They'll recognize me, but you, they don't know. And you'll be able to tell if it is her. All you have to do is go into the restaurant and order the house specialty. Then tell me if she's there." How could I be so stupid? I am suddenly certain she is there. "We can go right away, I'll have you back in an hour."

Quan sighs. "I suppose I have nothing better to do."

* * * *

I almost kissed a girl once when I was fifteen. She was thirteen, but very sophisticated in a feminine way, her red hair curled, her nails painted. She had just moved in that year to the house across the street and was due to start at my school in September. Our mothers conspired that we should socialize together. I followed her around like a puppy. I loved the way she smelled, the way her hair curled, her white skin like a porcelain doll. Before her first date with a boyfriend, she decided she needed kissing practice. So in her bedroom, all hung with pictures of unicorns and horses, she asked me to pretend to be her boyfriend. I agreed. But then we went on talking as usual, and we never kissed. I wondered if I was supposed to interrupt her, sweep her off her feet or what. I thought she'd stop at some point and say, okay, let's try it. But she never did, and we never mentioned it again.

* * * *

I am standing on a Boston street corner at sunrise, looking up at the reflected sky in a plate glass second floor window. Quan is back in New York with a gift from me of two more jade earrings over a thousand years old. The back streets are quiet, the steel grates down over shop doors, the waterfall sound of rush hour coming over the tops of the buildings. I make my way to the back of the building, where the kitchen door is propped open. Amid the clang of woks and the hiss of frying and running water, I hear Skinny Dou's voice. He is yelling at one of the kitchen workers, which one I cannot guess. He is busy, that is all that matters to me.

I open the door to step through, but it is not the kitchen I enter. With a shift of the universe, I emerge in Jin Jin's room.

I find her at the window, looking out at the sunset, her hair unbound in her lap and the comb idle in one hand. She crosses the room to me, a tiny smile wrinkles her eyes. I take her hands in mine.

"I'm sorry," I find myself saying. "I didn't know."

She nods.

"I'll take you where you want, when you want. You don't have to wait anymore."

She nods again. I am in a hurry to get us away, but she stops me with a few quick words in Mandarin, her voice sweet and high like a bird by a stream. She wants to be ready.

From a wooden chest she unearths a silk dress that covers her from throat to ankle. I help her to button it over her shoulder and down her back. Then she sits in front of the mirror and I take the black silk of her hair in my hands. There are so many things I want to know, and yet I cannot bring myself to squander these moments with chatter. My hands and hers move together over her hair, binding it up with two slender lacquered sticks.

* * * *

When I had first come to work for Skinny Dou, I had an idea in the back of my mind that I could fool people into thinking I was something I was not. My mother was ashamed of the "restaurant" side of the family, and had raised me to be as American as apple pie. But when I was fifteen and I learned I had come from the mainland, I began to undo that any way I could. I tried to teach myself to read Chinese and failed. When I went to college I tried again and succeeded, but I had thought it too late—it was too late to be who I had been meant to be. When I took the Chinese restaurant job, it was one more stab at grabbing a piece of the life I felt I had missed. But fate takes care of these things, and upstairs in Skinny Dou's restaurant I found a true piece of the past waiting for me like an piece of jade buried in a box of silk.

* * * *

I center myself and take a deep breath. All around us the hall of mirrors glitters, as if we stand at the center of mammoth diamond, every facet the entry to another world. "Look," I say. "Look." Like waltz partners we turn in a slow circle, the facets blossoming all around like a kaleidoscope.

Then her breath catches in her throat and she pulls me onto a street of packed earth. We huddle against a high wall and she cranes her neck around one corner. I crouch and peek also, into a shrine, where a young man is making his obeisance to his ancestors. Around him candles flicker and incense burns but he seems to glow with a luminescence of his own. Jin Jin covers her mouth and pulls back, one hand against her chest.

"Thank you," she tells me, "thank you."

"Is this goodbye?" I can barely speak. It feels as if a giant hand is squeezing my throat and my chest.

She leans forward, one crystalline tear in her eye, and brushes her silken lips against mine. Then she rounds the corner and is gone.

* * * *

My heart is a hall of mirrors. I stand at the center of being, at the center of everything, and look into the future, the present, and the past. I belong everywhere and nowhere, and know not where to go. One step and my destiny will be decided. I float between worlds and consider. There is no folktale in which the dragon's daughter dies of a broken heart. Stories end, but they are never finished. I go in search of a lucky red sky to call my own.

Pride/Prejudice: A Novel Excerpt

Ann Herendeen

"It is a truth universally acknowledged," Fitz said, "that a single man in possession of a good fortune is in want of a wife."

Charles blinked and sat up. "Lord, Fitz! It's the middle of the night. What do you expect me to make of that? Sounds like another of your epigrams."

"I suppose it is," Fitz said. "But its meaning does not seem particularly obscure."

"You and Caroline going to tie the knot at last? You sly dog."

Fitz grimaced and pulled Charles back down beside him. "My dear," he said, "you have a tendency to levity that, like any disproportion, can be tedious in excess."

"And you," Charles said, "have a way of talking to people as if you were a judge and they the prisoner in the dock."

"Guilty as charged," Fitz said, bestowing a kiss on the pouting lips. "My great uncle might have been pleased at my following his example. Now, what shall my penalty be? I know." He trailed his hand down Charles's slender body until he found what he was searching for, held tight and squeezed.

Charles groaned and arched his back. "God, Fitz, you're a devil. I wish you'd—"

"Don't talk," Fitz said. He moved lower in the bed, opened his mouth and paid his forfeit with an alacrity bordering dangerously on enthusiasm. He would consider it deplorable if he were not motivated by love. Love of the purest kind.

They woke to dawn light. "I'm only leasing the place," Charles said, picking up the argument as if there had been no interruption. "I haven't committed to anything permanent—a few months' tenancy, a year at most."

"The minute you take possession of the house," Fitz said, still groggy from sleep, "nay, the minute you ride into the village, you will be besieged by every fortune-hunting mama and her brood of hideous, squinting, gap-toothed, caterwauling daughters."

"How do you know they will be hideous?" Charles asked. "Or are all women hideous if you think I might find them agreeable?"

"In a way, yes," Fitz said, attempting a lightness of tone he could never feel on this subject. "You are modest in your assessment of your own charms, and too easily flattered by the pitiful arts of any barely respectable female."

"My word," Charles said. "You have a low opinion of my understanding. For someone who calls himself my friend—"

Fitz saw he had wounded where he had hoped merely to inspire wariness. "My dear," he said, kissing the cheek that presented itself as he approached the lips, and stroking the soft brown hair. "I don't question your intellect, merely your judgment, and only on this subject; one that has proven difficult for the wisest philosophers to master, back to antiquity, much less an English gentleman of twenty-two."

"Whereas from the vast experience of twenty-seven, all is revealed," Charles said.

"Twenty-eight, last month," Fitz said. "It is not my age but my temperament that gives me an advantage. I do not immediately assume, because a woman simpers and plies her fan, that she is in love with me, or I with her."

"At last the truth comes out," Charles said. "You don't like women. I've suspected it all along."

"Really?" Fitz said. "In other words, because I show some taste and discrimination, I am supposed not to care for women in general."

Fitz's voice had entered that supercilious register that ordinarily would have led Charles to concede the debate. This time he persevered. "When have you ever looked at a woman but to find fault? As far as marriage is concerned, my fundament is as close to a wife as you'll ever come."

"Don't be coarse, Charles," Fitz said. "If you believe that's all you are to me, your understanding is worse than I thought."

"Deny it all you like," Charles said. "But I begin to pity Caroline."

"And what, may I ask, has your sister to do with this conversation?"

"I am not to be coarse," Charles said, "but you are allowed to be dense. We've talked it over a hundred times. You're to marry Caroline and I'm to marry Georgiana—double brothers-in-law." He shrank back, seeing the truly alarming expression distorting the features of his friend's handsome face.

"Do not," Fitz said, "I repeat, do not bring my sister's name into this bed."

"Why not?" Charles said. "You think she's too good for me? I notice you don't scruple to pollute yourself."

Fitz caught himself on the verge of losing his temper and took several deep breaths. Why was it that this subject always upset him, when he knew it was inevitable? "I'm sorry, Charles," he said. "You see, Georgiana is just turned sixteen. With the difference in our ages, and especially since our father died, I am more of a parent to her than a brother."

Charles laid his hand on his friend's muscular chest. "I understand, Fitz. I'm sorry too. I just think you're making too much of this business. You know my father wanted to purchase an estate but died before he could accomplish it. It's the least I can do to follow through on his intentions. You may sneer, from your lofty perch atop the greatest property in Derbyshire—which, you may recall, you inherited—but I, like Lackland, must start from nothing—although I hope I'll do better than King John."

"You could do a lot worse than the Magna Carta," Fitz said.

Charles laughed dutifully. "I'm not rushing into anything. Surely you agree I'm behaving with all the circumspection and prudence you could require."

"My dear boy," Fitz said. "I agree that you think you are. You can't help it that you fell in love with the first house you saw with sufficient rooms, just as you fall in love with every woman who possesses all her teeth and whose hair retains its natural color." He rolled over on Charles, pinning him to the mattress with his larger, heavier form, and kissed him until he gasped for air.

"Brute," Charles said when he was allowed to breathe. "Overbearing, domineering brute." He licked his lips, moving his tongue in a slow circling motion. "Kiss me again, brute."

"If you're going to tease me like that," Fitz said, "I shall be obliged to do more than kiss you."

"Mmm," Charles said, "I was hoping you'd say that. Just try to take it easy. I want to ride over and look at the place today."

"I will be as gentle with you," Fitz said, "as with a woman."

"Lord help me!" Charles said. "I'm a goner. I won't be able to sit for a week."

And yet, a few hours later, as Charles Bingley rode through the village of Meryton to the manor house of Netherfield Park, he was permeated with a great sense of well-being. Fitz had allowed him to go alone, and to make all the arrangements without interference. "You are no longer the untried youth of our first acquaintance, but are on your way to becoming a man," he said. "I've known it for some time now. Bear with me if on occasion I find the transformation difficult to accept."

"Of course I will," Charles said. "Indeed, I hope—that is—I don't want to give up being your dear boy entirely."

The animation that this speech produced in Fitz's austere face and hard body almost led to a repetition of the dawn's activities, until the advancing hour and the possibility of the entrance of servants with shaving water brought things to an abrupt and unsatisfying conclusion.

"Tonight," Charles said, "I will tell you all about it, and you can criticize my decisions and inform me as to how much better you would have managed the business."

"How disagreeable I must be, to be sure," Fitz said. "I wonder you don't take the first chance to marry and seize your freedom."

"I could never be completely free," Charles said. "Just give me credit for some maturity."

"Isn't that what this tiresome conversation has established?" Fitz said, but smiling. "Go on, then. Sign the lease on your manor and invite every female in the neighborhood to a ball. I won't say a word."

"I will hold you to that, Fitz," Charles said. He just might, at that. A ball to celebrate the establishment of his own household. And if he met a pleasant, pretty young lady or two, where was the harm in that? He would have to marry sooner or later, however Fitz jibbed at every mention of the subject. In fact, it might be very nice to have a wife. But he would do nothing rash, nothing to make Fitz jealous or unhappy. The man had the devil's own temper, but he was the truest friend and there was no doubt he had Charles's interests at heart. And he made love like—like a demon and an angel, both, in one body.

Charles sighed and dismounted in front of the house. It was well kept, in good condition, only recently vacated. He could be happy here. He was sure of it.

That first ball in the Meryton assembly rooms lingered in Fitzwilliam Darcy's late-night torments for weeks. It had all gone as he had foreseen. Every family in the neighborhood had made a point of calling on Charles as soon as he moved in—even before. "I scarcely had my furniture unloaded and my trunks unpacked," he remarked in his cheerful, uncomplaining way, "when the local squires began riding up to 'get acquainted,' as they said."

The ball reflected the fruits of their labor, all the gentry for miles around attending, and worse, all the dreary, middling sort of people, the attorneys and the merchants, anyone who had acquired sufficient capital to retire from business or buy a tiny plot of land and could now call himself a gentleman. That in itself was bad enough, but naturally they all had families, and for some reason their progeny ran to daughters—at least that's how it looked to Fitz.

"My goodness!" Caroline Bingley said, gliding up to take his arm. "It's like a scene from some disreputable opera."

For once Fitz was in agreement, and grateful for her protection. He could only be thankful that he had had the good sense to stay in town until the previous evening and had not had a chance to be introduced to anyone; he could therefore claim to be unable to ask any of this enormous local harem to dance.

Charles was already dangerously entangled, with a plump, glowing girl, all smiles and lush curves, just the sort that would be considered the beauty of this benighted backwater. In London, of course, she'd be dismissed as a country milkmaid, but Charles conversed so spiritedly with her during the dance, and was on the verge of claiming her for an ill-advised second set, when Fitz attempted to intervene.

"Quite a prize, eh?" A vacuous old tradesman who had been elevated to the rank of knight took hold of Fitz's arm as he stepped forward to put a word in Charles's ear.

"I beg your pardon?" Fitz said, lowering his eyelids with disdain at the man's coarse, red face.

"Miss Bennet," Sir William Lucas said. "Our own native rose, you know. It seems your friend hasn't wasted any time. We may see some interesting developments soon, eh, what?"

Fighting the urge to plant the mushroom a facer, Fitz turned away and almost collided with Charles. "Not dancing, Fitz? How can you be so stupid?"

Fitz shrugged. "You are dancing with the only handsome girl in the room, other than your sisters."

"Oh, Miss Bennet is the most beautiful creature I ever beheld!" Charles exclaimed, his voice unnecessarily loud over the thin strains of music from the small orchestra. "But there's her sister forced to sit down, and almost as pretty. Why not ask her?"

Despite his best efforts, Fitz couldn't help sliding his eyes in the direction of the seated girl, curious as to how the sister of a country beauty would appear—buck teeth, perhaps, or a giggler, or spotty—and by the worst of bad luck his eyes met hers as, sensing his covert scrutiny, she turned her head toward his side of the room. Wide, dark brown eyes, fringed with delicate lashes;

expressive, humorous eyes, yet earnest; lively but honest. Gentle and innocent as a doe's but with the wit of a philosopher. Playful and seductive as a kitten's but with humanity and Christian grace to temper any impropriety...

Fitz felt himself blushing like a schoolboy, frowned and looked away. By God! He would not be made a fool of! "I'm afraid she is not handsome enough to tempt me," he said, ashamed of the words as soon as they left his mouth. "You had much better return to your charming partner and leave me to my uncharitable solitude." He watched Charles follow his advice, annoyed at being obeyed so promptly, and became aware of Caroline standing nearby, apparently having witnessed the entire disgraceful incident.

"Miss Bingley," Fitz said, giving a slight bow and attempting a smile. "Will you do me the honor?"

"Why, Mr. Darcy," she said, "I worried, for one breathless moment, that Cupid's arrow had pierced your heart."

"What the de—I mean, whatever are you talking about?" Fitz said.

"But then I recalled," Caroline continued, "that you do not possess a heart to be wounded."

Fitz was grinding his teeth as he led her out to form the quadrille.

That night was pure torture, and only the fact that mortals rarely possess the gift of foresight, and Fitz could not, thankfully, anticipate that worse was to follow, allowed him to bear his trials with gentlemanly composure.

"Wasn't it splendid!" Charles said, standing so temptingly naked in the center of the bedroom, arms out-flung in rapture, twirling slowly and tilting his head up to stare for some reason at the ceiling.

"Very nice," Fitz said.

"Nice?" Charles repeated. "Nice? That is the most mewling, pathetic, inadequate word in the English language. The ball shall be anything you say, except nice."

"Very well," Fitz said. "It was not nice in the least. It was horrid. It was hot, crowded, dreary, noisy—and noisome."

"You mean it stank?" Charles was diverted. "Now you're teasing. Explain yourself."

Fitz stretched his long limbs on the bed, artfully displaying the beginning of tumescence over the curve of a muscular thigh. "Come here, you provoking creature, and I'll explain at length."

Charles let his arms fall to his sides, and his mouth drooped. He was not hard—a disturbing and unwelcome development. "You know, Fitz, I've been wondering if we're getting too old for this."

Something pierced Fitz's heart, and it wasn't Cupid's arrow. He willed himself into control. "What do you mean, my dear?" he asked.

"Surely I don't have to recite your lessons back to you," Charles said. "This. Us. All that Achilles-and-Patroclus, Damon-and-Piteous stuff you talk about."

"Pythias," Fitz corrected. "What is it, Charles? Do you doubt my feelings for you?"

"No, never," Charles said. "But Fitz, you always called it a youthful love." He paused, looking down at himself, as if the question had arisen within his body, in his chest, covered with silky hair, or his slim waist with its trail of that same dark hair leading to the dense thatch at his crotch. When he spoke again, his words tumbled out in a nervous rush. "That beautiful girl tonight. Miss Bennet. She made me think that maybe it's time for me to put aside childish things."

Fitz took several breaths and counted to ten, then to twenty and backwards to one. "I see," he said, when he had his voice so modulated that his desire to commit brutal murder did not leak through. "A scheming, mercenary female, who from the look of her is on the cusp of becoming an old maid, finds that Providence has dropped a handsome, unattached young man with a considerable fortune into her sphere. Even before her first dance with this savior is finished, she has so poisoned her innocent victim's mind with thoughts of matrimony that he—"

"Stop it!" Charles shouted. "Just stop it! It's not amusing in the least." He strode to the door, yanked it open with such force that he almost struck himself in the face, remembered he was naked and slammed it shut again. "Just let me find my dressing gown and I'll leave you to your poisonous thoughts."

Fitz had already risen to the occasion. He wrapped Charles in a strong embrace, pressing what was left of his by now dwindling erection against his friend's equally flaccid member. "My dear," he whispered. "My dearest, sweet man. Forgive me. I think only of you, of your welfare. You know I never wish to hurt you."

Charles tried to free himself but was no match for Fitz's strength. "Let me go, Darcy," he said. His voice was icy, as Fitz had never heard it.

Fitz released Charles and stepped back, as one does instinctively from attack. "Please, Charles," he said. "Let's not quarrel over this."

"It's too late," Charles said. "We already have. Haven't we?"

"Not if we don't allow a trivial exchange to enlarge into a disagreement," Fitz said. "Whatever I said was meant in kindness to you. And I humbly and deeply apologize for any unintended affront to your beautiful Miss Bennet." This time his voice shook with the lie, but it worked to his advantage.

"Oh, Fitz," Charles said, remorse flooding him at last. "You know I can never stay angry with you." He lay down on the bed.

Hallelujah! Fitz thought, blasphemously and with Low Church vulgarity.

"She is lovely, though, isn't she?"

"What?" Fitz's hand was involuntarily arrested on its path to Charles's lovely thick cock.

"Miss Bennet. Isn't she the most beautiful lady you've ever seen? And do you want to hear what's even better?"

"Please," Fitz said, the last vestige of arousal draining from him like bilge from a beached ship's hold. "I'm all aquiver with curiosity."

"She has the sweetest disposition of any woman I've ever known," Charles replied, oblivious to any sarcasm.

"She would, naturally," Fitz muttered, but softly, so Charles heard nothing of the words.

"Let me tell you everything she said," Charles said, nestling into Fitz's embrace, resting his head on Fitz's shoulder as if they had already fucked themselves into exhaustion instead of having stopped everything dead from some sort of willful perversity.

"Yes, do," Fitz said. "Tell me everything." He might as well get it over with, he thought, giving the night up for lost. Dawn was almost here anyway, and they'd have only a precious couple of hours of sleep. Pity what little time they had was wasted on hearing that, amazing as it seemed, this aging country maiden was possessed of every virtue and free of every vice.

In the end, Charles allowed Fitz one quick romp before snuffing out the candle, but it was an unsatisfying, hasty business, and Fitz was so discomposed by the insipid narration preceding it that it turned into a dry bob instead of the real thing. He could tell Charles's heart and soul were far away, across the meadows in the neighboring village of Longbourn, where this damnable Miss Bennet was no doubt lying equally chastely in her sister's arms and enumerating dear Charles's considerable and genuine good qualities...

Which is what led to his body's failure, Fitz realized later. The sister's beautiful eyes had intruded on his mental vision just at what should have been the height of pleasure. Fitz imagined her watching him, those innocent but wise orbs staring unblinking while he groaned and sweated over Charles's firm buttocks, and he lost whatever meager strength he had regained.

"Never mind, love," Charles said. "It's late. You're tired, that's all."

"Yes," Fitz agreed, taking the path of least resistance. "But I am sorry."

"Don't be," Charles said, stroking Fitz's damp hair back from his high brow. "It's only what I said before. We're too old for this."

This time the voice in Fitz's brain rang its clarion warning, unmistakable: Get out now. Take Charles and get away.

He gave thanks every day since that he hadn't listened.

Glossary

Fundament: Rear end, butt
Mushroom (slang): Nouveau riche, upstart (analogy of someone who springs up overnight from the muck, like fungus)
Plant someone a facer (boxing slang): To punch someone in the face
Dry bob (slang): Dry hump; to have intercourse without ejaculation

Challenger Deep

Kathleen Bradean

Pop rode from Oakland to Guam in my lap. I put my vintage green and yellow A's baseball cap over him so that people wouldn't notice the plain cardboard box with the gold embossed stamp, "Williams and Sons Funeral Directors." A dusty cobweb clung to the back corner of the box. It had taken me a while to make good on my promise to him.

The first two days on the island, I let Pop sit on the dresser in the hotel room. Afraid that a maid might think he was trash, I decided I had to carry out his final request. Until I closed the past, the rest of my life was suspended.

I removed my hat as I ambled into the hotel lobby. By the time I reached the granite and glass reception desk, the hotel staff beamed expectant smiles.

"Hi. I need to find out how I can hire a boat."

They nodded, as if they understood everything. "Yes, Sir."

I grinned at them. It helped that I was so athletic and lanky, barely any hips or breasts. My look was boy next door—suntanned, with a white-toothed California smile. The short blonde haircut, the way I moved, the unisex clothes, worked magic. I passed as a man!

Then, recognition set in. "Um, Ma'am. Miss Erica." Fear that they'd offended me pulled at the corners of their eyes. They still smiled, but a little less certainly, less brightly.

My smile faded too. Funny how one little word had enough power to make me feel right with myself. But they snatched it away from me as quickly as they offered it. I wanted to be Sir. I wanted that magical word back.

"I need to hire a boat to take me out over the Challenger Deep." I set my A's cap on their polished counter.

The smiles drooped a bit more. The staff shrugged.

The hotel manager stepped forward to handle me. He wore a lei of waxy cream flowers over his dark green suit. The rest of the staff faded back, but their ears were tuned to the conversation and I saw their gazes slide away from their tasks to watch me. "No good fishing over the Marianas Trench," he told me with a tight smile. He folded his hands at his waist as if that closed the matter.

"I'm not fishing. I'm—." Who knew how many local laws I broke carrying around Pop's ashes, much less dumping them into the ocean? "I'm paying my last respects."

"It's all the same ocean. Same water. Why not take an island tour and pay your respects during that?"

He tried to hand me a glossy three-fold brochure of feral blondes on a sailboat, each clutching a tropical drink. I didn't accept it from him.

"I made a promise. My father was on the Trieste survey team that measured the Challenger Deep. He wanted to go back."

The manager's smile grew more fixed. "There's nothing out there. Just ocean." He decided a minor problem with the Japanese tourists at the far end of the desk needed his attention.

No one was interested in stories about Pop.

They didn't care that being on the team that measured the deepest place on earth meant something to him, and they couldn't understand how important it was to me to carry out Pop's final wish. I made a promise. Pop raised me to keep my word.

Pissed off, I shoved my A's cap over my cropped hair. My walk as I crossed the lobby had a definite female motion to it. I tried to get back into my male groove but couldn't.

I decided to explore past the fenced hotel grounds. The day before, I saw boats beyond the hotel's private beach. I figured I'd simply go hire one myself.

I reached for the brass handle on the lobby's glass doors.

A chubby, flirty doorman rushed to open the door for me. He was the one who always offered to bring me boys, girls, or smoke. "My brother has a boat," he whispered out of the side of his mouth.

"A big boat?"

The doorman shrugged his rounded shoulders, a common answer on the island, I was learning. No one wanted to say no.

"Last week, one of his customers caught a tuna! Big fish." He threw his arms wide, inviting me to imagine it.

Across the lobby, the manager cleared his throat.

The doorman scooted behind a potted palm. His dark green uniform blended with the plants.

"It's the distance I'm worried about." I felt silly, talking to a huge terracotta planter, but when I stood closer, the stiff palm fronds poked my face.

"My brother goes out there many times, I think."

And made it back apparently, which was my bigger concern. I shoved my hands into the pockets of my khaki shorts. "Can I meet him? See the boat?"

The doorman peered around the potted jungle. "I'll make the arrangements. Meet me beyond the security gate at five o'clock tomorrow morning."

"That early?" It felt so cloak and dagger for such a sunny, tropical island.

"The trench is very far. Better to start at daybreak so that it isn't dark when you come back." The doorman moved from behind the big planter. "Bring lots of water, three times what you think you need, food, and beer," he told me as he moved across the shiny marble floor. Then he trotted back. "Best prices, just for you, at the market in the blue building. Don't go into the other store. No good there. They rip you off. Charge you tourist prices. Go to the blue market. Ask for Gogui. My cousin. Tell him I sent you. You get a good price." He nudged my elbow then glided away to open the door for the Japanese tourists.

* * * *

The pure white sands of the hotel's imported beach gave way to Guam's domestic brown sand past the hotel's bamboo gate. It was just after dawn and the air was already torpid. Bright flags on ships' masts refused to flutter in the light breeze.

The doorman called out to me from behind a scraggly hibiscus bush. I wondered about him. Maybe skulking around playing games of intrigue made days of endless perfection seem more exciting.

Pop's box of ashes poked my back through the pack, prodding me on, or warning me, I wasn't sure.

Morning was rising, flat and harsh, over the sullen waves. Guam sat near the International Date Line, so we were among the first people on earth to witness the beginning hours of a new day.

"You went to see Gogui?"

I nodded.

"I told you. Best deal around."

Why we were whispering was beyond me.

The last high tide left a meandering line of tiny pink shells, seaweed, and dried foam along the sand.

"Tano!" The doorman greeted his brother as we trudged through the deep sand. "This is Miss Erica. She needs a boat."

Tano worked fishing line in his brown hands, his long fingers arcing high over his palm. He glanced up at us when the doorman hailed him but he didn't say anything. When we were a couple feet away, Tano set aside the knot he tried to tease out of the line.

Why was it that men always had the thick, long lashes that women wanted? His eyes were like tropical water over a shallow white sand beach. I could see the line of his hipbones above the low waistband of his shorts. A large hook, carved in bleached bone, hung between nipples like melted chocolate kisses.

I should have negotiated the price before I saw him. There had to be a premium for all that languid sex. He caught me looking, so I pulled the brim of my cap low over my eyes. Tano and his brother chatted in Chamorro, the island idiom. Whenever they laughed, as sparkly as sunlight on water, I felt as if it were about me. I shifted my backpack and dug the toe of my black Vans into the sand.

Tano's boat looked like shit, but all the sport-fishing boats along the beach were as weathered as the men who captained them. The metal fittings were speckled with rust. The dingy red stripe running along the hull was crusted with salt.

I looked past the surf to the ocean. It went on without end, and the boat seemed so small.

"No good fishing in the deep. Fish like warm, shallow water," Tano said to me.

I glanced up at him again. High cheekbones, thick lips, he was too incredible to look at straight on, like the sun. Sparse hairs on his chin curled wildly, one lighter brown than the others. A flush of heat hit my lips and cheeks, as obvious as a hard-on. I felt the welcome, warm tingle of interest between my legs.

"I'm not fishing. I want to release something."

The doorman tried to infect our half-hearted haggling over the price of the trip by baiting Tano and then me in turns, but we already reached an understanding between flitting glances.

* * * *

It took most of an hour to get the boat ready to go. The doorman disappeared when the work started. Tano told me what to do, sometimes showing me by covering my hands with his dark brown ones. By the time the boat was on the water, we had a casual flirtation going. It was easy. No forced chuckles, no posturing.

Tano asked, "What's with the hat? You touch it like a talisman every time you mention your father."

I caught myself touching the brim again and gave him an embarrassed grin. "Pop and I were big fans of the A's. He bought this cap for me when I was in seventh grade. We caught a foul ball that day."

"I touch a tree every time I return to shore. Superstitious, both of us," he chuckled.

I gave him a friendly little nudge with my shoulder as we bent to lift the cooler onto the deck. Tano bumped back, grinning and showing a gap in his front teeth.

We set sail as the sun broke above low clouds. Land slipped from sight and I felt as if the world went away.

"You don't get seasick, do you, Erica?" Tano asked as we hit open ocean.

We slammed up and down waves until he tacked enough to cut through the troughs. The side-to-side rocking was harder, but at least my teeth didn't clack together.

I patted my stomach. "Something I inherited from Pop. Sea legs. Sea stomach, I guess. He was in the Navy." The sun was already strong, so I put on my sunglasses and tugged at the brim of my cap when I felt the wind try to lift it. "He was stationed near here for a couple years."

"Good, because it's going to be hours of this," Tano warned. He squinted at the bright light bouncing off the white surfaces of his boat.

There were large padded captain's chairs at the back of his boat for fishers, but I settled onto the worn red cushion under the sun shade and propped my feet on a cooler. I sipped from a cold beer. "Your brother told me that you go out to the Mariana Trench a lot. If there's nothing there to see, as everyone keeps telling me, why do you go?"

Tano stared at the water. Damn, pissed him off, and I wanted to sweet-talk him into a little bump and grind. He was just my type—a jock. It was going to be a very long day if he wasn't going to talk.

Tano did talk though. His eyes focused past me as if he were remembering a distant, hazy past. "About three years ago, I was unhappy. I was in love. There was a man... He consumed my heart and soul. I lived for the sight of him. On the day he moved away, I sailed to the edge of the trench. I hung over the railing, staring into the deep, wondering if I had the balls to jump. Instead, my tears fell. Maybe, they are still falling."

"The trench is deep," I agreed. "Seven miles from the surface to the bottom of the Challenger Deep—the lowest spot along the trench. Pop told me that you could toss Mount Everest down it and still have a mile of water left." I almost touched the cap, but saw Tano's teasing smile and held onto my beer instead.

"Big enough to hold all the sorrow in the world."

Tano leaned far over the side of the boat. It was body poetry, the arc of his lean brown torso, the grip of his long toes on the railing of the boat, the way his hand slapped against the rising waves.

After he swung back onto the deck, he dragged wet fingers across my lips. I licked the drops away.

"Tastes like tears, doesn't it," he asked softly. Our bodies touched.

We stayed there, pressed together, staring down into the water as if it held answers.

"Pop once told me that the human body is mostly seawater."

Tano smiled slyly. "Does that mean we're mostly sorrow?"

It was my turn to stare off at the intensely blue water. I ran my fingertips over the lumpy white A on the front of my cap. "Some of us."

* * * *

We played his CDs of local technopop and danced like we were in a club. The unpredictable motion of the water made it hard to keep my footing, but Tano put his hands over his head and moved like curling waves. I wasn't as steady so I bumped against him a lot, but I closed my eyes and imagined I was a hot boy under the flashing lights of a foam pit, and everyone wanted to take me home. When his hands went to steady me, I pretended strangers couldn't stop themselves from reaching out to touch my boy flesh.

When the batteries died in his player, I collapsed onto the cushions, laughing. "I haven't danced like that in a long time. I expected, you know, a tropical paradise, people to be so much more open about their sexuality. But it's worse here than back home. When they think I'm a man, I can dance with a girl, but the moment they realize I'm," I gestured down to my body with contempt, "this, they get angry and move away."

Tano rested his elbows on the boat's console. He still panted from our dancing. "I have to be careful. That's why I couldn't tell him that I wanted him. I could only suffer, and want, and be silent."

"Sorry."

I wanted to tell him that I understood, but at Pop's funeral, people said, "I know how you feel," and I'd think, You can't even begin to guess what I lost. But I'd nod and stare down at the carpet until they moved on to the food laid out on the dining room table.

* * * *

I had to move under the faded red sun shade to stay in the short shadows. Noon already. He watched me out of the corner of his eye. "It's a strange thing to be doing, burying your father."

I shrugged.

"Usually the son does that, around here."

I peeled the label off my beer bottle with my fingernails, trying, as usual, to take it off in one piece. Another superstition. I wasn't even sure what curse a whole label blocked.

What the hell, he came out to me.

"I'm not a woman. I mean, not inside. Just on the surface." I got the big label off and worked on the smaller one at the neck of the brown bottle. "I was supposed to be a boy. I have two older sisters. They're girls."

I knew that sounded stupid. I set aside my beer.

"I mean, they're girly-girls. Real girls. Inside and out. Not me. See, everyone knows if the two older kids are the same sex, the third child is the last try for the other. Mom even told me that the only name they had picked out was Eric. In the hospital, they slapped the A on the end to make me Erica."

There was something about strangers that made confession so easy. Flash—expose my soul—flash—walk away with one less bur-den, confident that the intimacy was safely contained in that moment like toxic waste buried deep under tons of cement.

I pulled off my hat and worked my hands around it in an unending circle. "I would have made a great boy. I hung around Pop and helped him work on the cars. I was the only one who went to baseball games with him. We both liked gingersnaps and root beer." As if that described the bond we shared that excluded my Mom and sisters. I was Pop's son in every way but the one that mattered to me.

Tano asked, "Do you like girls?"

I gave him that frank look that I learned in bars, the one that got men to follow me to dark corners. "The individual person matters more than the gender. Men, I understand. Women are like a separate tribe with weird rituals and a different language. I don't get women, but I like making love to them. I like men too. Some of them."

"You like everyone except you." He sipped from his beer. "I only like men."

* * * *

The waves whooshed and hissed. It was a vast desert, the surface of the ocean. No birds overhead, no signs of life in the water. I drank more beer than I should have and watched Tano because there was nothing else to see.

Every movement he made was sure, slow. I envied the way his fingertips trailed over the boat's chromed steering wheel. His lips were so rough and cracked from the sea that I thought they'd feel great nibbling on my skin.

Sweat shone on Tano's slender neck. I wanted to lick it away. Sex surged through my blood, in my chest, in my belly, between my legs. I wondered if men felt that too, or if it was all in the dick for them.

Shit. I was dumping Pop's ashes, a funeral of sorts, and I was cruising the island boy. I was going to burn in hell.

* * * *

"Did you ever think of changing to a man?"

After hours of silence, his voice startled me.

"Yes." I drew my feet off the cooler and leaned forward with my hands clasped together. "I mean, I looked into the treatments. The stumbling block was that I had to live as a man for a year. Not that I didn't want to, but I didn't know when to begin. On the way home from the doctor's office? I got onto the bus as a man, but three stops later someone called me Ma'am and I was back to being female. The next morning I planned to start off fresh, but I couldn't escape my body. Every night I'd go to sleep swearing, "This is my last day as Erica," but then I'd get dressed and go to work and still be stuck in the twilight world between who I've been and who I want to be."

Tano smiled out at the waves. "You can't become who you already are. You can only accept it. Maybe you're not male; maybe you aren't female. Maybe you aren't straight; maybe you aren't gay. Maybe you're simply you." He made me see myself in a tilted mirror. "There are vast spaces in the between. There's more ocean than island."

"Maybe I'm the shore."

* * * *

The bottom dropped out of the world. I clutched the boat railing. I was falling, falling while we were floating. Dizzy, I gulped air.

Wave. Trough. White foam. In the distance, the water was unrelenting blue, but the crest curling off the bow of the boat was green and gray. Nothing was different, yet primal instinct told me that I was in danger.

Intense pressure squeezed my chest as if I dove into the depths. "What is it?"

He answered in a whisper, "We're over the trench." He cut the engines. Even the waves were hushed, as if we'd stepped inside a great cathedral.

The swells knocked the boat.

"Is it always like this?"

He nodded. His pale eyes were as wide as mine. It didn't seem possible, but we could feel it, the void below us. I stared up at the azure sky, afraid that if I looked down, like a cartoon character, I'd fall.

I didn't think I believed in such things, but I swore I felt the immense presence of god.

I wanted to run. I wanted to hide. I lurched to my backpack and pulled out the box of Pop's ashes.

"Maybe you shouldn't drop your father over the side. Maybe you should throw in your sorrow, like I did. Let it sink."

"It's not that easy."

Tano snatched my A's cap off my head. He tossed it onto the waves like a Frisbee.

"Hey!" I was too afraid to jump in after it even though I was a great swimmer.

That much water could drown you, I thought. The weight of it would drag you under the surface. You'd never see the sun again.

My hat bobbed on top of a far wave, disappeared on the rolling surface, reappeared even further away.

"That was the A at the end of your name. Now, you are Eric."

My mouth open and shut like a hooked fish.

"Your life as a man has begun."

He was an idiot. He didn't understand. "It isn't that easy. It can't be that easy."

"But what if it is? That hat was a gris-gris, a magic charm. Throw it away, and throw away the A that made you into a girl."

Anger welled up behind my eyes.

Tano pleaded with me. "Believe just enough to make it real. Go back to shore as a man. You don't know when to being? Begin now! Right now! Because the now is the only time you ever really have."

My throat was too tight to breathe.

"I let my moment pass. I'm stuck in a now that never ends, the man I want living with someone else. Before that happened, I should have acted," Tano told me, and I saw tears in the corners of his eyes. "Don't waste your now, your chance."

The hat slowly absorbed water, growing darker. The big white A on the front sank lower as it absorbed tears. When it was full of them, it fell below the surface. Feeling as if I were drowning, I gasped in salt air.

"You can only tread water so long before the misery will pull you under. It's not sink or swim. It's sink or fly."

The hat was gone. Could I cast off my outer self as easily as he cast away my hat? I inhaled again and relaxed my fists.

"I only like men," Tano reminded me.

He came to me, wrapping his arms around my waist. I felt his dick against my thigh. He kissed me, and it was like kissing the sea. I tasted the salt on his mouth and felt the tug of his chapped skin over my smooth lips. His skin was hot from the sun.

"Fly."

I was Eric. Kissed, suddenly I was a prince.

I shoved Tano to the floor of the boat. His shorts came off in a quick tug. I was more aggressive than he probably expected, but he didn't seem to mind. We fucked like men, raw energy wildly spent.

* * * *

Pop told me that the day he sailed to the edge of the Marianas Trench was a profoundly spiritual day for him. He didn't use those words exactly. Being a Navy man, he said something like, "God grabbed me by the balls and made me take a hard look at the man I was becoming."

Maybe Pop knew I needed to face it. Maybe he wanted it for me. Maybe that was why he made me promise to bring him there.

I was sorry that I wasted three years keeping that promise. The breeze ruffled my short hair like a friendly paternal pat.

Tano started the boat's engines.

Against the Challenger Deep, the hurdles ahead of me suddenly seemed like nothing. A drop in the ocean.

Tano turned the boat around.

Pop always said that the measure of a man was in how he kept his word. Out of habit, I reached for a cap that wasn't there, and, remembering, smiled a little.

I tipped Pop's ashes into the vast blue. The wind picked them up and scattered them further. Pop flew on gusts of wind, and then he fell, soft as tears, and is probably falling still, into the mourning wake. I felt every inch a man.

Mr. Greene

Ours M. Hugh

I don't think I'll ever forget the title of that painting. The only reason I even remember the name so clearly is because of the artist, Dorothea Koch. I used to imagine her in my mind's eye, some waifish first-year NYU student. She probably had outrageous hair, and an outspoken belief that she would prove to the world that she could make it as an artist, and that what she had to say had not been said before. Dorothea had scrawled the title of her piece next to her signature in the bottom left corner of the canvas. The luscious red paint she used to sign and entitle her work ran right on to the edge of Mr. Greene's left shoe. Perhaps the irony was intentional. I prefer to think it was not.

In the three years I was with Amelia, we never talked about where she got that painting. I always assumed it was something she got from an ex-girlfriend, or maybe haggled over for her first apartment. Maybe someone left it behind when she took her flat in Astoria. The piece certainly didn't belong in her bedroom. The frame was gilded and poorly tacked, probably salvaged from something someone threw away on the street. It didn't fit on the wall space she had available. The canvas hovered ponderously over the headboard like a pyrite zeppelin. I was the only guy Amelia ever went with in all her years. She picked me up off the street too. Maybe the picture came with the frame. There were lots of quirks about this Amelia. She was the kind of person who could never just get up and go somewhere. There were countless layers of makeup application, hair tweaking, and accessory picking. Amelia had to take a shower every time she went outside, which was always followed by an application of some sort of skin oil. Fuck all if I commented or cajoled. That was like shouting 'Jenga!' before the whole tower came down. Getting ready to go out to the grocery store took more time than walking there did. I never noticed all these things until a few weeks after we split, and I rolled out of bed to go buy a cup of coffee—something I hadn't done in years. I think part of the reason she went through all the rigmarole was that she was uncomfortable in her own skin. Lord knows I wasn't uncomfortable around her in her skin. In those three years I don't think we spent a night apart or fully clothed. If only satisfaction of the flesh were full satisfaction.

I can't say that I loved Amelia. I loved being with her though. Nights with her were feral and hungry; two predators stalking the same prey, but both ending up hungry. In the beginning, sex with Amelia was a contest of wills, to see which of us would get off first in a given romp—both vying to be the last. I would be lying if I didn't say I had to work on holding off. Eventually, Amelia realized she was missing out on a lot of orgasms by holding out until after she got me off. At that point, the game flipped to going for high counts on how many times I could get her off before I eventually let go. I am sure the upstairs neighbors loved the competition. I certainly did. I speak for the box spring when I say it did not. It never spoke up though, aside from its squealing protests while we were in the midst of the act, which were usually secondary noise to the usual opera of moans and groans that accompany the act. The neighbors never mentioned anything, but their stares said plenty when we passed each other by the mailboxes or on the way to the store.

Amelia never wanted to do anything alone, and never wanted me to do anything alone. Her insecurity was contagious. Co-dependency bloomed in me like malaria, to the point I would get feverish if I had to work overtime or missed my train. Those were busy days for me, in the early part of our relationship. The weekend she picked me up, I was celebrating landing my new job. Between the raise in salary, and the stress of seventy-hour weeks, it was a wonder I kept it as long as I did.

Sometimes, I'm amazed my addiction to her didn't kill me. While I had it, the job was the only acceptable excuse at my call to hold the dependence at bay. It was the other half of the competitive coin we flipped every night between the sheets. We needed that aggressive friction to make sparks fly, and, once cooled, that friction left us bonded. I cannot count how many engagements I skipped out on, simply because she couldn't make it. Amelia, on the other hand, would regularly schedule plans for both of us. Sometimes she cancelled, sometimes she didn't. The associates she kept seemed to be okay with her flakiness. It bugged the shit out of me, but I stuck with it anyhow. Amelia never had any friends though, only acquaintances.

We argued about her lack of friends, along with all the other banal things couples argue over. These arguments would often start or end in a baseless accusation. I was always accusing her of going back to women, and she was always freaking out about me getting ready to leave her. Neither of us ever joked about the twenty years in age between us. We didn't need to. It was apparent every time we lay next to each other; skin warm and slick, tight and saggy. I often wish I had met her when she was younger, before she decided she fancied cheeseburgers instead of protein shakes. I guess I should be pretty flattered that she spent so long on me, regardless of what she ate. At the time, I was too bothered by the constant self-doubts to realize that I was such a desperate commodity to her. Aside from me, her only other long-term had been her first guy in high school. Between him and me, she had nothing but women.

When I found all this out several months in, I asked her why she had broken her habits. Amelia admitted she had thought I was a woman when she saw me stumble out of the bar our first night. I guess with the long blonde hair and my slender build that possibility is not too unbelievable. It certainly wouldn't have been the first time someone made the mistake. Well, that is not entirely true. It is the first time a woman ever made the mistake. Amelia always hated that I could fit into her jeans better than she could.⊠⊠Man, am I off track; I was talking about the painting. The painting was noteworthy because of the content, rather than the artistry or the technique. Who the hell paints the back of someone's ankles and shoes? No walking, no action, no conflict. Five feet by seven feet of canvas depicting tranquil shiny heels peeking out from under two pinstripe pant legs, standing sentinel before a sea of sidewalk. Maybe that is the trick of the painting. You see the pant leg and your brain is expecting wingtips, but your eyes are giving you thick mannish feet jammed into thin leather stilettos, and you are supposed to laugh. I never found it funny. That painting used to be my solace whenever Amelia wanted it from behind. I would stare at that painting and try to stay hard, ignoring what was purring and gyrating below me between my legs. I would stare at the brushstrokes that added the luster to those sensuous heels, and I'd be able to hold on for another two minutes. The painting helped me win, some nights. I met Amelia the same way I left her: so drunk I could barely stand on my own. That first night she picked me up as I drunk-stumbled out of Cutty's, One of the few things I remember from that night was her going on and on about my hair, and the fact that my arms were so smooth as she poured me into a cab. I don't remember what I told her in response. Whatever it was, it was witty enough to have her hop in the cab after me, and take me back to her place. We clearly fucked that night, though I don't remember any of that any better than I could remember her name when I awoke the next morning. I didn't know where I was, who she was, or where my clothes were. It was just her bed, the painting, and me. It took her hours to wake up, and by then my hangover had dissolved into a dull throb in the back of my head, and a ravenous hunger. She introduced herself when she finally woke up, knowing, somehow, that I wouldn't remember. Maybe I never knew. Nobody knows but her.

It was funny that first morning, the awkwardness of intimacy; like freshly hatched chicks learning to walk. After showering, she had me oil her up, and then suggested we wander out to find some food. The planning and conversation over breakfast plans took place while she was in the midst of her hour of preparation, and I was perched naked, on the edge of her tub. That was the only time she ever talked to me while getting ready. She gave me a blowjob after she finished her lipstick, then told me to get dressed so she could straighten it up. From that exchange on, once I left the steamy womb of the shower curtains, I was banished from the bathroom until she was ready to get dressed.

That morning, the thin chill in the air was a clear indicator that summer was on the way out. The frost and colored leaves of fall had yet to arrive; opulently bedecked, as death often is. We went to some local joint and had eggs and toast and tea and coffee. I never drank tea. Amelia never drank coffee. After brunch, I was ready to go home, but she coaxed me back to her place. I didn't leave for another two days. Amelia's bedroom was too small for furniture other than her bed. Her dresser was in the closet in the hallway. The light switch was by the door, and there were heavy blinds covering the windows. Even if I did remember to bring a book, I could never read it, because turning on the light meant getting up to do so. Amelia had the annoying habit of sleeping on the side of the bed not against the wall, so I would have to climb over her if I wanted to take a piss or go get a drink. I would always wake her in the process, and we would have a fight, which would generally end with us fucking again. I never thought to just open the blinds. I spent a lot of time staring at that painting, while she snored next to me, the crows feet at her eyes smoothed away in her sleep. It was always visible through the dim light that filtered in around the edges of the blinds. Amelia could sleep away a Saturday like someone who had put in a sixty-hour week, then do the same thing on a Sunday. Amelia didn't work; instead, she lived off her inheritance. I shouldn't be too judgmental. For a while, I lived off her inheritance too.

Times were hard. The market was tough to break in to when you had been out of work for a while. I had been out of work for a while. People were crashing planes into buildings, and employers were moving jobs to India. How the hell were you supposed to fight those odds? Particularly when you lost your last gig due to excessive absence, as opposed to the company going under, like everyone else. It was much easier to lie around, drink away the weekend with other working stiffs, and alternate between staring at the painting and masturbating the rest of the time Amelia slept.

Everything ended abruptly when I found that box of dental dams. She swore they were old, but the receipt from Duane Reade was dated the week before. There hadn't even been a Duane Reade there when we started seeing each other. We never used protection. Maybe that is why it stung for months afterwards. It still stings.

Amelia did go back to women after I left her. I've been watching her for months, trying to figure out which of the freshman she would pick out, and which toy in her bag of tricks she would use to seduce them. She never stays with any of them very long, and generally ends up discarding them like twists of Kleenex. Amelia knows how to collect these little girls. She does it like a farmer's wife picking out eggs. Before the little experimenters have figured out what is going on, they are in the frying pan. She always leaves a few behind, so that there will be something to throw in the pan tomorrow or the next day.

It amazes me that all these taut little co-eds are so allured by an older woman, when, obviously, they could have their pick of other taut little co-eds. It must be the experience, and the security of an older woman. Maybe it's a mom thing. I don't know. I bet Amelia still plays her games for high score now, rather than holding out. I bet that much has changed.

She doesn't know what is coming. Hopefully, she won't until it is too late. I've spent a lot of time thinking about that damn painting, and what it might mean. She used to tell me, "Mark, you better give me what I need, or I'm gonna go look elsewhere." I tried to as Mark, and she went elsewhere anyway.

The straps on my stilettos bite my heels like puppy teeth. They are not quite sharp enough to break the skin, but sharp enough to let me know they are there. The fit of my silk pinstripe suit should dissuade anyone from spending too much time staring at my feet. The catcalls on the walk to the bar have been quite vociferous. It seems like construction workers will promise anything for a little wiggle of the hips. If only they knew.

By the end of the night, my ankles will probably be gashes.—raw and red, like that puppy spent all night gnawing. The price will be worth it if I can talk to her, introduce myself again, and maybe get her number. I know what lies in that bag of tricks. I know what she likes, and how she thinks. I made sure that I am wearing short sleeves, so my arms will be showing. I should be able to slip in past her defenses and have her lusting before she realizes I am not who she thinks I am.

My name will be Marci. Marci Greene.

Art Making
Kate Evans

Michelle has never lied to her lover, June, before—and for a moment she reconsiders. She stops on the lawn and turns to look back at the house. Glacier-like, the new house exudes a frosty aloofness, a blank-faced enormity.

June, smiling, peers out the upstairs window at Michelle. She holds their terrier, Ragamuffin, up to the window, waving his paw in her hand. The room glows, lamplight shedding gold on June and their dog—a small speck of warmth engulfed by the vast white house.

Michelle feels a rush of cold fall air. Perhaps she should just go back in the house and carry in the three pumpkins that slouch against the porch. They could make jack-o-lanterns this afternoon. Or Michelle could help June stencil pink and blue terrier silhouettes on the walls of the nursery while they watch the game.

Instead, she turns and walks, her throat tightening, her body moving away from the house. Her lie to June creeps into her bones, the lie that she is merely taking an afternoon walk.

As she steps to the sidewalk that is lined with the sentinels of slim, straight-backed trees, Michelle pulls her long, red hair from under the neck of her coat to let it sweep across her back. Tulle fog clings to the crew-cut grass that fans out from each house's colossal white portico. The cold air smells full, like rain is on the way. Michelle's heart thrums as she walks, her body charged. A fat, striped spider clings to a glossy web on the cement cherub that their neighbors, the Whites, installed just last week. The statue is surrounded with regulation redwood bark.

Michelle knows the Whites aren't happy with her and June. In the three months she and June have lived next door, they've put in their lawn but not the plants and retainer wall. Michelle knows the Whites want perfection—and fast—but it just isn't in her.

Things are tight since they're spending so much money and time with the fertility specialist. They didn't tell this to Georgia and John White, though, who apparently have no such problem since three little girls with all their pink accoutrements fill their vast house. And if June is right, Georgia looks to be gaining some weight. So perhaps another White is on the way.

Michelle was inseminated yesterday, for the eleventh time. The first few times the sperm arrived at their old one-bedroom house on Grant Street in its cryogenic capsule. June, wearing garden gloves and ski goggles, removed it carefully, defrosted it in its clear tube in a pan of bubbling water over the stove. Michelle fitted herself with the cervical cap and tube, lying back on their sagging burgundy couch, nestled against her grandmother's needlepoint pillow for luck. June and Michelle had giggled off and on for hours after the first insemination at the image of June, with her frizzy brown hair, wearing goggles and hunched over the stove like a crazy scientist. They giggled at the thought of a stranger's sperm wriggling up into Michelle's body, her body wondering what the hell this foreign substance was. June lit a few lemon candles then lay next to Michelle, pressing into her.

They took a break from the successive inseminations the month they moved into the new house in Whispering Winds development. Michelle didn't want to move; she wanted to remodel the Grant Street house and stay in the neighborhood with bungalows, buckled sidewalks, and full-grown willows. June, though, wanted a new house, a new neighborhood. They were building a family; why not go for it all in an unsullied space? Now that they had the money in equity, why not sell and move? A clean, new place for a fresh start. A clean, new place with no electrical problems (what if a spark lit a fire, did they want to put a baby at such risk?), no plumbing problems (gritty stuff came out of the old pipes; was that safe to drink, much less wash baby bottles in?).

June was sure there was mold in the walls, radon in the attic, rot in the foundation.

Michelle said all of that could be fixed in a full remodel.

But what about working on the baby, countered June? How could they work on a baby and undertake a remodel at the same time? It was more sensible to buy in this new development, where everything was already set, in its place, ready to go.

Now they were settled in the new house and settled in with Dr. Ray, who was inseminating Michelle in her antiseptic office each month.

Michelle watches her feet walk along the perfect sidewalk squares. She knows that all this spanking newness makes June happy. June emits an aura of satisfaction as she crochets blankets while watching the Sports Channel on the new big screen T.V. June is content, set for the introduction of a pink-skinned infant who will have her own freshly stenciled room in their unpolluted four-bedroom house.

Michelle rubs her hands together in the cold then shoves them in her pockets, her fingers touching her cell phone. Spread across a neighbor's front door is a cotton spider web housing a huge plastic spider that wears a pointed witch hat. She feels an ache in her gut—the ping of ovulation?—and a warm gush in her groin. For a moment she panics, thinking she can't remember his phone number. Then it comes to her.

It's so cold that she's sure no one will be at the mini-park at the end of the block, which would be a good place to make the call. The cement walkway to the park is lined with skinny trees tied to sticks. The play equipment—a plastic motorcycle on a spring, two bucket baby swings, and a twisted insect of a slide—is mounted over a springy, rubber surface.

If rubber surfaces had been in parks years ago, maybe Michelle would not have broken her arm when she was eight at the old park across town, the one with sloping slides, and swings that shot high, and round cement tubes where she would echo her name, over and over. The massive shade trees were almost better than the equipment: Michelle climbed as high as she dared, converting people on the ground into toys or ants. She fell when she was trying to hang upside down by one leg. She'd been testing her strength. Later, when Michelle gingerly approached the park equipment with her puckered, white arm recently released from the cast, her grandmother had scolded her. "Don't be so timid," she'd said. Michelle's grandmother died just two months ago, shortly after Michelle and June moved to Whispering Winds. In the hospital bed, her grandmother had been silenced by a stroke.

Michelle feels like she's losing her breath so she shakes away the image of her dying grandmother.

She guessed right. The park is empty. The nearby gray houses have their white blinds shut, and the tulle fog is gathering even more thickly in the cold. Michelle sits on a cement bench, frosty damp permeating her jeans to the backs of her thighs.

Roland answers the phone on the first ring.

"Hi," he says.

"I'm at the park."

"How are you?"

"Okay."

"I'll be right over to get you if you want."

"Okay."

"Are you sure?"

"Yes."

Her heart picks up its pace again. The low fog swirls and a raindrop stains the knee of her jeans. Roland has hung up, and she realizes she still has the phone to her ear. She clicks the phone shut and drops it back in her jacket pocket.

On the cul-de-sac across the way, just past the slide, a man in a black coat walks a white dog. If Michelle squints, the dog almost disappears in the pallid atmosphere, the leash leading to nowhere. Michelle does something she hasn't done since she was a kid—closes her eyes and pretends she's invisible. But she knows her long red hair is aflame in the white air.

A month ago, Roland began his comments to her about her hair. "Hey Red," he said. She was taken aback at first. But after Roland brushed by her a few times while he was shelving books or passing her on his way to the bookstore's rear cash register, she realized he meant the nickname not only playfully.

She was used to comments from men over the years—sometimes they stirred her a little, but usually they left her cold. There was something different about Roland, though. His soft brown skin, his chocolate eyes, the way one front tooth overlapped another.

During one of the many conversations they had during breaks, he told her his mother was second generation from India. Something about those teeth, and the way he moved his hands, reminded her of her best friend in tenth grade, the girl who had sent shockwaves through her body during surreptitious stroking in the middle of the night as they slept in sleeping bags zipped together on the floor of her bedroom.

Michelle and Roland began stretching their conversations beyond the ten minutes allotted for breaks. Michelle never asked Roland how old he was, but she figured he was in his mid-twenties, at least ten years younger than she. An art major at the local state university, he talked about slender-necked Modiglianis and puddle-eyed Lempickas in a way that made her crave... something. What? She wasn't sure.

"Look," he'd once said, pulling a book from his backpack and opening it on the table between them. A thick-thighed nude with a body like golden hills barely contained the space of the frame.

"Lempicka's excesses are magnificent," he said, pausing to sip his tea. "Even cars look like flesh in her paintings. You can just feel the overflow. A hallmark of Bohemia."

"I feel like I could reach out and touch her. It's like you want to be in that world," Michelle said, feeling awkward at her attempt to talk about art.

"That's both the artist's passion and technique. She's a master of shadow."

Michelle wanted to show Roland her grandmother's paintings. But she was apprehensive, not sure if they were good art and not wanting his opinion if they weren't. Glistening apples, gold pocket watches, walnuts on purple silk that looked like it would be smooth to the touch. At least thirty of these paintings were stacked in a closet in the guest room. June kept saying to Michelle that they should hang them; the paintings had covered almost every inch of the walls in the old Grant Street house. But to hang her grandmother's creations of glowing, old objects in the new house doesn't feel right to Michelle. The paintings would be undermined or contaminated, somehow, by the house's sleek silver carpet and faux brass fixtures.

The pace of raindrops begins to pick up. Michelle pulls her coat hood over her head. When she sees Roland's red truck approaching, she feels a pang, static shooting inside the cavern of her chest.

A blast of warm air greets her when she slides onto the bench seat. He smiles at her and turns on the windshield wipers. They don't say anything for a few minutes, just sit there staring straight ahead at the thud and squeak of the wipers. The truck pulls out of Whispering Winds and onto the slick main road, which is reflecting the stoplights. Roland turns on the radio to a whiskey-voiced woman singing about her lover standing under the moon. They pass three mini-malls crammed with quick marts and diet centers and video stores.

"I want you to see something," Roland says.

"Yeah?"

"Yeah," he says as he turns and follows the signs to the freeway and heads north.

"I need to make a call," Michelle says.

Roland turns off the radio as Michelle dials. When June answers, Michelle can hear the game in the background. She feels an odd wash of nostalgia.

"Where are you? Aren't you soaked?" June says in a voice that suggests she has one eye on the game.

"I ran into Leanne," Michelle says, her heart thumping. "She asked me if I wanted to go shopping with her, and maybe to get something to eat. It sounded like a good thing for my mood."

Michelle stops herself, concerned if she chatters on too long a false note will surface. She panics for a minute at the thought that June might ask to say hello to Leanne, a friend who lives across town. "Oh, yeah, hon, that sounds good. Hey, just don't drink anything, you know, because who knows if those wrigglers hit their mark. Maybe our little daughter is growing in you as we speak." Static crinkles over the line.

"I think we're cutting out," Michelle says, relieved for an excuse to hang up.

"Okay. Have fun."

Michelle clicks off, a kind of gloomy dread sweeping over her. She pushes aside a pinch of a thought: What if Leanne calls?

Turn this truck around, she almost says. As the windshield begins to cloud, Roland reaches over and turns on the defroster. She catches his profile out of the corner of her eye, his high, arched nose, his minky eyelashes, his hands soft against the steering wheel. She settles back as he drives, the gloom settling and electricity sparking her veins once more as they move down the road.

"That's my great-aunt," says Roland.

He and Michelle are standing warm and dry in a gallery, raindrops sliding down their coats. In the oil painting, a woman is draped in sheer, brown material. Her body overflows—rounded stomach, full breasts with salmon colored nipples, lush scarlet lips. Her shoulders, forearms, and thighs are thick and long, seeming to seep beyond the edges of the canvas in smoky fullness. Yet there is an angular quality to her softness: her collarbones protrude, her nose and eyebrows arc, and her slicked-back hair is run through with a stern pencil-straight part.

"She was one of Tamara de Lempicka's lovers," Roland continues, "Or at least that's the story. They knew each other in Paris in the 1920s. She was my father's aunt."

"Did you know her?"

"Only through this painting."

They continue through the exhibition of Lempickas, body after body exuberantly ballooning toward them, each supple yet slightly metallic in the contrast of shadow to skin. In one painting, four nudes intertwine, sienna flesh with sienna flesh, so that it's not clear where one body starts and another stops. In another, a fleshy man and woman embrace, his potent arms curving around the woman's gravid stomach.

It's in front of this painting that Roland places his hand in the sway of Michelle's back. Michelle reaches over and touches his arm, the bridge from him to her.

Michelle lies on her back, her hands on her stomach. She listens to the end of the storm, a few scattered raindrops on the roof. White light from a streetlight ekes in. From her place on the futon mattress, Michelle can see canvasses looming like shadows in the corners of Roland's studio apartment. One leans against the easel in the corner. The room has a greasy, spicy pungency: Roland's smells, and the scent of art making.

Roland sleeps on his side, his breath warm against her neck. During sex, she had been surprised at the sandpaper feel of his face, and the way he kept his eyes open, staring at her as he entered her. His hipbones had nudged insistently against hers.

And now her blood feels like it's smoothly flowing through her body, a kind of rested state she hasn't experienced in months. She feels ample and lush. Sated. If she were a painting, she'd be a Lempicka.

For a moment she entertains a fantasy of her grandmother as a young woman drinking wine in Paris with Roland's aunt and Tamara de Lempicka. They're in a studio cluttered with palettes for blending colors, an array of brushes and half-finished paintings and tubes of paint littering the warped wood floors and color-splattered tables. They talk about bodies, laugh about affairs, drink wine, and light each other's cigarettes. Atop silk-strewn blocks for models to pose, they disrobe.

Friends and Neighbours

Jacqueline Applebee

Oh hello Ink, can I come in for a bit? Ta. I thought you'd be watching the football—hasn't the game started yet?

Ah, you're a love, a cup of tea sounds great. You're too good to your old next-door neighbour.

You all right there? You look a little tired, all sweaty and rumpled... oh Ink, you scoundrel! What have you been up to?

Don't give me that, I know something's up. You've been having some naughty fun haven't you? My eyesight may be failing, but I can tell—wasn't I married for more than forty years? A man knows what a woman looks like when she's been well and truly ravished. Not that I did much ravishing towards the end. Gladys was always a shy girl, god rest her soul.

What's that? Of course you're a woman. You're not a boy, you're a fine lass.

Oh alright then, if that's what you want to call yourself, then be my guest. Actually I can see you as a boy now you mention it—you've got that cheeky-chap smile and you never do wear a dress. I can picture you in a school cap and shorts; you'd have so much fun.

How did you just spell it? B.O.I. Boi... bit of a strange spelling isn't it? I never will catch up with you youngsters. Blimey, if lesbians like football so much, do bois go crazy for it?

Thought as much.

So, who gave you that glow on your face? Was it that quiet lad, the one with long hair in the post office, who always stammers when he sees you? He should get that hair cut, makes him look like a bloody hippy. Now listen to me, I sound positively ancient. I suppose these thick glasses don't help much. I hate glaucoma. I can't work out if he's been winking at me, at you, or at both of us.

Remember when he called me your father? Oh Ink, I'd be proud to be your dad; you'd make a terrific daughter... or son, I should say. Of course my daughter Patricia would have a thing to say about that. Don't know why she gets so strange when I mention you.

That lad in the post office has good strong hands for someone so young, that's why I thought you might like him as one of your special friends. Short nails too. Didn't you tell me once that short nails were important? Or is that just with ladies? You're a lucky sod, I'll give you that; to be comfy with the lads and the lasses too. Wish I'd been bolder when I was your age.

Nah, don't say that. Sometimes it is just too late. Can you imagine me in a gay bar, with all that loud music and funny booze? Leave me down the working men's club any day. I can get a plate of fish and chips, a nice cup of tea and a couple games of dominoes. Now that's what I call a good time. Well, that's what I think of as a good time. I suppose when you compare it to some of your places, it doesn't quite measure up. Only thing I don't like about the working men's club is some of the old codgers who go there. I hate it when they get drunk and rowdy—they come out with some shocking things, and it hurts my ears to have to listen to those bigots.

When I was a young man, we may not have had queer celebrities flashing about, well apart from Cole Porter and Noel Coward, but it wasn't unheard of for ordinary folk to be that way inclined either. And if you thought someone was queer, well you kept your opinions to yourself—I was brought up to be polite, and I don't see any point in bad-mouthing people because of what they like. I know, you think your folk didn't exist until the nineteen-sixties, but let me tell you, some of the things I saw in the army—it would make you blush. The lads knew how to fight, but they knew how to enjoy themselves.

There was one fellow—a Scotsman name of Finbar. He was lovely, really was, and he would give you the last of his rations if you needed it. You won't believe me, but he almost seduced me once. We were on cleaning duty, just the two of us, when right out of the blue, he touched me. He was soft as any lady I've known—so smooth and gentle. He stroked my back and my hair, made me purr like a cat. I found myself responding, just moving up against him, and it wasn't dirty or shameless, like I thought it would be. He treated me like I was something special and not just another squaddie polishing boots in the barracks. Finbar was a real gent, said I was nice, and wanted to get to know me better and everything. But I was scared and I suppose I was stupid too. A stupid young man that grew into a stupid old codger.

Oh don't mind me Ink, but I do wonder what it would have been like? I bet he would have been lovely; so tall, and with ginger hair, like a true Scotsman—I think he was from Aberdeen. Do you know they deep fry bars of chocolate up there? Finbar was sweet. I miss the old sod.

What's that? That would make me a what? A bisexual? Sounds strange, sort of nice-strange. What football team do bisexuals support?

Any team they like?

Dear god, if Patricia knew we were having this little chat, she'd have a seizure!

Enough about me, how about you? Look at you? If it wasn't that young lad in the post office, then who was it?

I know! That pretty young thing at the supermarket. You know, the one on the tills last Saturday. Rachel... Rebecca? Roslyn! That's it. Ooh, she's nice, make you a good girlfriend, I'm sure of it. She's got lovely big bosom... I thought you liked big tits? What do you mean that's not all there is? Of course it is! Give me a good woman with a decent set of breasts and I'll be happy. And if she can make a good cuppa tea, then all the better. Why don't you ask her out? Go on, you're not shy are you? Thought not, what with all those dinky clubs that you seem to love so much.

What?

Oh I do beg your pardon. Kinky clubs. Excuse me, Ink. What's that one you told me about? No, not the one with the electrified floor, I mean the one in the basement of that pub in Kings Cross... where all the smoke comes out of the ceiling and there's camouflage netting on the walls.

Yes, that one! Sounds like Vietnam! You really like that one, don't you?

No, I don't want to go to a place like that. They'd never let an old sod like me in, and besides my Patricia wouldn't be too happy; she already gets in a huff when I spend too much time with you. I told her, Patricia, I said, that girl Ink is a good'un. She may have a strange name, but she's a decent sort.

Oh Ink, I love you too. You're a sweet boi. Did I pronounce that right? Going to take me a while to get used to it. A boi and a bisexual—what a pair!

So, are you going to tell me who put that smile on your face or am I going to have to beat it out of you? Ooh, you'd like that! I should say, tell me or I won't beat you—that would work.

Oh, you're having a laugh aren't you?

Are you serious?

You and my daughter? My Patricia? No, don't look at me like that. I'm just shocked that's all. I never knew... hang on—I thought she couldn't stand you? When did that change? Blimey, this glaucoma is worse than I thought. How could I have missed all the signs? My own daughter...

Dear sweet Ink, welcome to the family, son!

Memory Lane

Sheela Lambert

"You still in bed, Shirley? It's juice time. Okay now, let's open those blinds and get some light in here."

Shirley blinked in the bright light as the room slowly came back into focus.

"I think it's high time you got out of bed. It's been three days and I'm not taking 'no' for an answer this time," the nurse insisted.

She pressed the button activating the head riser until the frail old woman was sitting up, then peeled back the quilt, exposing her bare feet and slender frame swathed in a lavender tank-style gown.

"Here's your slippers," she announced, slipping them over the wrinkled toes. "Now I'm gonna swing your feet down and help you into your chair," she warned. She lifted the slender ankles, guiding them to the side of the bed then slid her arms under the bony shoulders, lifting her around and into her chair. With some patients she needed help, but this one was light as a feather.

"Let's get you into the sunshine," she said, wheeling the chair over to a rectangle of light on the floor. She brought over the rolling table and set down a small plastic container. "Here's your juice, and here," she said, rummaging in the night table drawer, "is your brush," she declared, holding it aloft for effect, then placing it on the rolling table away from the juice. "If you're not careful, your hair will turn into a rat's nest. You'll have birds perching up there and we'll have to cut those tangles out," she warned as she headed out the door.

Shirley could always tell from the color inside the translucent plastic cup what kind of juice it was. Yellow equals apple and red equals cranberry... they knew better than to bring her orange. At home, yellow would have meant white-grape-peach and red would have been raspberry-cranberry. She could taste the fruity sweetness and her mouth watered. She peeled back the plastic film over the juice cup and took a sip, but the bitter taste of apple was a disappointment and she put it back down.

She reached for the brush and began listlessly running it through the long, tousled ends resting on her left shoulder; bleached white in the glare of old age. She gazed down at her gnarled and swollen fingers, the age spots scattered across the back of her hands, the white scars from where the melanomas were removed and the lump on her right wrist that ached most of the time and wondered...Whose hand is that? How did I get here? And who is this old lady with the white hair?

My hands are smooth and my hair is red, she declared to no one in particular.

Who is this old lady who sits in my chair and brushes her hair? She smiled slightly at the unexpected rhyme as she continued brushing out the tangles and knots.

A sound rose up from the street below. She wheeled herself closer to the window and looked out on the street. The sidewalk was bristling with wall-to-wall people from the curb to the buildings.

That's strange, she thought. It's not usually like that. Usually people are walking back and forth, up and down—now they're packed in like sardines. Wonder what's going on?

What was that sound? A sound like a distant roar swelled up and the crowd below became more restless. A piercing shriek made her glance up. On the building across the street was a balcony full of festive-looking people leaning over the railing in the direction of the approaching roar. Most of the crowd below was leaning in the same direction as the partiers on the balcony. The sound got louder and louder until a pack of motorcycles burst onto the street. A cheer rose up from the crowd as the motorcycles whizzed past. Were the riders all women? A large banner marched into view proclaiming: "Pride is Our Heritage."

It's Pride Day? Today? How come nobody told me? Don't these people know it's a holiday? she grumbled. *They have Christmas out the ass around here but when it's my holiday, do they have as much as a rainbow cookie?* No! she exclaimed.

Groups were starting to march down the street holding brightly colored banners and wearing everything from t-shirts to colorful costumes to leather to sports-bras as they marched, danced or wiggled down the street. Cheers and applause from the crowd was constant but swelled up as each new group passed by. Marchers waved and blew kisses to the parade-goers who waved back, blew whistles and waved mini rainbow flags on sticks as the balcony party threw fistfuls of confetti down on the crowd.

It was a familiar sight, although not from this vantage point. She was used to being on the ground, in the street, marching and dancing and waving and blowing kisses with the best of them. At least back when she could do that sort of thing. She was never one to stand on the sidelines, she always had to be part of it because it was her holiday. Better than Christmas, Hanukah, Thanksgiving, or Halloween. Because it was hers, she had fought for it, she had worked for it and she claimed it as hers and theirs even when other people refused to grant the respect that she and they all deserved. Even the year that the banners and t-shirts and buttons all read: "What Part of Equal Don't You Understand?" but only said "Gay and Lesbian" (not Bisexual and not Transgender) Pride underneath. But they didn't get the irony! she fumed.

It had taken many years of fighting, organizing, strategizing and proposing. Going to Town Meetings and listening to people's horrible speeches like "Don't rain on our Parade!" "Get your own parade!" Newspaper articles that called them "dangerous" for wanting to be included. She finally had to join up and attend meeting after interminable meeting. Losing scarves and hats on subways and in cabs (her favorite expensive chenille scarf!) from exhaustion after meetings because "new business" was always at the very end of the meeting and it was always scheduled under "new business" or because she went to committee meetings even with a 102 degree fever so as not to appear unreliable because only members could vote and you had to go to committee meetings to become a member. Twelve years, to be exact, of beating her head against a wall and going to Pride and wanting to be ecstatic like everyone else, but crying on the inside at the same time. Extreme joy, bordering on ecstasy, with a deep pain chaser that ate away at her like a rat nibbling a hole in her heart just gnawing on it and sometimes it felt like a knife in her heart, or like a choking feeling... the betrayal of brothers and sisters and cousins from her own tribe.

Of course as soon as it changed, it was like it had always been that way. No press release issued, just quietly adding the two little words that had caused all that resistance and hostility to be rained down on them. And she would hear people say, "Oh, it was changed two years ago" or "five years ago" or "it's always been this way" and that's exactly what she had wanted and had always insisted, that it was no big DEAL but she knew, she always knew, exactly how many years it had been.

She hadn't stopped with the Parade—there was more that needed changing. But that was a major success.

Why are you still getting so worked up after all these years? She frowned.

THUMP THUMP THUMP. Outside, shiny and elaborately decorated floats sailed by, topped with gyrating dancers, THUMP THUMP THUMP. Blasting out music that demanded booty-shaking by all within earshot. THUMP THUMP THUMP.

She picked up her forgotten brush and began rhythmically brushing her hair in time to the music until she snagged another tangle and was thrown off sync.

A loud cheer went up from the crowd. Most of the women on the float below had taken off—not only their tops but their bras as well—and were dancing bare-breasted much to the delight of the lesbians in the crowd who were hooting and hollering and falling off of balconies to get a better view. It's official, you know that Pride is really here when you see breasts out on the street, she chuckled.

She remembered back to the Pride when her best friend Becky had sidled up to her sans shirt, her only covering, two strips of duct tape over her nipples like pasties. They strolled through the

Village holding hands to the cheers, hoots and hollers of all the butches who deeply, or at least loudly, showed their appreciation. Later, she bought Becky a chunky black chain-link necklace at the festival —by special request—that she had to admit looked appropriate paired with the duct tape pasties. She was proud to be holding hands in the Parade with a girl who had the balls to walk around like that, even if she thought it was crazy and wouldn't be caught dead half-naked on the street herself.

Then she remembered the year that her ex, Darlene, showed up and stripped down to nothing but a Victoria's Secret satin bra and shorts and she couldn't believe how big her breasts were—and on such a slender girl—double D's! But you've seen them before, Darlene chided. Yes, but I just didn't remember they were this big, she marveled.

Below was a giant wedding cake float and decorating the top tier like a life-size wedding cake ornament were two guys in tuxes holding hands. Walking in front, to the strains of "Here Comes the Bride," was an assortment of bride & bride couples, groom & groom couples and a giant drag queen in a white wedding dress with big blonde hair and a poofy veil.

She thought back to her wedding date with Darlene. She'd been invited to Margaret's double bisexual ecumenical wedding in a borrowed Upper West Side apartment. The brides wore matching white tuxedos, Margaret's with a lavender cummerbund and Annie's white-on white. A Dignity priest and a straight but open-minded Rabbi officiated. Ironically, it had been harder to find a Rabbi willing to perform an interfaith wedding than a same-sex one, according to Margaret. Darlene arrived in a vintage black lace dress that clung to her curves and showcased her long shapely legs. What an entrance they had made! Walking in with this blonde, gazelle-like goddess on her arm, she felt like the world was hers.

She put the brush down on the table and parted her hair down the back with her fingers. She divided the left half into three sections and began to weave the colorless strands into a slender braid. Her hair was no longer as thick as it used to be. During the years she had worked in Harlem, on humid days her hair would get so puffy that their receptionist used to say, "Shirley, your hair just wants to be a fro." Since it turned white, it had become straighter and more manageable and there was a lot less of it.

Dean had started out as a Gay Pride fling. She had introduced herself to the tall punky boy during the March but when he lit up a cigarette she quickly moved on, avoiding him in favor of other old and new friends. At the parade's endpoint, however, the friends melted into the throng and she was suddenly alone and blinking into the crowd. Feeling abandoned and annoyed that she now had an hour or two to kill before meeting Margaret and Annie for dinner, she was happy when the tall, gangly, punky boy with a blonde Mohawk wandered over to ask where everyone had gone. He followed her around like a puppy while she was killing time at the Festival; flitting from booth to booth collecting bisexual buttons, lesbian pulp fiction refrigerator magnets and free condoms until it was time to meet her friends.

They commandeered a window table at the Pink Teacup and waved to random bi friends who wandered by, waving them in and expanding into the soul food restaurant until they had taken half of it over. Margaret and Annie came and went as did the rest of the crowd but Mohawk boy had stuck it out. She took him home expecting a Gay Pride fling and ended up with a boyfriend. However, by the end of the summer, the charm of dating someone younger and punkier turned into the weirdness of dating someone who was still in college, living at home with his mother, sleeping in a bunk bed and managing to be 20 minutes late for every date. She took him to the Jersey Shore for Labor Day weekend. But faced with his naked body in bed she was reminded of her gangly high school son and that was the end of it. Pride Day to Labor Day, the perfect parentheses for a bisexual summer romance.

She fished around in the table drawer until she found two lavender hair thingies to match her nitedress. It really irked her if the colors didn't match. She picked up the brush and gave the right side a few good strokes, just in case they had gotten out of line while braiding the left. She once again divided it into three, but half-way down the braid, one strand became skimpy, while another was fat so she had to shake it out and start over.

There was another Pride fling, wasn't there? Her elusive and painfully thin friend TJ, a workaholic cameraman for CNN with a transgender streak. She had never been attracted to him until the day he showed up to the BiGroup with cute little breasts. He pulled her into a dark corner during the break and lifted up his shirt to show them off. "Feel them," he urged. She cupped them, squeezed them gently a few times, testing their feel. They were a perfect handful, small but round and spongy. His hard, thin frame now had something soft and round on it. He seemed happier and squeezing his home-grown boobs made her tingle. But his usually long blonde hair was in a crew cut and he had three-day stubble on his face.

"It seems kind of odd that although you're taking hormones and you have these new breasts, with your shirt down you actually look more macho than usual."

"You know it's funny, now that I'm on the hormones I feel more female on the inside. I feel much calmer and more balanced... and more myself. I don't feel as much need to cross dress or look fem on the outside. I'll probably grow my hair out again, though. And I did try the laser hair removal thing, but it all grew back! I'm a lazy shaver," he admitted, batting his eyes. They agreed to meet the next week in the Bisexual Section of the Pride March.

Although they were hanging out with the whole bi contingent, they kept track of each other all day making eye contact, holding hands here and hugging there, sitting together at dinner and when the time came to go home he offered her a ride. Miraculously, there was a parking place right in front of her building. TJ just had to show off the new breasts again and the next thing you know they were breaking open one of the free condoms that flowed like water at the Pride Festival. TJ said his penis had been shrinking and might some day "peter out" in its usefulness as a sex toy but it was still in good working condition that night and considering its current size she was glad it had shrunk a bit. Breasts or not, he one-night-standed her just like a guy. Why had she slept with him despite his disclaimer that he "wasn't really looking for a relationship right now?" Pride Day never seemed fully celebrated without Pride Day sex. The holiday just seemed to demand it. So if she wasn't dating anyone and was at loose ends, so to speak, she was casting about for someone with whom to celebrate properly.

Was any other holiday like that? Just not the same without a sexual encounter to cap it off?

In the suburbs, Halloween was mostly a children's holiday involving costumes and the pursuit of candy. Not very sexy. But New York City was famous for its fabulous Halloween parties for adults, not to mention the legendary Halloween parade. Some might feel inspired by the alter ego of their costume to act out fantasies in the bedroom after an exciting Halloween bash or to become frisky even before leaving said party. Wasn't there an incident in a dark corner of a bisexual Halloween party with a very sexy pirate and a naughty nurse? Didn't that pirate, after a series of long delirious kisses while entwined in sandwich-like embraces between him and the naughty nurse, run his hand up her thigh, under her long velvet skirt and give her the only orgasm she had ever achieved standing up? Yet sex on Halloween was never obligatory, only dressing up in costume really was.

Christmas was a family holiday. A Christmas tree, Christmas stockings and Santa Claus were essential but present-opening was the real orgasm.

Hanukah, a spiritual holiday, commemorated a miracle by the lighting of Menorah candles while singing Hanukah prayers, maybe spinning a dreidl or peeling the gold foil off some Hanukah gelt and popping the chocolate coin in her mouth. Sex just didn't come into it.

Valentine's Day started with the distributing of valentines in grade school accompanied by eating heart-shaped pastel candies inscribed with love-notes and progressed to the romantic candlelight date in the traditional red dress, with flowers, dinner and hopefully: jewelry. Sex would most likely follow, but the symbols of Valentines day were cupids and red hearts: love and romance were at the "heart" of it. No pun intended! One of her cherished rituals was the valentine she always received in the mail from her Dad, assuring her that she was still his special girl. Or used to...She was now older than her dad was when he died.

St. Patrick's Day involved the wearing of green, parades, shamrocks, bagpipes and kilts, getting sloppy drunk, and for queer folk: annual parade protests because they weren't allowed to march in it. But by the end of the pub crawl or the jail visit, people were in no condition to get laid.

Easter was another kids' holiday... waking up to an Easter basket brimming with Easter grass and pastel colored bunnies, chicks and eggs—some edible, some stuffed and furry. There was also the dipping of eggs in vinegary smelling Easter-egg dye with special wire dippers and fizzy dye tablets that came in a bunny-decorated box. She used to play a game with her son, hiding pastel colored foil-wrapped chocolate eggs all over the house the night before, and playing "find the Easter eggs" on Easter morning.

Passover was also a spiritual holiday: an extended-family ritual around a long dinner table involving yarmulkes, prayer books that were read backwards, and an interminable story, punctuated with food rituals, that had to be finished before they could eat dinner. Recounting the history of the Jews' slavery and exodus from Egypt, which inevitably led to a discussion of the Holocaust. Definitely not sexy.

There had to be one. She racked her brain. What about Mardi Gras? She had never been to New Orleans or Brazil for that week-long celebration. But who didn't know about the parades, the extravagant floats adorned with half-naked float queens in elaborate headdresses and sequined thongs, the bender-in-a-glass Hurricane cocktails, the flashing of breasts for beads, the dancing in the streets, and the "Girls Gone Wild" videos. Mardi Gras most certainly cried out for some hotel-room debauchery.

But she was never interested in traveling just to pursue debauchery, no matter how colorful or exotic. Her idea of vacation was always something healing, like lying on a warm beach being soothed by the sound of the ocean (which she had done) or inspirational, like doing an art museum tour of Europe (which she had never been able to manage—too expensive and too far away.)

When you are young there are things you think you just haven't done yet. Like parachuting out of a plane, being a rock star or having a pet monkey. Later, you have a list of things you've been putting off or are just beyond your reach like an art tour of Europe or opening a natural foods restaurant. But at a certain point you realize that there are things you will never do. *I will never go parachuting or bungee-jumping. I'll never see the Louvre or the Frida Kahlo Museum. I never had my own restaurant. Never was a rock star. Never put out my own line of natural body products or my catalog of organic cotton clothes. But sometimes you can still surprise yourself.*

She remembered the year she turned 50. It had been raining on and off all day. She was walking down the March route with Debbi, the blonde angel, holding hands. As they turned onto 8th Street in the Village, where the crowd turned decidedly queer, she spontaneously pulled down the rain-soaked shoulder strap of her lavender tank dress, exposing her left breast, leaving the other strap to hold up the dress. She may have been 50, but her breasts were still 35. She walked to the end of the March with breast bared, which was enthusiastically appreciated by all the women in the crowd and even a few of the gay men. But mainly, she felt free.

I did live my life without putting off being myself. I was never afraid of my feelings—I embraced them. And I fought for those who couldn't fight for themselves. It was a small cause, as causes go—certainly not ending world hunger. But then world hunger hasn't ended and most of what I set out to change—like the name of this parade. . .did.

For many years, it had been the New York Lesbian and Gay Pride March and after 11 long years of hard work, the name had been changed and Bisexual and Transgender had been added. Ditto for the Lesbian, Gay, Bisexual and Transgender Community Center... *that one only took 10 years,* she chuckled. And ditto for the LGBT

Film Festival, which took 13. It had all happened after the new century.

She smoothed out the ends and tied off the braids with the lavender hair thingies. She picked up the all-wood brush and put it back in the drawer. Feeling tired from the effort of all the brushing, braiding and nostalgia, she closed her eyes but could still hear the celebration below; muted by the thick glass window.

A loud cheer rose up from the crowd. She looked down and saw a banner marked BiGroup NYC coming toward her with the bisexual flag, in pink, purple and blue, appliqued on top of a rainbow flag. The group had chosen a theme this year and many of them were wearing matching pink satin togas draped over their march outfit. Some of the women were wearing only a bra under their toga and some were completely bra free. The crowd's excitement over the assortment of beautiful bisexual breasts was reaching fever pitch. As the bi group pulled up in front of the nursing home, a whistle blew and the parade stopped. They must be letting the cars through on the Avenue, she thought...that's gonna take awhile.

She released the brake on the wheelchair, spun around and started rolling herself towards the door. She rolled out in the hallway and turned left toward the elevator. As she approached, the doors opened and an orderly got off, but stopped to hold the door for her. She wheeled herself in and pushed the button for the ground floor. When the doors opened, she made her way towards the front entrance, glancing at the security desk. It was empty! She glanced down the hall and saw a security guard bent over the snack machine, struggling with the levers. She darted over to the mechanical assist door and pushed the button. The door opened outward and real air washed over her for the first time in months—replacing the artificial atmosphere of the home. She was at the top of the ramp looking out on the crowd. Miraculously, police barriers cut a path through the crowd from the ramp to the curb... *probably in case one of us decrepit leftovers has to be rushed to hospital,* she thought. Problem was, another police barrier stood like a fence across the curb, blocking her escape. Nevertheless, she started wheeling her way down the ramp towards the barrier.

Hey! Hi! she shouted at the bi group, waving to get their attention. Some heads turned and a few people broke off and ran over to her at the barrier. "*Shirley, hi!*" they greeted, "*Happy Pride! How are you?*" they inquired, sizing up the wheel chair. They looked familiar but she couldn't quite call up their names. She had been cooped up in this place far too long.

Suddenly, a piercing whistle blew, signaling for the marchers to move out. Most of the kids ran back leaving one dusky young man with multiple earrings and a head bristling with braids. "Want to join us?" he asked. "It's only a few more blocks." She nodded vigorously. He glanced from side to side, checking for cops, then pulled back one end of the barrier, making an opening just wide enough for her to squeeze through. She rolled into the street and he quickly pushed the barrier back into place—then grabbed the handlebars of her chair and wheeled her up to the Bi-Group banner.

The music started back up and the parade lurched forward as the crowds cheered, rainbow flags waved and glitter and confetti rained down on the dancing marchers. The celebration continued... and she was in the midst of it one more time.

Naked in the World

Geer Austin

Craig led me into the front foyer of his house. There was silver foil paper on the walls and black and white linoleum tiles on the floor. The phone, a slim white Princess, sat on a black Parsons table.

"I'm pretty sure my parents won't allow me to go," I said.

"Don't tell them," Craig said. "Just say you're spending the night here."

He dialed my number and put the phone up against my ear. While I waited for someone to answer, he danced a jittery dance, and his hair fell over his eyes.

My mother picked up the phone.

"Craig's mother invited me to spend the night," I said.

At first there was silence on the other end. Then my mother said, "I don't know, Danny. I hope you're not getting in over your head with this Craig."

"No, Mom," I said. "Anyway, his parents will be here the whole time."

"Craig is not my cup of tea," she said. Her voice rang hard and metallic in my ear. "We are a different kind of people than his family. You understand that, don't you?"

I hated when Mom acted like a snob. She had tried to send me to boarding school two years earlier to prevent me from hanging out with people like Craig. People she thought weren't good enough for me. "Yeah Mom, we're different," I said. I glanced around the foyer, thinking Craig's family lived in a cool new house with modern furnishings while we lived in a creaky old house decorated with antiques. So, I thought, they were not only different, but better than us.

"You can stay there this one time, but don't ask again." I signaled thumbs up as I hung up the phone.

"Groovy," Craig said, and he pushed his black hair away from his face.

It was 1968, the summer of love. Craig was wearing his usual outfit, ragged bell bottom jeans, a faded T-shirt and a few strands of beads. His black curls tumbled down to the middle of his back. He looked the way I wanted to look. Only my parents wouldn't allow it. My blonde hair was neatly cut above my ears, and I wore a starched, pale blue button-down shirt, white jeans and penny loafers. But we were exactly the same size, medium height and thin like two spindly-legged deer.

We had met in gym class shortly after I moved to Bryn Mawr almost a year earlier, in the beginning of eleventh grade. We were the boys who were chosen last for touch football. We bonded in gym class, and over the course of the school year become best friends. Then summer started. I hadn't seen him since school had let out the previous June. My parents had filled my summer days and nights with activities—tennis lessons and dances at their country club, and a teen group at their church. But finally I had been given a night off, and to celebrate; I had headed over to Craig's house.

We made salami sandwiches for dinner and ate them standing up beside the refrigerator. Some mustard dropped from my sandwich onto my shirt, and I dabbed at it with a wet sponge.

"Leave it alone," he said. "You don't always have to be so neat."

I threw the sponge into the sink.

"We have to walk to the train station," he said. "My parents went out somewhere, I guess." In the half dozen or so times I'd visited Craig at his house, I'd never met his parents. His room was next to the back door, and we walked in and out without passing through the rest of the house.

"The walk will be worth it, though. We're gonna see a new band everyone's been talking about. I hear they're really amazing."

In Philadelphia, we walked from 30th Street Station to the Electric Factory, a new club, and waited among a group of mostly older hippies until the doors opened. The club was a big open space with no seats, and the music was so loud I could barely think. After the opening band finished their set, a wild looking woman skipped onto the stage, sang her heart out, then paused to swig something from a paper cup.

"Who is that?" I shouted to Craig over the din.

"That's Janis Joplin," answered a guy standing next to us.

A man stood on a platform in the middle of the audience and fiddled with an overhead projector. Swirling colors splashed over the band and hit the wall behind them. Craig and I stood together in the crowd, transfixed by the sound of the singer's voice and awed by the light show.

After the concert, on the train back to Bryn Mawr, we sat on the metal platform between the cars, hanging onto the hand rails over the steps that led down to the track bed, with our heads stuck out into the wind. At Bryn Mawr we hopped down and walked toward Craig's house. A bright white full moon hung high in the sky and lit our way along the hedged streets of the town.

"Janis was so great," I said.

"I might go back tomorrow night. But you won't be able to get out again, right?"

"Not a chance in hell," I said.

I knew Mom wouldn't let me stay over at Craig's house two nights in a row, and if I didn't stay at Craig's, I'd have to explain to her that I was heading into Philly to go to a rock club. She'd say no to that. She specialized in overprotection. Anyway, I had a date with my girlfriend Darcie the next night. Mom liked Darcie. She didn't go to my school, but her family belonged to the same country club as we did, and she and I often met there to go swimming in the pool or play tennis together. Occasionally we went to a movie.

Around two o'clock, Craig and I strolled down the street where I lived and passed my house where my mother and my father must have been slumbering in their twin beds, never dreaming that I was out roaming the streets of the town. Even though the house was set well back from the road at the end of an expanse of lawn, it loomed large and white in the moonlight. All the windows were dark, and for a moment it reminded me of a gigantic cemetery monument.

"We better not talk," Craig whispered. He knew my parents well enough to worry that they'd sense our presence as we walked along the street in front of their house. "They'd kill you if they knew you were out this late."

I kept my mouth shut until we left the house well behind. Then I said, "What about your parents? Won't they be mad when we come in so late?"

"Oh, they don't care," Craig said. "It's summer. Anyway, they're probably asleep."

"They give you a lot of freedom," I said.

"They're just waiting for me to grow up and leave. My dad's pretty cool, but I have a stepmother, and she doesn't like me very much. Dad says my real mom ran away to live in Paris, but I think she killed herself."

We walked for a few moments in silence. The thought of Craig's mother killing herself was almost impossible for me to comprehend. My mother seemed so formidable and indestructible. I couldn't imagine her taking her own life. Finally I spoke. "Maybe your real mother really is living in Paris. Maybe you could go there and find her."

"Maybe," he said, and he walked a little faster.

When we reached his house, a snappy little split-level, it was as dark and quiet as my house had been. Craig led the way up the front path, but instead of tiptoeing inside, he stopped and said, "Let's go swimming."

There was a swimming pool behind his house, set in a small patch of lawn. We stripped off our clothes and slipped into the dark water. I started swimming laps underwater, taking quick breaths at either end of the pool. Finally, I surfaced at the shallow end and rested for a moment. Craig whispered something I couldn't quite hear, so I breast stroked over to where he was clinging to a ladder in the deep end near the diving board. In the harsh white moonlight, I could make out the fine features of his face, his broad shoulders and one long delicate arm draped over the top step of the chrome ladder.

He rested the other arm on my shoulder. "I didn't know you were such a great swimmer," he whispered close to my face. His arm snaked around my back, our chests touched together, and we clung to each other for a few seconds with our lips pressed together. Something like an electrical current passed between our bodies. Craig lost his grip on the ladder, and we sank below water. He pushed away from me, and we popped up like a pair of corks and hoisted ourselves out of the pool without saying a word. I turned away from him and slipped on my underwear. We crept into the house and fell asleep in separate beds.

The next morning at my tennis lesson, I missed even more balls than usual. At home, I listened for the sound of the phone ringing, like one of my sisters waiting for a boy to ask them on a date. I knew the other kids would call Craig and me queer if they found out we had kissed, but that didn't stop me from wanting to do it again. Several days passed without hearing from him. So I telephoned him and asked him out.

"Want to go to the movies?" I asked.

"What's playing?"

"Barbarella."

"Can you pick me up?"

Craig's parents never let him use their car, and I often chauffeured him around town.

In the theater, we didn't touch or even look at each other. We watched Jane Fonda cavorting in outer space with a cast of characters including a hirsute caveman and a lesbian queen. Afterward, I drove Craig home in my mother's station wagon.

"That movie was out of sight," Craig said. "I'd ball Barbarella in a heartbeat if I got the chance.

"Yeah. Me too," I said, but truthfully, Barbarella was not the type of woman who attracted me. I was more drawn to my girlfriend Darcie with her short dark hair, boyish athletic body and small breasts. I thought Barbarella was too flashy and obvious with her masses of blond hair, big cleavage and clinging costumes. But I wanted Craig to think I shared his tastes. "Barbarella's really sexy," I said.

I pulled up in front of his house. My curfew was midnight, and we had barely a half-hour before it was time for me to leave.

"Come inside for a minute. I want to show you a picture I drew on my bedroom ceiling," he said.

"Your parents let you draw on the ceiling?"

"They don't know about it."

He switched on the lamp in his room, and I looked up.

"I don't see anything," I said.

"It's phosphorescent. Hang on for a minute. It takes time to soak up the light."

A few minutes later, he switched off the lamp. We fell on our backs on one of his twin beds and looked up at a large greenish glimmering face embellished with a beard and long hair, surrounded by dozens of tiny stars and several smallish moons. I wondered for a moment if the painting was supposed to represent God. Then I rolled over and kissed Craig on his mouth, this time using my tongue. He responded by opening his mouth and throwing his arms around me. Without breaking our kiss, he rolled me onto my back and lay on top of me. His tongue pushed into my mouth, and his body pressed against my body through the fabric of our shirts and blue jeans. I slid my hand underneath his T-shirt and brushed my fingertips up his spine and down again to the waistband of his jeans. When I poked under the elastic of his underwear, Craig pulled away as if he had awakened from a dream, switched on the light and stared at me as if I was a stranger.

"Hey, Danny," he said, trying to catch his breath. "I'm not into this. I'm into chicks."

"Yeah, me too," I said, and I got up off the bed, mumbled goodnight and left his house.

In the car on the way home, I wondered why Craig had pushed me away instead of holding onto me. He had seemed to be enjoying himself. Had I ruined our friendship when I stuck my hand down his pants? Would he be friendly the next time I saw him, or would he dismiss me? When I pulled into the garage behind my parents' house, I glanced in the mirror. I looked distressed and confused. Exactly the way I felt. I wanted to sneak into the house without seeing anyone, but my mother, as usual, had waited up for me. I put neutral thoughts in my head and a neutral expression on my face, and hoped she wouldn't sense my underlying mood. She glanced at me and then looked at her watch. I checked my watch too. It was midnight. I had squeaked in under my curfew.

"You'd better go to bed," she said. "You have to mow the lawn tomorrow morning, and you have a tennis lesson in the afternoon."

"Yeah Mom," I said. "I remember."

I went upstairs to my room, climbed into bed, and fell instantly into the heavy sleep of adolescence. I didn't think or dream about Craig, or at least I didn't remember dreaming about him when I woke up the next morning.

That weekend, Darcie and I went to see The Swimmer at the movie theater in Wayne, a couple of towns up the Main Line. Friends of her parents had recommended it. Afterward, I drove to an unpopulated cul-de-sac in an unfinished development and parked. Darcie scooted over to my side. I put my arm around her and kissed her lightly on the lips. She pulled back and smiled at me.

"What did you think about that movie?" she asked.

"Why was that man going from swimming pool to swimming pool?" I asked. "I didn't get it."

"I think his life was falling apart. He'd lost his money and his family. It was some kind of breakdown. Probably symbolic of something."

"He looked like somebody's father. Somebody we'd know. It was depressing."

"Yeah, a lot of parents we know are depressing," she said, then she snuggled closer to me. She smelled good, like fresh laundry and shampoo. I kissed her again, and this time she leaned into the kiss. I took a chance and slid my hand under her blouse and she let me unhook her bra and caress her breasts for a couple of minutes. Her skin was warm and silken. I wanted to kiss her breasts, and I shifted my position and hunched over so they were with reach of my lips, but she pulled down her blouse and slid away from me. "I think you should take me home," she said. "My mother will be worried."

A couple of days later my parents took my sisters and me on a weeklong tour of the historic sights of Mount Vernon, Williamsburg, Arlington and Washington. After they brought us home, they shipped me off to tennis camp. By the time I returned, the summer was over.

I ran into Craig in the hallway outside my homeroom on the first day of school.

"Let me see your schedule," he said.

I pulled it out of the pile of books slung across my hip.

"You're in all the smart classes again. But we're still in the same gym class." He grinned and handed me my schedule. "Did you go away somewhere for the second half of the summer?" he asked. "I called a few times, but your mom said you weren't there."

"Yeah, tennis camp. What about you?"

"I was here all summer. I have a girlfriend now."

"Who?"

"Sue Hancock. She goes to private school."

I shifted my books on my hip and headed down the hall. Craig walked alongside me.

"You want to do something this weekend with Sue and me?" he asked.

"Okay. I'll drive," I said, "and I'll ask Darcie to go with us."

"Cool. I like Darcie," Craig said. "Danny and Darcie, D&D," he said with a grin, then turned and strolled away.

I watched him walk down the hall. His black curls were neatly tied with a length of rawhide into a ponytail that fell between his shoulder blades. He wore faded jeans and a royal purple shirt with oversized sleeves. A couple of girls stared at him as he walked by them. There weren't any other boys in our school who looked like him.

In gym class later that day, we stood together while all the other boys were chosen for touch football, until finally we were picked for opposing sides. After the scrimmage, we kept each other company in the locker room. I avoided staring at his body in the showers, and he didn't look at mine.

Throughout our senior year, he treated me like a hipster pal, despite my short hair and conservative clothing, and I followed in his footsteps to rock concerts and head shops. I became friends with his girlfriend Sue, and he and Sue seemed to like Darcie. He jokingly referred to us as D&D, when we were together. At school, he and I hung out together in gym class and at lunch. I stopped eating with the smart kids and hung out at Craig's table of freaks and druggies. Even though we both had girlfriends, we got called queer by the jocks and the greasers. Craig said they called him queer because of his long hair. I worried that I actually might be queer, and to cover up, I tried to walk and talk like Steve McQueen.

On the night of our senior prom, I left the house clad in my father's tuxedo and picked Darcie up at her house. She was wearing a long black dress. Our parents had given us permission to stay out all night; they thought we would attend the prom and a chaperoned after party. Instead, we drove to Craig's house—his parents had gone away for the weekend—and changed into jeans and t-shirts we'd stashed in the trunk of the car and went out to a local bar, where they let us in as long as we didn't drink, to hear a garage band fronted by an acquaintance of Craig's. After the concert, we returned to Craig's house. Craig and Sue lay down on one of his twin beds, and Darcie and I lay on the other. We passed a joint back and forth, listening to Jimi Hendrix's new album, Electric Ladyland, and munching on Oreos and potato chips. We were anti-alcohol—that was our parents' vice—so we washed our snacks down with Coke. After we finished the joint and had our fill of cookies and chips, Craig and Sue began to make out. Darcie and I followed suit, our tongues darting in and out of each others' mouths and our hands exploring each other in the dark. We could hear whispering, soft moans and creaking noises from the other side of the room. I glanced over at Craig and Sue's bed and saw the motion of Craig's butt moving under the covers. I felt a rush of electricity surge through my body and I started tearing off my clothes and ridding Darcie of hers. We slipped under the covers, kissing, our bodies pressed together and our hands roaming blindly. I kissed down her neck, heading for her breasts like a heat seeking missile, then went to town, licking and sucking and rubbing my face on her smallish but firm mounds while her hands squeezed my butt. The moaning and creaking from the other bed grew louder. I sneaked one hand down to her thighs while continuing to suck her breast, distracting her while I slid my hand up between her legs until my fingers got wet and rubbed my fingers up and down in the dark until there was moaning coming from our bed as well. I felt Darcie's body shudder, then she rolled toward me, reaching out and holding me tight. The rhythmic bed-squeaking from Craig and Sue's side of the room sped up and I could hear him slapping against her as he drove into her. I rubbed myself against Darcie's leg until my breath got ragged, there was a muffled cry from the other side of the room, and I exploded into a thousand pieces.

We dozed off for a while... then Craig got up, and leading Sue by the hand, called out "D&D, lets go jump in the pool," so the four of us stumbled out to Craig's backyard for a swim. I remembered the night almost exactly one year earlier when Craig and I had swum alone in the pool and surprised each other with a kiss. That night had been bright with moonlight, and I'd seen Craig clearly from across the pool, but the night of the prom was moonless. We paddled slowly across the pool in the dark, taking care to avoid bumping into one another. The water was chilly, and we soon went back inside. There was a funny old movie on the Late Late Show, and we watched it to the end. Then the national anthem played and a pattern appeared on the screen, signaling the end of the broadcast day.

At daybreak I woke up and smiled when I saw Darcie's head next to mine on the pillow. I kissed her eyelids, and she giggled.

"I wish we could stay here all day," I said. I wanted to lie with her in bed for hours, breathe in her scent and feel the warmth of her body next to mine. But both of us had parents waiting for us at home so I got out of bed. I put on my tuxedo, Darcie put on her prom dress, and I drove her home, keeping one hand on the wheel and one in hers. "Thanks," I said when I kissed her goodbye. I considered telling her I loved her, but I didn't want to lie to her. "I'll miss you," I admitted, and I was telling the truth.

After graduation, Craig traveled out to California, hoping to settle in the Bay Area. Darcie also left town to stay with a host family in the south of France for the summer, part of a program designed to help her perfect her French. She sent me a couple of letters telling me about her host parents and the town where they lived. I began to suspect she was also perfecting her lovemaking technique with the help of a French guy, because in the beginning of August, she stopped writing to me. All summer long, I worked at our town's recreation park teaching little kids how to play tennis. For me, it was a boring few months. My best friends had abandoned me. I felt lonely without them; they left a gap in my life that wasn't filled by other people. I missed Craig. I missed Darcie. I didn't know what to do with myself in the evenings after work so I stayed home and watched stupid shows on TV with my parents. In September, I started my freshman year at Boston University. Darcie, who had gone to college in Virginia, resumed her correspondence with me. We sent chatty letters back and forth about our lives at college. In November, Craig sent me a postcard of a cable car making its way up a steep hill with the San Francisco Bay in the background. On the message side, he had printed his new address in San Francisco. I wrote him a long letter describing my life in Boston. I told him I missed him, and I signed the letter, "Love, Danny." He didn't write back. I sent him another letter, but the letter was returned by the post office. I wondered if he had gone to look for his mother in Paris.

For a couple months, he and I were out of touch, but I couldn't stop thinking about him and all the fun times we had together in high school. How good it felt to spend time with him.

I thought about him even more than I thought about Darcie. I couldn't forget our swimming pool kiss on the night of the Janis Joplin concert or our embrace under the phosphorescent stars on his bedroom ceiling. I started keeping a journal, and along with musings on my daily life, I composed notes to Craig in it. Then one day I suddenly felt stupid writing in a notebook to someone who had left no forwarding address, and I resolved to forget all about him. But despite my resolve, I couldn't put him out of my mind.

I spent Christmas vacation at home with my parents. Between Christmas Day and New Year's Eve, I went on a date to a drive-in theater near Bryn Mawr with Darcie. The theater management had thoughtfully installed heaters on poles next to the parking lots so moviegoers would be toasty warm even when it was thirty degrees Farenheit outdoors. I hooked the speaker and the heater over the car window, and Darcie and I hopped in the back. She cuddled up to me, and I kissed her and slipped my hand up her turtleneck, unhooked her bra and fondled her breasts. Then she slithered down my body, unzipped my fly and gave me the first blowjob of my life.

"Where did you learn how to do that?" I asked as soon as I came.

"I should have told you," she said. "I have a boyfriend at school. It's getting pretty serious. I really shouldn't be doing this."

"He'll never know," I said, thinking a boyfriend in Virginia was an abstract concept to two people sitting in a car in Pennsylvania.

"That's not the point. I'm supposed to be faithful."

The movie was "Once Upon a Time in the West." We watched it for a half hour trying to make sense of the plot.

"Claudia Cardinale is so fucking beautiful," I said.

"Don't look at her, you creep," Darcie scolded. "Look at me." She kissed me and blocked my view of the screen.

I caressed her breasts again and then pushed up her shirt and kissed them. "Let's make love one time," I said. "And in the New

Year, you can start being faithful to your boyfriend."

"It'll be my New Year's resolution," she said. "No more Danny interludes."

We each pulled one leg out of our jeans, thinking we could slip on the other leg quickly if someone passed by the car. Darcie straddled me, and we each kept one eye on the windows, just in case the cops decided to pay a visit to the drive-in. But Darcie's legs cramped up, so we decided to risk lying down. Probably everyone else at the drive-in was having sex too, I thought. The cops would have had to arrest 100 people before they got to us. So I forgot about the rest of the world, stripped off my jeans, and moved slowly inside her, stopping when I got close to orgasm. I wanted our last time together to last as long as possible, and she seemed to want the same thing. Eventually we came and lay in each other's arms not really focusing on the movie. Only when the credits rolled did we pull on our clothes.

I felt sad when I dropped her off at her parents' house. It seemed like a breakup, though without the anger that accompanies most breakup scenes. We sat in the car and chatted about our respective colleges, and she talked a bit too much about her boyfriend. Then out of the blue, she said, "I meant to ask. What happened to Craig? You haven't mentioned him all night. In high school, you guys were so tight, sometimes I felt like the other woman." She laughed as if she was making fun of high school concerns from the superior vantage point of freshman year in college.

"He moved to California and completely disappeared."

"And was it him or me you wanted?" she asked. She tilted her head to one side and smiled. "Be honest. I really don't care anymore."

"To tell you the truth," I said, "maybe him a little more than you."

"That's what I thought," she said. She jumped out of the car and ran toward her front door. I rolled down the window and yelled, "But I liked you too. It's complicated!" But she had already disappeared into the house.

* * * *

After that I lost touch with Darcie. There were no more letters and no phone calls. Back at college, I concentrated on my studies, tried to make a few friends, and decided to become a philosophy major. But I often thought about the night at the drive-in with Darcie. The muddle I had made of my relationship with her made me realize I needed to figure myself out. What positions had the two of them, Darcie and Craig, occupied in my life? It was true that I had been so obsessed with Craig that I didn't really fall in love with her. I didn't blame her for being angry with me for admitting that my relationship with her was secondary to my friendship with Craig. But I knew that my attraction to her had been real. Our night at the drive-in had been exciting, until we had a fight about Craig.

In my philosophy class, we discussed Plato and Socrates, and the Greek concept of love between men, which the professor implied might have a sexual connotation. Also the Greek tradition of every man marrying and siring children. Melanie, the woman who always sat next to me in class, and I walked down Commonwealth Avenue together one evening after class.

"I don't really understand the Platonic concept of love," I said.

"I think it's about bisexuality," she said, "but the professor can't bring himself to use that word."

"It seems as if there was an entirely different social construct back then," I said. "You can't really compare it to modern times."

"I think everyone must be a little bisexual," she said.

"I don't think so," I said. I thought of my parents and their rigid adherence to contemporary social norms. "Not my parents."

"Ewww," she said, and she cringed. "Don't even make me think about my father with a man."

That evening I met Melanie for dinner at her dormitory dining room. We sat at a long, beige, Formica-topped table. The walls of the room were painted a matching shade of beige. It occurred to me that Boston was full of rooms like these, and inside them were other students like us, all grappling with the same questions.

Melanie sat opposite me at the picnic-style table. She had long honey blond hair. My hair was almost the same shade, but my eyes were blue and hers were pale brown. I stared at her as she told me a story about going to India as an exchange student, living with a family of actors, and eating food so fiery that it gave her the hiccups. "It was an entirely new reality," she said.

"What is reality?" I asked. I thought maybe she knew more than I did about the world since she had seen more of it, and could explain it to me.

But she refused to take on the role of leader or guide. She laughed at me. What was reality? We were only nineteen years old, and neither of us knew the answer to that question.

* * * *

In early May after I had almost stopped thinking about Craig and had given up all hope of seeing him again, the phone rang in my dorm room.

"It's Craig," the caller said.

He didn't sound the same.

"Craig? I can hardly believe it's you."

"Yeah, Danny boy, it's me."

"How did you get my number?"

"B.U. has directory assistance," he said.

"Are you calling from San Francisco?"

"No, I'm in Cambridge. But I'm at a phone booth and I can't talk. There's a guy who needs to use the phone. I'll tell you everything when I see you."

"Where?"

"Come to the Cambridge Common. I'll look out for you."

Normally I avoided Cambridge Common because the street people who congregated there aggressively panhandled and then shouted obscenities if you passed by without tossing them a coin. And they looked and smelled as if they never showered or bathed. Although I now tried to look like a hippie, I still smelled fresh and clean like a nice boy from the suburbs.

I walked upstairs from the MTA station into Harvard Square just as the sun broke through the chilly New England afternoon and warmed the air. I took off my purple Shetland sweater and tied it around my waist, and then glanced down at my freshly laundered oxford cloth shirt, the same kind of shirt I had worn in high school, my faded and patched blue jeans and my scuffed cowboy boots.

I found Craig sitting on the grass next to a ragged young woman.

"Spare change?" she said and held out her hand.

"That's Danny," Craig said. "Danny, this is Crocus."

I plunked down on the dusty lawn next to Craig.

His fingernails were edged in grime, and his hair hung in greasy ringlets down to his waist. His tattered clothing drooped around his frame. His eyes were almost the same as I remembered, soft and brown, but they seemed to look at everything but me.

A hundred yards away a rock band that seemed to be stuck in the middle of an interminable rendition of "Satisfaction" occupied the space under a huge oak tree. Their guitar cases lay open on the ground, and a few coins had been thrown in them.

"I'm going over to Jerry," Crocus said. She walked over to the band and sat at the feet of one of the guitar players.

"She has a thing for Jerry," Craig said.

"She's not your girlfriend?"

"I'm not really with anyone right now."

"Me either," I said.

He flopped onto his back and shut his eyes.

"How long have you been here in Cambridge?" I asked.

"A couple of weeks. I meant to call you, but—"

"Where are you living?"

"Right here." He sat up and spread his arms wide to encompass the park.

"You mean you're a street person?" I heard the insult in the tone of my voice, and I wondered now to retract it.

He looked at me for a moment with hurt in his eyes, and then lay down on his side and drew his legs toward his chest.

"I mean, that must be cool, living in the park," I said. "No school, no parents, and it's free." I thought about patting him on the shoulder, but he smelled as if he hadn't taken a shower or washed his clothes for a few days, and I didn't want to touch him.

"Actually living in the park has gotten a little old. And it's cold, not cool," he said. He sat up and laughed, and then he started coughing. When his coughing fit subsided, he said, "This really isn't my scene. Things were going well for me in San Francisco until I met this guy who brought me back east for a gig. He was in a band that opened for the Moody Blues. I was helping out with the equipment and shit, but it didn't last."

I pulled a dusty blade of grass out of the lawn and twisted it around my finger while I searched for something to say. I couldn't imagine living without a home or money or food, and I wondered how he could handle being homeless. I remembered the shiny little house he'd grown up in and its foil wallpaper and modern furniture. It seemed as if he had left the world we had once both occupied, and a gulf had opened between us. But still, I felt a connection to him. After all, he was Craig, the co-star of my fledgling journal.

"Hey, I like the hair." He tugged at the tips of my hair, which had finally grown past my shoulders.

"Thanks," I said. "I always wanted hair like yours, but my parents wouldn't allow it." I wondered if Craig's dirty hands were coated with germs and whether the germs had started a colony in my hair. But I reminded myself again that in addition to being a filthy street person he was my beloved friend Craig. It seemed intolerable that he would have to sleep in the park that night. "You can stay in my dorm tonight if you like," I said. "I got a single this semester. You can take a shower if you want."

"Oh yeah, a college dorm. I've stayed in a few of those. You like college, Danny boy?"

"It's either college or Vietnam," I said.

"Oh right, the draft. They can't draft me because they wouldn't be able find me, but they probably wouldn't want me anyway."

"They'll take anybody," I said.

"I go crazy when I have to," he said. "Scares the shit out of people. Army wouldn't like that." He looked directly at me, bulged out his eyes and twirled them in their sockets. Then he flung his head back and forth. His hair flew in all directions.

For a moment I wondered if he really had gone crazy. But I kept thinking, this is Craig, not some insane street person. I laughed to show I got his joke, and I flung my hair around in the air and bulged my eyes out. He laughed too, and his laugh again dissolved into a cough.

When we walked into my dorm, an acquaintance, a business major from New Jersey, passed us on his way out the door. He stared at Craig in horror, as if he had never seen a street person before.

"This is my friend Craig from high school," I said.

The guy just nodded his head and kept walking.

Craig stayed in the shower for about a half-hour, and afterward, I gave him some clean clothes. At dinner, I sneaked food from the cafeteria, and he gobbled it down like he hadn't eaten in days. After he finished eating, he sat cross-legged on my bed listening to records and looking at album covers while I studied for finals at my desk.

"I know the drummer in this band," he said. He held up a Commander Cody album I particularly liked.

"How'd you meet him?" I asked.

"Oh, I know a lot of people in the music scene in San Francisco. It's pretty cool out there."

Craig leaned back and rested his head on my pillow. I kept glancing at him out the corner of my eye. He had stopped coughing and after his shower and meal looked miraculously healthy and fit. His clean hair fanned out in soft ringlets around his head, and he seemed to relax for the first time since we had connected in the Cambridge Common. He stared at me while I scribbled notes in my notebook and underlined half the words in my copy of Plato's Republic.

"Why don't you put your books away, and come over here and smoke a joint with me," he said. He reached into the pocket of the dirty jeans he had thrown into a corner of my room and pulled out a sooty roach. With a flip of a Zippo, he lit it. "Is it okay to smoke in here?" he asked.

"Half the people on this hall are drug dealers," I said. "This is the third-most druggy dorm on the East Coast."

"No shit?"

He sat back down on the bed, and I sat next to him. We each took a hit off the roach, which was so small it singed our fingertips. Craig snuffed it out on the floor and stashed it against one of the legs of my bed.

"I'm tired," he said. "Let's crash. We can both fit in your bed, right?" He slipped out of the clothes I had given him and stood for a minute, displaying his tawny skin and his long black curls. His ribs and his knees jutted out of his body, but he was still the fine-featured Craig I remembered from the night of the swimming pool. "Your turn," he said.

I stripped off my clothes and stood facing him, forcing myself to think about the nasty green medicine my mother dosed me with when I had the sniffles, the stuff that tasted so bad just the memory of it drove all thoughts of pleasure from my mind. I didn't want to get hard in front of Craig.

"You first," he said. He gestured toward the bed.

I slid under the covers and jammed my face against the wall. Craig got in next to me. Without hesitation, he pressed his body up against mine and tugged at my shoulders until I turned around and touched my chest to his. He pressed his lips against mine and slid his tongue into my mouth. His hands slipped down my body, and I began to tremble. He pulled away from our kiss and looked me in the eyes. "You're shaking like a leaf. Haven't you done this before?" he whispered.

"Only with Darcie. Not with a guy."

"I thought you were into guys."

"You're the only guy I ever wanted," I said. I trembled ever more violently.

"Don't be afraid, Danny," he said. "It doesn't matter whether it's a guy or a chick. Love is all that matters. Just try to relax."

He kissed his way down my body, but I continued to tremble. "I'm sorry," I said. "I just can't stop shaking."

"Don't apologize," he said. "Sex is natural. Guilt is the only downer."

He kissed me again, and soon I calmed down and fell into a rhythm with him that seemed familiar, as if we'd made love many times before. We didn't talk much, except we both murmured "I love you." I wasn't sure whether this meant we were in love like a boy and a girl or if it meant we loved each other like best guy friends. When we came, our bodies jolted as if we had been electrocuted, and both of us cried out at the same time. Afterward, we fell asleep and didn't wake up until the alarm clock rang in the morning. I got out of bed, but Craig turned over and went back to sleep.

I put on my clothes, slipped out of the room, went downstairs to the cafeteria, and appropriated some food for our breakfast. Craig was still asleep when I came back to the room. I sat down next to him and nudged his shoulder. He opened his eyes and said, "Hey man," and sat up in bed. I cut open mini boxes of Rice Krispies and poured milk over the cereal. Each of us ate a banana in addition to the cereal, and I ate a couple of pieces of raisin toast, but he set his toast aside and wrapped it in a napkin.

"I was thinking when I was in the cafeteria," I said. "Did your mother ever come back from Paris?"

"She killed herself when I was a baby. My dad finally told me. She hung herself in the kitchen. Just she and I were in the house. When my dad came home from work, I was all alone in my crib."

"And I thought for sure she had gone to Paris," I said. "I thought she'd come back for you someday."

"Not everyone has parents like yours," he said.

I sat down beside him and stroked his hair. He shut his eyes and leaned against me. I pictured him as a baby alone in his crib. I wanted to take care of him for the rest of his life, so he would never have to be alone again. I held him closely against my chest, but after a few minutes, he opened his eyes and pulled away from me.

"While you were downstairs, I decided." he said. "I'm hitching back to San Francisco today."

"But it's 3,000 miles."

"I should get there in a week or so."

"You could stay here with me if you want."

"Things were better for me in California. I had an apartment and a girlfriend out there. Actually, she reminds me of you. I'm going to try to get back together with her. Things fell apart after I went on the road."

I didn't feel jealous when he mentioned his girlfriend. Just sad that he was going to leave so soon after we'd reconnected.

"Will you be here when I get back from class?" I asked.

"It would be nice to stay with you for a while," he said. "Believe it or not, I think about you all the time. You were the best thing about high school."

"What about Sue?"

"She was great too, but you were my best friend." He wrapped his arms around me and leaned his head on my shoulder. "I always wanted to be together with you like this, but I was scared. I didn't understand how I could be attracted to both you and Sue. It seemed like I should want one or the other."

"To be honest, a lot of the time I only wanted you."

"I sort of knew that, and that's part of what scared me. Because I will always need to be with a chick. So it wouldn't be good for you if I stayed here. Anyway, it's past time for me to go back to California."

"I like women too," I said. "It's just that I think I can only love one person at a time, and in high school that person was you. It really wasn't fair to Darcie." I glanced over my shoulder at my alarm clock. "I'm already late for philosophy class," I said. "Why don't we talk about this later?" I thought maybe I could buy a little more time.

If he stayed until the afternoon, he might stay for another night.

He threw his arms around me, but when I tried to kiss him, he turned his head away. "I'm going to leave when you go to your class," he said. "I've already made up my mind."

I didn't know what to say to convince him to stay that wouldn't make me look too needy. We were still a couple of guys who had been friends in high school. Having sex with each other hadn't transformed our relationship. I picked up my pile of schoolbooks, and we left the building together. Outdoors, we stood on the street corner, up the block from my dorm, and stared out at the traffic on the avenue without saying anything for a few moments. Then I put my arm around his shoulder, and pulled him toward me, and he kissed me right on the street corner. Melanie chose that moment to walk past us on her way to philosophy class. When Craig pulled his head away, he said, "Come out and see me in California," and he walked into the street and stuck out his thumb. A battered Volkswagen van stopped for him. I could see him talking to the driver as the van sped away, probably telling her he was heading for San Francisco and asking her how far she was going. I stared at the back of the van until a truck blocked my view.

It was a fifteen minute walk up Commonwealth Avenue from my dorm to the liberal arts school. I bowed my head and studied the sidewalk as I walked. When I reached the classroom, I estimated Craig must have been crossing the city line, heading west on the Massachusetts Turnpike toward California.

I sat down next to Melanie in my usual place. She avoided looking at me.

After class, I followed her out of the building. "I guess you saw me on the street," I said.

"I didn't know you were gay," she said. "I mean, it's okay with me. I'm just a little surprised."

"I'm bisexual," I said. "Isn't that what you said everyone is? Except our parents of course."

"I was just talking off the top of my head," she said. "I've never actually dated a girl."

"That guy you saw me with was my best friend from high school. I guess I was in love with him. He was leaving for California when you saw us together."

"So we can go out sometime?" she asked. "Maybe go to a movie or something?"

"Yeah I'd like that," I said.

* * * *

That night, I found the roach Craig had left on my floor. Singed on one side, stained on the other and gummy with resin, it might have given him another high had he remembered to take it with him. I held it for a moment in my hands like a talisman, and then raised it to my lips and imagined a kiss. He'll call me from California, I thought. And I'll talk on the phone with his girlfriend. She and I will become friends. Maybe I'll spend the summer with them in San Francisco. It would be like "Triad," my favorite Jefferson Airplane song, with two guys and a girl, all three in love with each other. So I wrote him a letter proposing the visit, mailing it to the only address I had for him, the one he'd scribbled on the postcard he'd sent me months earlier, but the letter was returned by the post office.

I went home for the summer, hoping that he would call me at my parents' house, but he never did. I began to compose notes to him in my journal again and daydreamed about him for the next year or so, but I never heard from him again. Finally, there was nothing left for me to do but to move into the future. My first lover and my first love were receding into the past. My memories of them stopped with the image of Darcie running into her house and slamming the door behind her in the last days of 1969, and Craig stepping into the Volkswagen van on Commonwealth Avenue at the beginning of the 1970s. What remained was me, naked in the world.

Alex the Dragon

Jan Steckel

Alex inspected the space between her front teeth in the bathroom mirror. Years ago a college T.A. had told her (in a graduate student's idea of a come-on) that in Chaucer's time, gap-toothed women were thought to be lecherous. Alex didn't have that gap before puberty. As she got older, her two front teeth gradually spread apart. After her marriage exploded in a ball of flame, she discovered that dental drift had given her a newly sibilant "s." Perhaps, she thought, there lay the clue to the etiology of her long-standing gender identity problem. She was actually a gay man.

That night she ran to the corner video store and rented "A Star is Born" and "The Wizard of Oz." She plopped down in front of the VCR with a glass of Evian and tried to sing along with Judy. Halfway through "Somewhere Over the Rainbow" she got bored and switched on "The L Word." After a while, she became aware of a murderous craving for chocolate warring with an impulse to masturbate wildly with the back of her electric toothbrush.

Uh oh, she thought. She was not a gay man at all. She must be a lesbian.

She scratched behind her ear. The skin back there was starting to flake. Stress from her divorce proceedings was making her eczema act up. She wandered into the bathroom and squirted some thick, creamy moisturizer into her palm. She massaged from her scaly elbows up to her itchy shoulders. She kneaded the muscles in her neck, rubbing along the prominent knobs of her vertebrae. They seemed to stick out even more than usual. Age? She sighed and grabbed the toothbrush. The chocolate could wait.

She decided she was going to be the best little lesbian in the whole wide world. She bought a leather jacket and high-topped black tennies, chopped off all her hair, and wore asymmetrical earrings with backwards baseball caps. She started smoking in dyke bars. She drank Dewar's and water, splattered her speech with expletives, and slept her way through every single lesbian in New Haven. There were only four. All the other wimmin were in lifetime committed relationships with the ex-lover of their best friend's girlfriend's softball buddy, with whom they had been in a lifetime committed relationship two lifetime committed relationships ago.

She had a one-night stand with a bizarrely body-pierced bi-curious anthropology student who never washed her hair. She flirted with and then dumped a deeply disturbed quality-control chemist with the same name as her mother. She tried to let an office manager with the alluring thighs of the Venus of Willendorf down easily, and disentangled herself with difficulty from a windsurfing nymphomaniac hospital chaplain.

"You don't look well," said her straight best friend Selene on the rare occasions that she still saw her. "You need to slow down, get some exercise, pay attention to what you eat. You look—I don't know, sallow. Like you're coming down with the flu."

Alex inspected herself in the mirror. Her eyes were a little bloodshot, and her skin had developed a greenish cast. Maybe it was the cigarettes and the drinking. She'd lighten up a little, go to the health food store, buy blackberries and broccoli. All she had wanted lately was steak, burgers, ribs. Her cholesterol must be through the roof. She had read somewhere, though, that you needed cholesterol to make sex hormones.

What made a person straight or gay? She had always appreciated Selene's beauty. The smooth bronze of Selene's eczema-free skin and the curve of her neck had attracted her even when she was married, but she had explained it away as an outgrowth of their emotional intimacy, the closeness one feels with a best friend. It was only men who could feel turned on just by the sight of a breast or thigh, without even knowing the person to whom it was attached. Men—and maybe butch lesbians. Is that what she was?

She was starting to notice women's bodies in a different way, divorced from their personalities. She felt carnal, even predatory. When the phrase "KNOCKER ALERT!" began to sound in her head whenever well-endowed female chests passed her on the street, she realized she had reached the point where she could totally sexually objectify other women. At last, she thought, I am a real dyke.

Then the unthinkable happened. She developed a monstrous crush on George, the clerk in the video store. He was years younger than she, with the same golden hair and friendly blue eyes as her ex-husband, but without the stubble and the body odor. You could tell he was going to tend to fat as he got older, but he wasn't fat yet. Just sort of—juicy. He saved special videos for her and knocked off late fees, but she didn't think he was just being nice to her to get into her pants. He seemed to be nice to everybody—teenagers, kids, old ladies—a regular knight in shining armor.

At first she hoped he was gay. Then she might still be a dyke, and her crush on him might have a weird logic of its own, like a double negative. But he turned out not to be gay, just engaged to be married. So as she lay awake all night writhing her way through erotic fantasies about George the Video Saint, she realized she must really be a bisexual.

Ssh.

Did she actually exist?

Or did she wander, like the dragon, somewhere in that realm between rumor and myth?

She got up and switched on the fake gas fire in her living room fireplace. She lit a mentholated Virginia Slim from the gas jet and took a few short puffs, then a long drag. Her naked toes broiled before flames that glowed more blue than orange. She had let her toenails get so long, they were beginning to curve like talons. She smiled, and smoke rose curling from her nostrils.

Face to Face

J.R. Yussuf

I had one thought as I watched her sleep; she was crazy as hell, and so was I. She was completely uninhibited, a ball of energy and readily available emotion. A swift smooth fox. The type to wake in the middle of the night, springing up deciding she suddenly wanted to go for a three mile run or do twenty minutes of calisthenics.

I had flashbacks of meeting her at this rooftop party Tony was throwing to celebrate getting promoted to financial curator at the IT Company he worked for, just one week before. Tony and I had already been good friends for just over a year. The night we met we'd both just graduated from Dartmouth College but hadn't met until after graduation at one of those summer graduation parties out in Hanover, New Hampshire.

The multicolor, Christmas light-studded rooftop overlooked Brooklyn on one side, and the borough that never sleeps on the other. Brooklyn and Manhattan were like night and day in scenery, vibe and quite literally with the amount of light emitted after dusk.

There were lots of guys on the rooftop and a decent amount of girls. All races represented, like a big bag of trail mix, most were in their late 20s and just a few over 30. Most guys were casual and wore fitted caps, Sperry's, Jordans or the tanks from H&M that every guy seemed to own. There were guys with dark wavy caesars, curly fros, locs, fades, box cuts, buzz cuts, bowler cuts, long curly hair, straight hair pulled into a ponytail and quite a few baldy's like me. Most girls wore short shorts, dresses with flowers on them or those long frilly skirts with the waistband worn just under the bust, either to mask the pudge from the guys or make themselves appear taller. The ladies rocked long luscious locs and patient short ones too, pixie cuts with highlights, silky straight hair, long multicolored box braids, blown out fros, tightly coiled fros, high buns, Bantu knots, low-cut hair dyed red, straight permed hair, weaves and a few other ones that I had no idea about but I loved nonetheless. As a boy I thought only black girls could be sexy. Bushwick, the neighborhood I grew up in, was predominately black: West Indian, African, Afro-Latino and just plain African-American. I learned the word sexy with a black girls' body as the example. I've learned to double back on that thought and look closely, to admire how much work women of all races put into their appearance. I pay attention to it all.

Tony and I were on the right side of the rooftop by two large ficus plants, overlooking other Brooklyn neighborhoods while he let me in on his newfound perspective on men.

"This nonstop roundabout also known as 'dating' is tired. Men are only good for sex. If I need anything else, I can get it from a friend."

Tony always said the craziest shit. You know, the shit most people thought, but would never say aloud. That was one of the things that was so dope about Tony. Tony stood at 6'0" slim athletic build, soft and short, curly light brown hair, with light brown skin the color of a peanut to match, a peanut head, high cheekbones with red undertones, large light brown eyes, thin mustache, full lips and a wide child-like smile when he was in a good mood and lastly, a strong prominent jaw. Tony was Native American and African American although people always assumed he was Dominican and even spoke to him in Spanish occasionally. He had lots of family living on the Unkechaug reservation on Long Island, NY and the rest living in Gainesville, Georgia. Tony wore a black leather cap, backwards of course, a long, fitted short sleeve black Raiders jersey, all black drop crotch harem pants, and neon green Nike Roshe sneakers, a gold Casio watch, a gold chain with the matching gold bracelet and a gold two fingered ring on his right hand. Tony could never wear something like this to work, but he was known as the guy with the brow-raising, brightly colored, sock-tie-handkerchief collection.

"How did dating get to be so fucking impossible?"

Tony continued on like this for a little while until I told him he should consider looking for different kinds of men in different kinds of places. Tony called me a "wise-ass" and maybe he was right, hell what did I really know? Shit, I was still single. I was just like my late 20-something peers trapped in their monotonous lives of routine going straight from home to the gym, from the gym to work, from work to a friend's crib to burn, from burnin at a friend's crib to back home to sleep, from sleeping to doing it all over again the next day. The online thing wasn't for me; something about it screamed thirsty. There were times like this however, that I veered from my regular routine and could potentially meet a girl, but sometimes it feels like I'm never going to find anybody.

Tony and I talked about everything from sex to politics to belief to the absence of belief to how Black Americans are conditioned to think to group think to finding freedom in eastern philosophies to music to the music industry and back to sex again. There were levels to this shit.

Then there was this sound, animal-like in that it was feral, impulsive, and attention-grabbing. She wore a red and gold mardi gras mask, a feathered rainbow colored fan which she wielded like a weapon, a swirling orange skirt complete with embroidery topped with a fitted vest that flashed her dewy and inviting cleavage, which came together with bare feet. Her skin glowed a nice olive color. Long, pretty eyelashes, oval shaped hazel eyes, rosy pink, plump lips, a soft slender neck, and a sexy, devilish grin. She was about 5' 6" and stacked like an athlete, highlights of dirty blonde intertwined with milk chocolate brown hair; I was hoping she was dirty in other ways too.

"Brrrrrrdakakakakai!" She was at it again, doing handstands that became cartwheels which melted into belly dancing which morphed into an interpretive dance to "Click" by Big Sean; the current song playing on the booming sound system. All eyes in the vicinity were on her, we were in a trance. Her arms moved and our breath stopped, her hips jerked and our hearts shook, she stomped, we jolted. She wasn't just a dancer, she was an acrobat, I was sure of it. I wondered if she'd be willing to climb me.

We locked eyes a couple times and each time it was crazy conversation.

Hello stranger
Wassup sexy, lets be friends
I'd like that very much, but are you sure you can handle me?
Finding out is part of the fun
No truer words have been spoken. I can tell we're going to have fun
For sure, lets.

I was intrigued and couldn't help myself, she's a thrill seeker and I had no problem playing my role as "the thrill." We winded up audibly speaking somewhere in between her impromptu performances. She was never really done and had never really stopped moving, from her hip rolls to her need to punctuate her points with a tap of her fan on my shoulder. She was an actress, a dancer and had even performed aerial dance on a couple of concert tours, I made sure to ask. She heard about the party from a friend of a friend who said they'd show up, and didn't. But here she was alone, mingling and the topic of more conversations than Tony at his own party.

She told me she lives for good music and conversation. She admitted to finding me interesting. Maybe it was the bald head, full beard and all the ink. I stood at 6' 4" medium athletic build, brown skinned the color of an almond with almond shaped, bedroom eyes, dark brown irises, long dark eyelashes, a thin top lip, a full bottom one, fully tatted arms and a sly smile. I wore rolled up white pants with the sleeves also rolled up on my midnight blue button up shirt, which I tucked into the white pants, and a caramel colored belt to go with my caramel colored Sperry's.

We talked about life and how it should be enjoyed regardless of how much money you have or where you currently are, in it. She'd just finished getting her bachelor's degree in theatre arts with a minor in philosophy. Her philosophy on love was: "do it as much and as hard as you can." Her philosophy on life was: "Travel every chance you get, meet new people, see the culture, eat the food, then find another place to explore." I love travel. A new experience with a different culture keeps the mind sharp. I told her how I was itching to eventually vacation somewhere in Central America. She mentioned her family back home living modestly in the mountains of Pico de Neblina. She was from Brazil but had roots in Colombia and Argentina. I was from Queens but had roots in the south of America and Botswana, the south of the continent of Africa.

"Ah! You could be related to royalty!"

She was very blunt, which I appreciated; I was very touchy-feely, which she didn't seem to mind. Being around her I felt there were no rules. Just the laws of attraction.

Hours had passed and we were the last ones there other than Tony. He was cleaning up while we chatted all whilst the sun began its early morning ritual. I mentioned to her that we'd watched the moon brilliantly streak across a dark sky and now we were going to watch the sun do cartwheels all morning together and how this was the stuff of romance novels and first dates. Now that there was more light, it became even more noticeable that she was barefoot. She had small pretty feet, a different color polish on each toe, both things I found to be peculiar since she was a dancer and dancers tend to have feet like cauliflower. She told me it was because she wasn't really a dancer but a "mover." We'd talked all night and I just realized I hadn't asked her why she was barefoot. "Your feet look like they could use a good foot rub, you wanna get up outta here?" I asked through a sly grin.

She ran off as soon as the question left my lips and hit her ears. While helping Tony clean up, I remember weighing just how offensive my question could have been to cause a 25 year old woman who flirted with me half the night to literally run away from me. I kept glancing wistfully at the door, hoping she would wave her fan just once more and saunter back in. "Who was that?" I mumbled and kept shaking my head. "She's amazing, and sexy as hell." Unfortunately, Tony didn't know her and I wondered if I'd ever see her again.

Her name was Katilla Riveros and she was a goddamn individual. The energy, the temperament, the fire under her ass.

She wound up finding me on Facebook a few days later and sent me a message, "Sorry I ran off like that. I hope we can be friends." Three mutual friends; Kerra Frantz a girl I went to college with who was into theater and acting, Dan Johnson a guy I barely remember meeting at a party last summer, and Clay Robinson; one of Tony's old "dates," as he euphemistically calls them.

Our topsy-turvy beginnings ran through my mind as I half laid up, half sat up in bed waiting for Katilla to get out of the shower and come back to bed to get sweaty all over again, after her impromptu midnight workout. One week later and here we were in my room, soon to be spread out on my twin mattress. She had a fat, juicy, Latin ass and a flat, stomach like she belonged on a far off beach somewhere. She was Brazilian, Argentinean and Colombian. Brazil is known for having the sexiest women, while Argentina's and Colombia's women are known for being as beautiful as they are crazy. Men from the south are known for our manners and making women feel safe, while Botswana is known for having the kind of men who adore women and that I did. But it didn't matter where she or I were really from, sex, and even love, is universal.

She got back into bed as swiftly as she'd gotten up and I couldn't keep my hands to myself. They had a mind of their own, although they were ever in sync, one making up where the other lacked, both doing a waggle dance much like bees, instructing Katilla's body where to go and what to do once it got there. She moaned deeply in this uncontrollable alto way and my mouth watered. You see 'cause I love to eat and feast and when I'm done there's never ever nothing left.

Don't get me wrong, she was no docile sheep in the bedroom she was more like a powerful panther right at home in its colorful labyrinth that is the jungle. She knew exactly what she wanted and exactly how to get it. She gripped, sucked and pulled until she had me right where she wanted me; she climbed on top and fucked me stupid. That surprised me, which she enjoyed: she loved seeing me sweat. We both purred as we ceased. Our duet made up for where words may have lacked. The room was spinning. Was I falling for her?

I had this gnawing feeling inside. Like cupid was inside my chest relentlessly pounding away at my heart or like forgetting what it was you forgot at home but knowing you forgot something. *What was it?*

Tiredness finally took over, then down, down, down into healing rest which carries lovers to new mornings' dawn. My left arm under her neck, her right leg on top of my left leg, my right hand on her right titty, her right hand palming my privates, we were a spider's web of limbs. We drifted off to sleep that way, caught in each other's lust-filled clutches. I woke up the next morning expecting another round in our erotic roundabout. Katilla was gone. All that was left was her scent on my pillowcase and my clothes everywhere: evidence of a night well spent. She was fun. Best sex I've had in…ever. There was that goddamn tugging feeling in my chest again.

I called her, and she took her sweet time calling me back, but then she demanded to see me right away. We'd get together, talk, eat, flirt, fuck, and fall asleep in each other's arms; but her mysterious disappearances were confusing. After our nights together, most mornings, she was already gone when I blinked awake, with nothing but wrinkled sheets on her side of the bed. When I asked her why she was always MIA, she looked at me like I was a lead weight, dragging her down. "Because I've got ambition. I can't sit around here all day waiting on you." Being questioned or pinned down wasn't her thing. She was a "fuck the rules" kinda girl and it was none of my business what she was doing or who she was with when she wasn't around.

The next time I called, she was happy to hear from me, but said she couldn't see me. Between auditions, rehearsals and bartending she couldn't squeeze me in. She was too busy. I fumed for a week but then I got a Facebook message from her personally inviting me to a one-act play she was in that was showing in a church basement in the East Village in a little less than a week. I won't lie and say I didn't feel a pang of excitement, until I realized she probably sent the same personal message to at least 50 of her other Facebook friends.

When the day came I went anyway, and bought a small bouquet

of flowers from a local deli that gave them to me for eight bucks. I sat through the painful one-act that consisted of lots of crying and betrayal but as I approached her afterwards, I noticed another tall black guy in the audience, carefully eyeing Katilla too and patiently waiting with a single rose. He was 6'2" the color of a dark chocolate Hershey's bar, with a fresh fade, a full beard and mustache. He wore a navy blazer which upset me because I did too.

When she finally hugged me, for a moment, I was right back to our weeks together. Now that the show had ended, I figured we could go out to dinner and then back to my place, back to my twin bed. But she said she was going out with her cast and that she'd call me the next day.

I never heard from her. Instead, a week later she posted pictures of herself and other performers touring and performing through Connecticut, Baltimore and DC via Facebook. Lots of smiling and hand-holding. I had that gnawing feeling inside again. Time to let go.

I planned on watching DVD after DVD to get through the whirling vortex of emotion Katilla left behind. I went over to Tony's place to borrow some DVD's that night, and for a little sympathy, but he was getting ready to leave out for a night on the town. He had a beige trench coat on over a crisp white v-neck which was tucked into forest green pants, belted by cream leather and accented with forest green suede slip-on loafers. I'd noticed he'd just gotten a shape up too because of how clean-shaven he looked. The only razor he ever let touch his face was the barber's. He had smooth skin, no ingrown hairs, no razor bumps, flaw-free.

It was supposed to be a quick exchange, since he was headed out, but I guess he took pity on me, realizing I needed to vent, because he blew off his plans, to listen to my dissonant love song. After that we wound up getting into a really good conversation about gender as a construct rather than just a biological fact, the sheepishness of masculinity worshippers, as well as the ongoing power struggle that exists amongst assigned gender roles. After a long night of talking, which eventually turned into Tony ranting about men, and me ranting about Katilla, we were both slumped on the black leather couch in the living room drunk off of feeling understood.

Tony slowly looked over at me. I'd never considered or thought of guys as anything more than friends, or enemies in some cases, but Tony was the shit. Thinking back, I could always tell Tony had a little crush on me but he was always respectful and besides some harmless flirting here and there, he never tried anything. And that was the spark that ignited my curiosity. My mom always scoffed that once you gain a man's curiosity you can gain just about anything else.

We were right next to each other practically touching. My mind started racing. I wanted to see what it was like, so I slowly looked at him and with my low-lying, bedroom eyes, I asked him for a kiss. *Woah.*

It was explosive, like a power surge.

Kissing him lasted forever. Wet warmth. We couldn't stop. It's like everything we ever wanted to say to each other was being said through our tongues. His lips were so soft and full, but it freaked me out a bit because he was an aggressive kisser and I felt his strong jaw pressing back up against mine which was new. Also, his face was smooth but large compared to a female's not to mention his mustache, which pricked me twice. It was completely foreign: tapping into a part of myself I never knew existed.

Overall, kissing him was just wow, you know. My draw to Tony however, had more to do with how close we were and how much respect I had for him. People say all the time that falling for someone is all about the compatibility between the individuals involved. I just never pictured my individual even remotely being a "he."

Thinking back, even though I couldn't admit it to myself then, I was drawn to Tony when we first met. More than that, I had a crush on him. It was just an unexplored part of myself that at the time was too foreign and didn't speak clearly enough for me to understand what it was saying, what it was whispering to me.

The gnawing feeling has gone. No more longing for true intimacy—I have it. No more routine for me. This is all new.

XESSEX

KATHERINE FORREST

Templeton asked hesitantly, after a glance at the unpronounceable five-word name on the manifest, "What may we call you?" In the dim light of the Station control room he smoothed a self-conscious, scarred hand over his forest green uniform jacket.

"You may call me Raj." The voice was light, musical, the words formed with awkwardness.

The Phaetan had come aboard Aries Station with proper credentials so far as Templeton could see; but he could concentrate on verification scan for only a few seconds at a time. Farlan, assigned to check the computer spec sheets, also stood transfixed and staring, boots seeming rooted to the stalamac floor.

"Raj," repeated Templeton.

"Yes, Commander," said Raj, supernaturally blue eyes drifting over to fix burningly on Farlan. "Monitor from Phaeta, by order of Godden, for one rote." The words were uttered as if memorized.

Released from the Phaetan's gaze, Templeton said with more assurance, "Everything has passed scan."

"Yes. And what are you called?" Raj inquired of Templeton's partner.

"N... Neal Farlan." Farlan cleared his throat and clasped his hands behind him, shiny black boots scuffing harshly on the metallic floor. "Neal Farlan, ma'am."

"Ma'am? What is ma'am? I was not taught such a word. My name is Raj."

The Phaetan was distinctly female in appearance, and surpassingly beautiful, the most beautiful creature Templeton had ever seen. Clad in a simple gold-edged scarlet tunic—perhaps a ceremonial costume as were their own green Space Service jackets—Raj was slender, statuesque, exquisitely curved. Cobalt blue eyes were fringed with thick blond eyelashes; shoulder length spun gold hair framed high cheekbones, a thin straight nose, and lips as tenderly shaped as the tiny ferns Templeton grew in the humid greenhouse of Aries Station.

"Excuse—I didn't mean to offend—" Farlan, mottled red with embarrassment, stammered further apology, wide dark eyes fastened on the golden apparition.

Templeton, realizing that Raj had not asked his name, looked on with a grin. Then he stared incredulously as the Phaetan's silken skin flushed from its pale ivory color into glowing peach. He found his voice as Farlan, also gaping, faltered into silence. "We've heard little of your planet, other than it recently sealed agreement with ExxTel as a primary source of biurnium ore."

"Yes," said Raj, and continued in a pleasing lilt. "We do not travel much, or for long. Our lovely planet is dark. We do not react well to light. In light we are... as you, when you are in water. That problem can easily be solved, of course. But being off our world for longer than a rote or two at very most seems to cause within us—" Raj paused and gestured gracefully. "—psychic damage."

"I see," Templeton said, and grinned again in the twilight dimness of Aries station. "Do many others on your world... look like you?"

Raj considered him for a moment and then responded as if to an utterly preposterous question, "Of course." With an ineffably sweet smile at Farlan, Raj extended a slender hand with long tapering fingers tipped with, silver fingernails. "Nealfarlan, would you bring me to my... quarters?"

"Of... of course." Farlan took the delicate hand as if he had been given an egg shell to hold. "Neal, call me Neal."

The Phaetan turned roseate pink, and gazed at Farlan with rapidly blinking gold eyelashes. Templeton thought, If Raj isn't flirting I never saw flirting before in my life. Good luck, he thought with amusement. You'll need it with a Trad like Farlan.

Farlan asked in a voice that crackled with anxiety, "Sir, may I have your permission to escort our guest?"

"Have I... gone against custom?" Raj asked, blue gaze enveloping both men.

As Commander of Aries Station, it was Templeton's prerogative to accord the hospitality of ExxTel to its guests—the few there ever were. He said, "Not at all, Raj. Customs here are no matter. I'll finish up the specs," he added to Farlan, and dropped one eyelid in a half-wink.

Farlan scowled in response and turned away, to Raj.

Closed-minded young fool, Templeton thought for an innumerable time, and watched them, Farlan tall and lean and broad-shouldered, dark hair fluttering around the collar of his green jacket as he strode down the corridor; and Raj, slender and golden, an arm through Farlan's, swaying with the grace of a willow on Earth, the Earth Templeton had put out of his mind.

He finished up the specs, concentrating on his task, and limped over to the monitors. From the status readouts he could see that the Comstock was almost loaded, a matter of a dozen or so hours before it would automatically disengage and journey to Moon Station. It would take approximately one rote—equivalent to not quite seven Earth days—to unload the twenty ExxTel transport ships from Phaeta, including the command ship which had carried Raj, and reload the biurnium on the Kimberly.

Odd, he thought. Odd that such a responsible command should be entrusted to so delicate a creature. But then he knew very well that there were many permutations in the galaxy. Perhaps the "male" equivalent on Raj's planet was similar to the ethereal intellectual elite on Nexus-five, totally lacking in corporeal substance except for the means and will to procreate through selected brood partners. Perhaps that was the reason for Raj's immediate and unmistakable interest in the youthful, virile Farlan.

Flashing red light from a screen caught his eye. He had evaluated the problem before the soft hooting of the trouble siren echoed in the control room. Shifting cargo had knocked one of the unloading robots into such a position that it could not right itself. He tapped instructor keys with certainty, and an extractor claw deftly removed offending bars of spilled biurnium so that an android could right the robot and reset its controls. The red light vanished; the siren cut off.

He took little satisfaction in his accomplishment, reflecting placidly that the simplest computer could have activated the same assembly line repair. Indeed, a simple computer would have prevented the only major production "accident" that had ever occurred on Aries Station. From ExxTel's point of view, the accident that befell Templeton could only have happened to a man. True, a basic defect in the Station's construction had allowed seepage of fantacid, but a robot or android would have completed the repairs in a fraction of the time; no damage would have been done like the infection in his face and leg.

"Symbiotic organism," the doctors had said of his fantacid-infected body when he had finally been treated. "Harmless, unless we disturb it."

And so Aries Station had become his home. He had reasoned that if he took ExxTel to court and won all the money on Earth, what good would it be to him? As the ancient nursery rhyme so aptly said, all the king's horses and all the king's men couldn't put Gray Templeton back together again. And in exchange for waiver of his legal rights, ExxTel was willing to leave him here, provided he passed the biannual psych tests.

Here he was insulated from the emotional blows he would have suffered on Earth from his disfigurement; he was comfortable, sufficiently amused by the entertainment modes, well-taken care of. Other wants and needs he had put firmly out of his mind.

He knew he performed a function of some value, although he was cynically aware that men and women were no longer really needed in space. Alien contact and the resulting severe convulsions had ensured that. With interplanetary travel almost entirely trade, and accomplished by robot ship with communication and data transmitted by computer, a Station Commander's prime function was fulfilled when aberrant worlds occasionally declared themselves enemy and launched attack; then the Commanders transmitted early warning information until they were flamed into oblivion.

ExxTel did not publicize the fact that Aries Station had had to be rebuilt nine times in the two century interval before Templeton's arrival. But ExxTel lavishly praised its Space Service:

YOU ARE ELITE, YOU ARE HEROES, YOU WHO WEAR THE FOREST GREEN OF EARTH AND WORK IN THE VASTNESS OF SPACE...

Templeton smiled ruefully. He was a brightly plumaged security guard who watched over a glorified warehouse. He would some day probably die out here, his name his only legacy, etched somewhere on a list of forgotten heroes.

He took some satisfaction from overseeing the bright young people assigned here for various reasons by ExxTel. Bright, promising young people. Except for Farlan. Templeton winced, thinking about Farlan and the Trads.

Other world civilizations had reverted to their own versions of dark ages upon alien contact, reviving ancient rites and customs in fierce determination to maintain their identity and the moral history of their worlds; and so also on Earth such a sect had formed. The Traditionalists. Patterned in behavior and belief after an era Templeton considered barbaric: pre-twentieth century.

Farlan had been recruited into the Service in spite of his fanatical beliefs, because of his mathematical genius. But Templeton was convinced that the intolerant Trads were misfits anywhere in the Space Service, whatever their gifts. Midway in his three month tour of duty, Farlan was a stalamac-headed bore and a constant irritant as far as Templeton was concerned; but he intended to be fair. He had seen no reason thus far to turn in anything but a favorable report.

Templeton returned his thoughts to a more pleasurable concern, the Phaetan visitor. As usual, ExxTel had supplied a paucity of information. The laconic message from headquarters at Pacifica had read:

PHAETAN EMISSARY. APPROVAL GODDEN. ETA 0250301. EARTH TYPE. USUAL COURTESIES.

Earth-type indeed, snorted Templeton, and punched in a

computer query. Impatiently but thoroughly, he read the voluminous chemical and mineral data blipping down the screen, and extracted the facts that Phaeta was Earth-size, heavily clouded, with ivory vegetation, high H_20 content and almost constant misty precipitation, no ocean covering equivalent to Earth's but multitudinous large bodies of water. The high land mass was heavy in biurnium element, ranging from six to ten percent.

CULTURAL DATA read the next heading. Lines of print flowed down the screen.

MATURATION LEVEL NINE

LIFE EXPECTANCY LEVEL EIGHT

TECHNOLOGY LEVEL TEN PLUS

RESTRICTED POPULATION LEVEL STABLE FIVE

NON-MONOGAMOUS HUMANOID TO FACTOR NINETY-FOUR POINT TWO

"Hmpf," said Templeton, rubbing his damaged face.

VEGETARIAN

TELESTHESIA DEVELOPMENT LEVEL THREE

Now that is damn interesting, thought Templeton. Raj read feelings—not thought—and from a distance. Interesting.

THEOLOGY LEVEL ONE

"Pantheists," Templeton interpreted, nodding approval.

POLITICAL ACTIVITY LEV-

He cancelled the program. "Seems like a nice little planet so far," he said aloud, grinning at the screen. "Why ruin my illusions?"

At dinner Templeton made laborious conversation. Raj, bare-shouldered in a clinging pale green garment, had brought food, of course, and ate an assortment of ivory-colored leaves and bean-shaped vegetables with two curved implements reminiscent of ancient Chinese chopsticks, wielding them with dexterous grace. Farlan was monosyllabic, scraping his fork unseeingly over the contents of his plate as he stared at Raj; his face was pale and drawn with tension, mottling with red when the caressing blue gaze flowed over him. Raj's silken skin blended through shades of amber. Templeton picked his way carefully through simple subjects, mostly the topical features of Phaeta.

Farlan blurted unexpectedly, "Do you have a husband?" Raj's gold eyelashes blinked in bewilderment.

"Mate. Uh, partner." Farlan groped for other synonyms as Raj gazed. "Does someone... stay with you, live with you?"

"Ah." Raj brightened to a cherry pink. "No. But we do not live as you live... together. It is different."

"Yes. I expect it is. It doesn't matter anyway." Farlan rose and said unhappily, "Please excuse me. I have... duties. Forgive me." He walked stiffly from the room, squaring his broad shoulders. Templeton looked at him with a mixture of pity and disgust.

"I do not understand," Raj said, reverting to pale ivory, which seemed to be the Phaetan's normal quiescent color.

"I don't wonder. Yes," he added, seeing that Raj would not comprehend his colloquialism.

"Neal desires me. I am able to know that is true."

"Yes," Templeton, remembering the Phaetan's telesthetic capacity.

"Why does Neal not permit me to grant desire?"

He said astounded, "You're willing to?"

"I know of your body structure. It was part of my briefing. I am able to."

"With an Earthman? You're willing to?"

"Neal has desire."

"It doesn't always work quite that way on our world. Desire doesn't always lead to..."

Tinkling silver laughter expressed Raj's derision for this peculiar behavior. "This is part of your... courtship pattern?"

"Not always." Templeton leaned his head to one side, thrust his good leg forward at a cocky angle, and grinned. "I'm willing. I have desire for you too, even if I'm ugly."

"Not ugly." With an elegant gesture at Templeton's disfigured face and leg, Raj said, "Hurt: not ugly. But you do not have the desire like Neal. It is... interest only. You are content as you are."

Silenced, Templeton contemplated Raj, tucking his leg back under him. My face and leg aren't the only dead parts of me, he thought.

The cobalt eyes, objective, held his. He realized that Raj had not altered in color since Farlan had left.

"The changing tones of your skin," he said to deflect Raj's disturbing attention. "Is that part of your courtship pattern?"

"What we feel is spoken truly with the colors of our bodies," Raj said simply. "We have no need for some of your words."

"I see." Templeton felt oddly chastened.

"Explain to me please about Neal."

"I'll try." He searched for simple words, concepts. "It's our culture, but a step backward into our past culture. A sect on my world called Traditionalists. They demand that all people have one way of living, one way of belief, one mate, one God which judges and condemns."

"Do you think—" Raj paused. "Do you think Neal... will become well?"

As Templeton roared with laughter, the Phaetan appeared taken aback.

"Perhaps," he said. "I don't know. He's young."

Raj rose, willow-graceful. "I will go to Neal."

"Good luck."

Raj turned back inquiringly.

"A wish that good things will happen," Templeton said. Raj smiled.

Before he turned in, Templeton went as usual into the greenhouse. Through the leafy ferns and plants he saw Farlan with Raj's slender body clasped in his arms, his dark eyes sulphurous with desire. Raj's arms were wound around his shoulders, fingers stroking his neck, his hair. Raj's body pulsated waves of deepening rose.

Raj murmured indecipherably. "Yes," said Farlan in a husky rasp.

Templeton ducked behind a row of ferns as they left, an arm around each other, Farlan's hand caressing down over the voluptuous curve of hip. Templeton grinned, and limped over to inspect his newest ferns. That damn alien is right, he conceded. I've finally managed not to need a thing. Not a damn thing.

The next day Farlan did not appear. There was a note in the control room:

Have advised Pacifica am returning on the Comstock.
Farlan

The freighter had already departed; Templeton switched on the communicator, dialed the Comstock's frequency. The figure on the screen was in space gear; there was no reason for ExxTel to provide oxygen atmosphere in its robot-manned freighters.

"I have nothing to say," Farlan said with cold finality.

Templeton demanded, "I have a right to know what happened between you and Raj, whether that creature is dangerous."

Farlan did not respond, his dark imperviglas headgear motionless.

"You've ruined your career." Templeton's voice was harsh, factual.

"I don't care. I've decided Trads don't belong in the Space Service anyway."

Templeton thought, I hope you make ExxTel realize that.

But he argued with the unresponsive Farlan, feeling it was his duty, until the Comstock was outside recall frequency. He could not have recalled the Comstock anyway for other than a Phase IV emergency, and the return of a misguided young genius could hardly qualify. But it would look better for the young man's future if his report could state that Farlan had changed his mind or at least regretted his act.

He signed off and sought Raj in the command cabin of the transport vessels. The Phaetan, clad in a tunic of ice blue, sat in motionless austere beauty, gazing into the star-specked blackness.

Templeton dropped heavily into a seating module. "What happened?"

"I do not know," Raj said sadly.

Templeton smothered a snort of impatience. "I saw you in the greenhouse, how the two of you were. What happened?"

"In my quarters there was a merging of our naked bodies," Raj said in a musical voice. "The rapture of Neal took me to the furthest spectrum of color."

"I see," Templeton said, disconcerted. He cleared his throat. "Then what happened?"

"I said to Neal that such complete fusion between bodies was rare on my world and resulted in the begetting of young."

"Aaahhh," breathed Templeton, his gaze sweeping in alarm over the elegant female form before him.

"Neal said the same. Neal was—" Raj's hands made motions of agitation.

"Upset. Disturbed," supplied Templeton. "I can well imagine."

"Truly. He asked then would I be procreating." Raj trilled with laughter.

"But you said—"

"It is the other members of my species which are in appearance like you who procreate."

Templeton leaped to his feet. "You mean you're a man?"

Raj's forehead knitted faintly. "Yes, I am by your definition male. Neal also asked that question and was—" Raj's hands again made agitated motions.

Templeton sat down again.

Raj said, "Male. Female. This is important... in your culture?"

"To a Trad. Don't concern yourself."

"I have been... in sorrow."

"Don't be, anymore. I'm sure... I'm sure—" Templeton stumbled over his words. "Well, you're a very special—you're kind."

"You are also... kind."

The cobalt blue eyes on his seemed molten. Templeton asked haltingly, "Do you think... that's all I can ever be?"

"No," Raj said, and turned from him to again contemplate the starry universe.

He went back to his quarters, and sat on his bed. And laughed for a while because he didn't know what else to do. Then he lay back, hands behind his head, and reflected, and imagined, releasing the aspect of his being he had frozen away for many years. His thoughts became more and more vivid.

He sat up and dialed the command vessel. "Would you have dinner with me, Raj?"

"Of course." Raj added softly, "I believe I can also arrange to come to Aries Station for a rote or two from time to time."

Templeton looked more closely at his vidiscreen and with a rush of joy saw that Raj was a warm shade of blushing pink.

Inland Passage

Jane Rule

"The other lady..." the ship's steward began.

"We're not together," a quiet but determined female voice explained from the corridor, one hand thrust through the doorway insisting that he take her independent tip for the bag he had just deposited on the lower bunk.

There was not room for Troy McFadden to step into the cabin until the steward had left.

"It's awfully small," Fidelity Munroe, the first occupant of the cabin, confirmed, shrinking down into her oversized duffle coat.

"It will do if we take turns," Troy McFadden decided.

"I'll let you settle first, shall I?"

"I just need a place to put my bag."

The upper bunk was bolted against the cabin ceiling to leave headroom for anyone wanting to sit on the narrow upholstered bench below.

"Under my bunk," Troy McFadden suggested.

There was no other place. The single chair in the cabin was shoved in under the small, square table, and the floor of the minute closet was taken up with life jackets. The bathroom whose door Troy McFadden opened to inspect, had a coverless toilet, sink and triangle of a shower. The one hook on the back of the door might make dressing there possible. When she stepped back into the cabin, she bumped into Fidelity Munroe, crouching down to stow her bag.

"I'm sorry," Fidelity said, standing up, "But I can get out now."

"Let's both get out."

They sidled along the narrow corridor, giving room to other passengers in search of their staterooms.

Glancing into one open door, Troy McFadden said, "At least we have a window."

"Deck?" Fidelity suggested. "Oh, yes."

Neither had taken off her coat. They had to shoulder the heavy door together before they could step out into the moist sea air. Their way was blocked to the raised prow of the ship where they might otherwise have watched the cars, campers, and trucks being loaded. They turned instead and walked to the stern of the ferry to find rows of wet, white empty benches facing blankly out to sea.

"You can't even see the Gulf Islands this morning," Troy McFadden observed.

"Are you from around here?"

"Yes, from North Vancouver. We should introduce ourselves, shouldn't we?"

"I'm Fidelity Munroe. Everyone calls me Fido."

"I'm Troy McFadden, and nearly everyone calls me Mrs. McFadden."

They looked at each other uncertainly, and then both women laughed.

"Are you going all the way to Prince Rupert?" Fidelity asked.

"And back, just for the ride."

"So am I. Are we going to see a thing?"

"It doesn't look like it," Troy McFadden admitted. "I'm told you rarely do on this trip. You sail into mist and maybe get an occasional glimpse of forest or the near shore of an island. Mostly you seem to be going nowhere."

"Then why...?"

"For that reason, I suppose," Troy McFadden answered, gathering her fur collar more closely around her ears.

"I was told it rarely gets rough," Fidelity Munroe offered.

"We're in open sea only two hours each way. All the rest is inland passage."

"You've been before then."

"No," Troy McFadden said. "I've heard about it for years."

"So have I, but I live in Toronto. There you hear it's beautiful"

"Mrs. Munroe?"

"Only technically," Fidelity answered.

"I don't think I can call you Fido."

"It's no more ridiculous than Fidelity once you get used to it."

"Does your mother call you Fido?"

"My mother hasn't spoken to me for years," Fidelity Munroe answered.

Two other passengers, a couple in their agile seventies, joined them on the deck.

"Well..." Troy McFadden said, in no one's direction, "I think I'll get my bearings."

She turned away, a woman who did not look as if she ever lost her bearings.

You're not really old enough to be my mother, Fidelity wanted to call after her, Why take offense? But it wasn't just that remark. Troy McFadden would be as daunted as Fidelity by such sudden intimacy, the risk of its smells as much as its other disclosures. She would be saying to herself, I'm too old for this. Why on earth didn't I spend the extra thirty dollars? Or she was on her way to the purser to see if she might be moved, if not into a single cabin then into one with someone less... more...

Fidelity looked down at Gail's much too large duffle coat, her own jeans and hiking boots. Well, there wasn't room for the boots in her suitcase, and, ridiculous as they might look for walking the few yards of deck, they might be very useful for exploring the places the ship docked.

Up yours, Mrs. McFadden, with your fur collar and your expensive, sensible shoes and matching bag. Take up the whole damned cabin!

All Fidelity needed for this mist-bound mistake of a cruise was a book out of her suitcase. She could sleep in the lounge along with the kids and the Indians, leave the staterooms (what a term!) to the geriatrics and Mrs. McFadden.

Fidelity wrenched the door open with her own strength, stomped back along the corridor like one of the invading troops and unlocked and opened the cabin door in one gesture. There sat Troy McFadden, in surprised tears.

"I'm sorry... " Fidelity began, but she could not make her body retreat.

Instead she wedged herself around the door and closed it behind her. Then she sat down beside Troy McFadden, took her hand, and stared quietly at their unlikely pairs of feet. A shadow passed across the window. Fidelity looked up to meet the eyes of another passenger glancing in. She reached up with her free hand and pulled the small curtain across the window.

"I simply can't impose..." Troy finally brought herself to say.

"Look," Fidelity said, turning to her companion, "I may cry most of the way myself... it doesn't matter."

"I just can't make myself... walk into those public rooms... alone."

"How long have you been alone?" Fidelity asked.

"My husband died nearly two years ago... there's no excuse."

"Somebody said to me the other day, 'Shame's the last stage of grief.' 'What a rotten arrangement then,' I said. 'To be ashamed for the rest of my life.' "

"You've lost your husband?"

Fidelity shook her head, "Years ago. I divorced him."

"You hardly look old enough..."

"I know, but I am. I'm forty-one. I've got two grown daughters."

"I have two sons," Troy said. "One offered to pay for this trip just to get me out of town for a few days. The other thought I should lend him the money instead."

"And you'd rather have?"

"It's so humiliating," Troy said.

"To be alone?"

"To be afraid."

The ship's horn sounded.

"We're about to sail," Troy said. "I didn't even have the courage to get off the ship, and here I am, making you sit in the dark..."

"Shall we go out and get our bearings together?"

"Let me put my face back on," Troy said.

Only then did Fidelity let go of her hand so that she could take her matching handbag into the tiny bathroom and smooth courage back into her quite handsome and appealing face.

Fidelity pulled her bag out from under the bunk, opened it and got out her own sensible shoes. If she was going to offer this woman any sort of reassurance, she must make what gestures she could to be a bird of her feather.

The prow of the ship had been lowered and secured, and the reverse engines had ceased their vibrating by the time the two women joined the bundled passengers on deck to see, to everyone's amazement, the sun breaking through, an ache to the eyes on the shining water.

Troy McFadden reached for her sunglasses. Fidelity Munroe had forgotten hers.

"This is your captain," said an intimate male voice from a not very loud speaker just above their heads. "We are sailing into a fair day."

The shoreline they had left remained hidden in clouds crowded up against the Vancouver Mountains, but the long wooded line of Galiano Island and beyond it to the west, the mountains of Vancouver Island lay in a clarity of light.

"I'm hungry," Fidelity announced. "I didn't get up in time to have breakfast."

"I couldn't eat," Troy confessed.

When she hesitated at the entrance to the cafeteria, Fidelity took her arm firmly and directed her into the short line that had formed.

"Look at that!" Fidelity said with pleasure. "Sausages, ham, bacon, pancakes. How much can we have?"

"As much as you want," answered the young woman behind the counter.

"Oh, am I ever going to pig out on this trip!"

Troy took a bran muffin, apple juice and a cup of tea.

"It isn't fair," she said as they unloaded their contrasting trays at a window table. "My husband could eat like that, too, and never gain a pound."

Fidelity, having taken off her coat, revealed just how light bodied she was.

"My kids call me bird bones. They have their father to thank for being human size. People think I'm their little brother."

"Once children tower over you, being their mother is an odd business," Troy mused.

"That beautiful white hair must help," Fidelity said.

"I've had it since I was twenty-five. When the boys were little, people thought I was their grandmother."

"I suppose only famous people are mistaken for themselves in public," Fidelity said, around a mouthful of sausage; so she checked herself and chewed instead of elaborating on that observation.

"Which is horrible in its way, too, I suppose," Troy said. Fidelity swallowed. "I don't know. I've sometimes thought I'd like it: Mighty Mouse fantasies."

She saw Troy try to smile and for a second lose the trembling control of her face. She hadn't touched her food.

"Drink your juice," Fidelity said, in the no-nonsense, cheerful voice of motherhood.

Troy's dutiful hand shook as she raised the glass to her lips, but she took a sip. She returned the glass to the table without accident and took up the much less dangerous bran muffin.

"I would like to be invisible," Troy said, a rueful apology in her voice.

"Well, we really are, aren't we?" Fidelity asked. "Except to a few people."

"Have you traveled alone a lot?"

"No," Fidelity said, "just about never. I had the girls, and they're still only semi-independent. And I had a friend, Gail. She and I took trips together. She died last year."

"I'm so sorry."

"Me, too. It's a bit like being a widow, I guess, except, nobody expects it to be. Maybe that helps."

"Did you live with Gail?"

"No, but we thought maybe we might... someday."

Troy sighed.

"So here we both are at someday," Fidelity said. "Day one of someday and not a bad day at that."

They both looked out at the coast, ridge after ridge of tall trees, behind which were sudden glimpses of high peaks of snow-capped mountains.

Back on the deck other people had also ventured, dressed and hatted against the wind, armed with binoculars for sighting of eagles and killer whales, for inspecting the crews of fishing boats, tugs, and pleasure craft.

"I never could use those things," Fidelity confessed. "It's not just my eyes. I feel like that woman in the Colville painting."

"Do you like his work?" Troy asked.

"I admire it," Fidelity said. "There's something a bit sinister about it: all those figures seem prisoners of normality. That woman at the shore, about to get into the car..."

"With the children, yes," Troy said. "They seem so vulnerable."

"Here's Jonathan Seagull!" a woman called to her binocular-blinded husband, "Right here on the rail."

"I loathed that book," Troy murmured to Fidelity. Fidelity chuckled. "In the first place, I'm no friend to seagulls."

Finally chilled, the two women went back inside. At the door to the largest lounge, again Troy hesitated.

"Take my arm," Fidelity said, wishing it and she were more substantial.

They walked the full length of that lounge and on into the smaller space of the gift shop where Troy was distracted from her nerves by postcards, travel books, toys and souvenirs.

Fidelity quickly picked up half a dozen postcards. "I'd get home before they would," Troy said.

"I probably will, too, but everybody likes mail."

From the gift shop, they found their way to the forward lounge where TV sets would later offer a movie, on into the children's playroom, a glassed-in area heavily padded where several toddlers tumbled and stumbled about.

"It's like an aquarium," Fidelity said. "There aren't many children aboard."

"One of the blessings of traveling in October," Fidelity said. "Oh, I don't feel about kids the way I do about seagulls, but they aren't a holiday."

"No," Troy agreed. "I suppose I really just think I miss mine."

Beyond the playroom they found the bar with only three tables of prelunch drinkers. Troy looked in, shook her head firmly and retreated.

"Not a drinker?" Fidelity asked.

"I have a bottle of scotch in my case," Troy said. "I don't think I could ever... alone..."

"Mrs. McFadden," Fidelity said, taking her arm, "I'm going to make a hard point. You're not alone. You're with me, and we're both old enough to be grandmothers, and we're approaching the turn of the 21st not the 20th century, and I think we both could use a drink."

Troy McFadden allowed herself to be steered into the bar and settled at a table, but, when the waiter came, she only looked at her hands.

"Sherry," Fidelity decided. "Two sherries," and burst out laughing.

Troy looked over at her, puzzled.

"Sherry is my idea of what you would order. I've never tasted it in my life."

"You're quite right," Troy said. "Am I such a cliché?"

"Not a cliché, an ideal. I don't know, maybe they're the same thing when it comes down to it. You have style. I really admire that. If I ever got it together enough to have shoes and matching handbag, I'd lose one of the shoes."

"Is that really your coat?" Troy asked.

Fidelity looked down at herself. "No, it belonged to Gail. It's my Linus blanket."

"I've been sleeping in my husband's old pajamas. I had to buy a nightgown to come on this trip," Troy confided. "I think it's marvelous the way you do what you want."

Fidelity bit her lip and screwed her face tight for a moment. Then she said, "But I don't want to cry any more than you do."

The waiter put their sherries before them, and Fidelity put a crumpled ten dollar bill on the table.

"Oh, you should let me," Troy said, reaching for her purse.

"Next round," Fidelity said.

Troy handled her glass more confidently than she had at breakfast, and, after her first sip, she said with relief, "Dry."

"This is your captain," the intimate male voice asserted again. "A pod of killer whales is approaching to starboard."

Fidelity and Troy looked out the window and waited.

No more than a hundred yards away, a killer whale broke the water, then another, then another, their black backs arching, their bellies unbelievably white.

"They don't look real," Fidelity exclaimed.

Then one surfaced right alongside the ferry, and both women caught their breath.

"This trip is beginning to feel less like somebody else's day dream," Fidelity said. "Just look at that!"

For some moments after the whales had passed, the women continued to watch the water, newly interested in its possibilities for surprise. As if as a special reward for their attention, an enormous bird dropped out of the sky straight into the sea, then lifted off the water with a strain of great wings, a flash of fish in its talons.

"What on earth was that?" Fidelity cried.

"A bald eagle catching a salmon," Troy replied.

The ship had slowed to navigate a quite narrow passage between the mainland and a small island, its northern crescent shore fingered with docks, reached by flights of steps going back up into the trees where the glint of windows and an occasional line of roof could be seen.

"Do people live there all year long?" Fidelity asked. "Not many. They're summer places mostly."

"How do people get there?"

"Private boats or small planes."

"Ain't the rich wealthy?" Fidelity sighed. Troy frowned.

"Did I make a personal remark by mistake?"

"Geoff and I had a place when the boys were growing up. We didn't have money, but he earned a good deal... law. He hadn't got around to thinking about... retiring. I'm just awfully grateful the boys had finished their education. It scares me to think what it might have been like if it had happened earlier. You just don't think... we didn't anyway. Oh, now that I've sold the house, I'm perfectly comfortable. When you're just one person..."

"Well, on this trip with the food all paid for, I'm going to eat like an army," Fidelity said. "Let's have lunch."

Though the ship wasn't crowded, there were more people in the cafeteria than there had been for breakfast.

"Let's not sit near the Jonathan Seagulls," Fidelity said, leading the way through the tables to a quiet corner where they could do more watching than being watched. Troy had chosen a seafood salad that Fidelity considered a first course to which she added a plate of lamb chops, rice and green beans.

"I really don't believe you could eat like that all the time," Troy said.

"Would if I could."

Fidelity tried not to let greed entirely overtake her, yet she needed to eat quickly not to leave Troy with nothing to do.

"See those two over there?" Fidelity said, nodding to a nondescript pair of middle-aged women. "One's a lady cop. The other's her prisoner."

"How did you figure that out?"

"Saw the handcuffs. That's why they're sitting side by side."

"They're both right handed," Troy observed critically.

"On their ankles."

"What's she done?"

"Blown up a mortgage company," Fidelity said.

"She ought to get a medal."

"A fellow anarchist, are you?"

"Only armchair," Troy admitted modestly.

"Mrs. McFadden, you're a fun lady. I'm glad we got assigned to the same shoe box."

"Do call me Troy."

"Only if you'll call me Fido."

"Will you promise not to bark?"

"No," Fidelity said and growled convincingly at a lamb chop but quietly enough not to attract attention.

"Fido, would it be both antisocial and selfish of me to take a rest after lunch?"

"Of course not," Fidelity said. "I'll just come up and snag a book."

"Then later you could have a rest."

"I'm not good at them," Fidelity said. "I twitch and have horrible dreams if I sleep during the day. But, look, I do have to know a few intimate things about you, like do you play bridge or Scrabble or poker because I don't, but I could probably scout out some people who do... "

"I loathe games," Troy said. "In any case, please don't feel responsible for me. I do feel much better, thanks to you."

A tall, aging fat man nodded to Troy as they left the cafeteria and said, "Lovely day."

"Don't panic," Fidelity said out of the side of her mouth. "I bite too, that is, unless you're in the market for a shipboard romance."

"How about you?" Troy asked wryly.

"I'm not his type."

"Well, he certainly isn't mine!"

Fidelity went into the cabin first, struggled to get her case out from under the bunk and found her book, Alice Walker's collection of essays.

"Is she good?" Troy asked, looking at the cover.

"I think she's terrific, but I have odd tastes."

"Odd?"

"I'm a closet feminist."

"But isn't that perfectly respectable by now?" Troy asked.

"Nothing about me is perfectly respectable."

"You're perfectly dear," Troy said and gave Fidelity a quick, hard hug before she went into the cabin.

Fidelity paused for a moment outside the closed door to enjoy that affectionate praise before she headed off to find a window seat in the lounge where she could alternately read and watch the passing scene. An occasional deserted Indian village was now the only sign of habitation on the shores of this northern wilderness.

The book lay instead neglected in her lap, and the scenery became a transparency through which Fidelity looked at her inner landscape, a place of ruins.

A man whose wife had died of the same cancer that had killed Gail said to Fidelity, "I don't even want to take someone out to dinner without requiring her to have a thorough physical examination first."

The brutality of that remark shocked Fidelity because it located in her her own denied bitterness, that someone as lovely and funny and strong as Gail could be not only physically altered out of recognition but so horribly transformed humanly until she seemed to have nothing left but anger, guilt, and fear, burdens she tried to shift, as she couldn't her pain, onto Fidelity's shoulders, until Fidelity found herself praying for Gail's death instead of her life. Surely she had loved before she grew to dread the sight of Gail, the daily confrontations with her appalled and appalling fear. It was a face looking into hell Fidelity knew did not exist, and yet her love had failed before it. Even now it was her love she mourned rather than Gail, for without it she could not go back to the goodness between them, believe in it and go on.

She felt herself withdraw from her daughters as if her love for them might also corrupt and then fail them. In the way of adolescents, they noticed and didn't, excused her grief and then became impatient with it. They were anyway perched at the edge of their own lives, ready to be free of her.

"Go," she encouraged them, and they did.

"I guess I only think I miss them,"Troy said. Otherwise this convention of parent abandonment would be intolerable, a cruel and unusual punishment for all those years of intimate attention and care.

And here she was, temporarily paired with another woman as fragile and shamed by self-pity as she was. At least they wouldn't be bleeding all over the other passengers. If they indulged in pitying each other, well, what was the harm in it?'

Fidelity shifted uncomfortably. The possibility of harm was all around her.

"Why did you marry me then?" she had demanded of her hostile husband.

"I felt sorry for you," he said.

"That's a lie!"

"It's the honest truth."

So pity, even from someone else, is the seed of contempt. Review resolutions for this trip: be cheerful, eat, indulge in Mighty Mouse fantasies, and enjoy the scenery.

An island came into focus, a large bird perched in a tree, another eagle no doubt, and she would not think of the fish except in its surprised moment of flight.

"This is your captain speaking..."

Fidelity plugged her ears and also shut her eyes, for even if she missed something more amazing than whales, she wanted to see or not see for herself.

"Here you are," Troy said. "What on earth are you doing?"

"Do you think he's going to do that all through the trip?" Fidelity demanded.

"Probably not after dark."

"Pray for an early sunset."

It came, as they stood watching it on deck, brilliantly red with promise, leaving the sky christened with stars.

"Tell me about these boys of yours," Fidelity said as they sat over a pre-dinner drink in the crowded bar. "We've spent a whole day together without even taking out our pictures. That's almost unnatural."

"In this den of iniquity," Troy said, glancing around, "I'm afraid people will think we're exchanging dirty postcards."

"Why oh why did I leave mine at home?"

Fidelity was surprised that Troy's sons were not better looking than they were, and she suspected Troy was surprised at how much better looking her daughters were than she had any right to expect. It's curious how really rare a handsome couple is. Beauty is either too vain for competition or indifferent to itself. Troy would have chosen a husband for his character. Fidelity had fallen for narcissistic good looks, for which her daughters were her only and lovely reward.

"Ralph's like his father," Troy said, taking back the picture of her older son, "conservative with some attractive independence of mind. So many of our friends had trouble with first children and blame it on their own inexperience. Geoff used to say, 'I guess the more we knew, the worse we did.'"

"What's the matter with Colin?" Fidelity asked.

"I've never thought there was anything the matter with him," Troy said, "except perhaps the world. Geoff didn't like his friends or his work (Colin's an actor). It was the only hard thing between Geoff and me, but it was very hard."

The face Fidelity studied was less substantial and livelier than Ralph's, though it was easy enough to tell that they were brothers.

"We ought to pair at least two of them off, don't you think?" Fidelity suggested flippantly. "Let's see. Is it better to put the conservative, responsible ones together, and let the scallywags go off and have fun, or should each kite have a tail?"

"Colin won't marry," Troy said. "He's homosexual."

Fidelity looked up from the pictures to read Troy's face. Her dark blue eyes held a question rather than a challenge.

"How lucky for him that you're his mother," Fidelity said. "Did you realize that I am, too?"

"I wondered when you spoke about your friend Gail," Troy said.

"Sometimes I envy people his age," Fidelity said. "There's so much less guilt, so much more acceptance."

"In some quarters," Troy said. "Geoff let it kill him."

"How awful!"

"That isn't true," Troy said. "It's the first time I've ever said it out loud, and it simply isn't true. But I've been so afraid Colin thought so, so angry, yes, angry. I always thought Geoff would finally come round. He was basically a fair-minded man. Then he had a heart attack and died. If he'd had any warning, if he'd had time ..."

Fidelity shook her head. She did not want to say how easily that might have been worse. Why did people persist in the fantasy that facing death brought out the best in people when so often it did just the opposite?

"How does Colin feel about his father?"

"He always speaks of him very lovingly, remembering all the things he did with the boys when they were growing up. He never mentions those last, awful months when Geoff was remembering the same things but only so that he didn't have to blame himself."

"Maybe Colin's learning to let them go," Fidelity suggested.

"So why can't I?" Troy asked.

There was Fidelity's own question in Troy's mouth. It's because they're dead, she thought. How do you go about forgiving the dead for dying? Then, because she had no answer, she simply took Troy's hand.

"Is that why your mother doesn't speak to you?" Troy asked.

"That and a thousand other things," Fidelity said. "It used to get to me, but, as my girls have grown up, I think we're all better off for not trying to please someone who won't be pleased. Probably it hasn't anything to do with me, just luck, that I like my kids, and they like me pretty well most of the time."

"Did they know about you and Gail?"

"Did and didn't. We've never actually talked about it. I would have, but Gail was dead set against it. I didn't realize just how much that had to do with her own hang-ups. Once she was gone, there didn't seem to be much point, for them."

"But for you?"

"Would you like another drink?" Fidelity asked as she signaled the waiter and, at Troy's nod, ordered two. "For myself, I'd like to tell the whole damned world, but I'm still enough of my mother's child to hear her say, 'Another one of your awful self-indulgences' and to think maybe she has a point."

"It doesn't seem to me self-indulgent to be yourself," Troy said.

Fidelity laughed suddenly. "Why that's exactly what it is! Why does everything to do with the self have such a bad press: self-pity, self-consciousness, self-indulgence, self-satisfaction, practices of selfish people, people being themselves? "

"The way we are," Troy said.

"Yes, and I haven't felt as good about myself in months."

"Nor I," Troy said, smiling.

"Are we going to watch the movie tonight, or are we going to go on telling each other the story of our lives?"

"We have only three days," Troy said. "And this one is nearly over."

"I suppose we'd better eat before the cafeteria closes." They lingered long over coffee after dinner until they were alone in the room, and they were still there when the movie goers came back for a late night snack. Troy yawned and looked at her watch.

"Have we put off the evil hour as long as we can?"

Fidelity asked.

"You're going to try to talk me out of the lower bunk." "I may be little, but I'm very agile," Fidelity claimed.

The top bunk had been made up, leaving only a narrow corridor in which to stand or kneel, as they had to get at their cases. Troy took her nightgown and robe and went into the bathroom. Fidelity changed into her flannel tent and climbed from the chair to the upper bunk, too close to the ceiling for sitting. She lay on her side, her head propped up on her elbow.

It occurred to her that this cabin was the perfect setting for the horrible first night of a honeymoon and she was about to tell Troy so as she came out of the bathroom but she looked both so modest and so lovely than an easy joke seemed instead tactless.

"I didn't have the courage for a shower," Troy confessed.

"Really, you know, we're too old for this."

"I think that's beginning to be part of the fun."

When they had both settled and turned out their lights, Fidelity said, "Good night, Troy."

"Good night, dear Fido."

Fidelity did not expect to sleep at once, her head full of images and revelations, but the gentle motion of the ship lulled her, and she felt herself letting go and dropping away. When she woke, it was morning, and she could hear the shower running.

"You did it!" Fidelity shouted as Troy emerged fully dressed in a plum and navy pant suit, her night things over her arm.

"I don't wholeheartedly recommend it as an experience, but I do feel better for it."

Fidelity followed Troy's example. It seemed to her the moment she turned on the water, the ship's movement became more pronounced, and she had to hang onto a bar which might have been meant for a towel rack to keep her balance, leaving only one hand for the soaping. By the time she was through, the floor was awash, and she had to sit on the coverless toilet to pull on her grey and patchily soggy trousers and fresh wool shirt.

"We're into open water," Troy said, looking out their window.

"Two hours, you said?" "Yes."

"I think I'm going to be better off on deck," Fidelity admitted, her normally pleasurable hunger pangs suddenly unresponsive to the suggestion of sausages and eggs. "Don't let me keep you from breakfast."

"What makes you think I'm such an old sea dog myself?"

Once they were out in the sun and air of a lovely morning, the motion of the open sea was exciting. They braced themselves against the railing and plunged with the ship, crossing from the northern tip of Vancouver Island to the mainland.

A crewman informed them that the ship would be putting in at Bella Bella to drop off supplies and pick up passengers.

"Will there be time to go ashore?" Fidelity asked.

"You can see everything there is to see from here," the crewman answered.

"No stores?"

"Just the Indian store... for the Indians," he said, as he turned to climb to the upper deck.

"A real, lived-in Indian village!" Fidelity said. "Do you want to go ashore?"

"It doesn't sound to me as if we'd be very welcome," Troy said.

"Why not?"

You're not aware that we're not very popular with the Indians?"

Fidelity sighed. She resented, as she always did, having to take on the sins and clichés of her race, nation, sex, and yet she was less willing to defy welcome at an Indian village than she was at the ship's bar.

They were able to see the whole of the place from the deck, irregular rows of raw wood houses climbing up a hill stripped of trees. There were more dogs than people on the dock. Several family groups, cheaply but more formally dressed than most of the other passengers, boarded.

"It's depressing," Fidelity said.

"I wish we knew how to expect something else and make it happen."

"I'm glad nobody else was living on the moon," Fidelity said, turning sadly away.

The Indian families were in the cafeteria where Troy and Fidelity went for their belated breakfast. The older members of the group were talking softly among themselves in their own language. The younger ones were chatting with the crew in a friendly enough fashion. They were all on their way to a great wedding in Prince Rupert that night and would be back on board ship when it sailed south again at midnight.

"Do you work?" Troy suddenly asked Fidelity as she put a large piece of ham in her mouth.

Fidelity nodded as she chewed. "What do you do?"

"I'm a film editor," Fidelity said.

"Something as amazing as that, and you haven't even bothered to tell me?"

"It's nothing amazing," Fidelity said. "You sit in a dark room all by yourself, day after day, trying to make a creditable half hour or hour and a half out of hundreds of hours of film."

"You don't like it at all?"

"Oh, well enough," Fidelity said. "Sometimes it's interesting. Once I did a film on Haida carving that was shot up here in the Queen Charlottes, one of the reasons I've wanted to see this part of the country."

"How did you decide to be a film editor?"

"I didn't really. I went to art school. I was going to be a great painter. Mighty Mouse fantasy number ten. I got married instead. He didn't work; so I had to. It was a job, and after a while I got pretty good at it."

"Did he take care of the children?"

"My mother did," Fidelity said, "until they were in school. They've had to be pretty independent."

"Oh, Fido, you've done so much more with your life than I have."

"Got divorced and earned a living because I had to. Not exactly things to brag about."

"But it's ongoing, something of your own to do."

"I suppose so," Fidelity admitted," but you know, after Gail died, I looked around me and realized that, aside from my kids, I didn't really have any friends. I worked alone. I lived alone. I sometimes think now I should quit, do something entirely different. I can't risk that until the girls are really independent, not just playing house with Mother's off-stage help. Who knows? One of them might turn up on my doorstep as I did on my mother's."

"I'd love a job," Troy said, "but I'd never have the courage... "

"Of course you would," Fidelity said.

"Are you volunteering to take me by the hand as you did yesterday and say to the interviewer, 'This is my friend, Mrs. McFadden. She can't go into strange places by herself?'"

"Sure," Fidelity said. "I'll tell you what, let's go into business together."

"What kind of business?"

"Well, we could run a selling gallery and lose our shirts."

"Or a bookstore and lose our shirts... I don't really have a shirt to lose."

"Let's be more practical. How about a gay bar?"

"Oh, Fido," Troy said, laughing and shaking her head. The ship now had entered a narrow inland passage, moving slowly and carefully past small islands. The Captain, though he still occasionally pointed out a deserted cannery, village or mine site, obviously had to pay more attention to the task of bringing his ship out of this narrow reach in a nearly silent wilderness into the noise and clutter of the town of Prince Rupert.

A bus waited to take those passengers who had signed up for a tour of the place, and Troy and Fidelity were among them. Their driver and guide was a young man fresh from Liverpool, and he looked on his duty as bizarre, for what was there really to see in Prince Rupert but one ridge of rather expensive houses overlooking the harbor and a small neighborhood of variously tasteless houses sold to fishermen in seasons when they made too much money so that they could live behind pretentious front doors on unemployment all the grey winter long. The only real stop was a small museum of Indian artifacts and old tools. The present Indian population was large and poor and hostile.

"It's like being in Greece," Fidelity said, studying a small collection of beautifully patterned baskets. "Only here it's been over for less than a hundred years."

They ate delicious seafood at an otherwise unremarkable hotel and then skipped an opportunity to shop at a mall left open in the evening for the tour's benefit, business being what it was in winter. Instead they took a taxi back to the ship.

"I think it's time to open my bottle of scotch," Troy suggested.

They got ice from a vending machine and went back to their cabin, where Fidelity turned the chair so that she could put her feet up on the bunk and Troy could sit at the far end with her feet tucked under her.

"Cozy," Troy decided.

"I wish I liked scotch," Fidelity said, making a face.

By the time the steward came to make up the bunks, returning and new passengers were boarding the ship. Troy and Fidelity, out on deck, watched the Indians being seen off by a large group of friends and relatives who must also have been to the wedding. Fidelity imagined them in an earlier time getting into great canoes to paddle south instead of settling down to a few hours' sleep on the lounge floor. She might as well imagine herself and Troy on a sailing ship bringing drink and disease.

A noisy group of Australians came on deck.

"You call this a ship?" they said to each other. "You call those cabins?"

They had traveled across the States and had come back across Canada, and they were not happily prepared to spend two nights in cabins even less comfortable than Fidelity's and Troy's.

"Maybe the scenery will cheer them up," Fidelity suggested as they went back to their cabin.

"They sound to me as if they've already had more scenery than they can take."

True enough. The Australians paced the decks like prisoners looking at the shore only to evaluate their means of escape, no leaping whale or plummeting eagle compensation for this coastal ferry which had been described in their brochures as a "cruise ship." How different they were from the stoically settled Indians who had quietly left the ship at Bella Bella shortly after dawn.

Fidelity and Troy stayed on deck for the open water crossing to Port Hardy on Vancouver Island, went in only long enough to get warm, then back out into the brilliant sun and sea wind to take delight in every shape of island, contour of hill, the play of light on the water, the least event of sea life until even their cloud of complaining gulls seemed part of the festival of their last day.

"Imagine preferring something like The Love Boat," Troy said.

"Gail and I were always the ferry, barge, and freighter types," Fidelity said.

Film clips moved through her mind: Gail sipping ouzo in a cafe in Athens; Gail hailing a cab in London; Gail... a face she had begun to believe stricken from her memory was there in its many moods at her bidding.

"What is it?" Troy asked.

"Some much better reruns in my head," Fidelity said, smiling. "I guess it takes having fun to remember how often I have."

"What time is your plane tomorrow?" Troy asked.

The question hit Fidelity like a blow.

"Noon," she managed to say before she excused herself and left Troy for the first time since she had pledged herself to Troy's need.

Back in their cabin, sitting on the bunk that was also Troy's bed, Fidelity was saying to herself, "You're such an idiot, such an idiot, such an idiot!"

Two and a half days playing Mighty Mouse better than she ever had in her life, and suddenly she was dissolving into a maudlin fool, into tears of a sort she hadn't shed since her delayed adolescence.

"I can't want her. I just can't," Fidelity chanted.

It was worse than coming down with a toothache, breaking out in boils, this stupid, sweet desire which she simply had to hide from a woman getting better and better at reading her face unless she wanted to wreck the last hours of this lovely trip.

Troy shoved open the cabin door. "Did I say something...?"

Fidelity shook her head, "No, just my turn, I guess."

"You don't want to miss your last dinner, do you?"

"Of course not," Fidelity said, trying to summon up an appetite she could indulge in.

They were shy of each other over dinner, made conversation in a way they hadn't needed to from the first few minutes of their meeting. The strain of it made Fidelity both long for sleep and dread the intimacy of their cabin where their new polite reserve would be unbearable.

"Shall we have an early night?" Troy suggested. "We have to be up awfully early to disembark."

As they knelt together, getting out their night things, Troy said, mocking their awkward position, "I'd say a prayer of thanks if I thought there was anybody up there to pray to."

Fidelity was praying for whatever help there was against her every instinct.

"I'm going to find it awfully hard to say good-bye to you, Fido."

Fidelity had to turn then to Troy's lovely, vulnerable face.

"I just can't..." Fidelity began.

Then, unable to understand that it could happen, Fidelity was embracing Troy, and they moved into love-making as trustingly as they had talked.

At six in the morning, when Troy's travel alarm went off, she said, "I don't think I can move."

Fidelity, unable to feel the arm that lay under Troy, whispered, "We're much too old for this."

"I was afraid you thought I was," Troy said as she slowly and painfully untangled herself, "and now I'm going to prove it."

"Do you know what I almost said to you the first night?" Fidelity asked, loving the sight of Troy's naked body in the light of the desk lamp she'd just turned on. "I almost said, 'what a great setting for the first horrible night of a honeymoon.'"

"Why didn't you?"

"You were so lovely, coming out of the bathroom," Fidelity explained, knowing it wasn't an explanation.

"You were wrong," Troy said, defying her painful stiffness to lean down to kiss Fidelity.

"Young lovers would skip breakfast," Fidelity said.

"But you're starved."

Fidelity nodded, having no easy time getting out of bed herself.

It occurred to her to disturb the virgin neatness of her own upper bunk only because it would have been the first thing to occur to Gail, a bed ravager of obsessive proportions. If it didn't trouble Troy, it would not trouble Fidelity.

As they sat eating, the sun rose over the Vancouver Mountains, catching the windows of the apartment blocks on the north shore.

"I live over there," Troy said.

"Troy?"

"Will you invite me to visit you in Toronto?"

"Come with me."

"I have to see Colin and Ralph. I could be there in a week."

"I was wrong about those two over there," Fidelity said. "They sit side by side because they're lovers."

"And you thought so in the first place,"Troy said. Fidelity nodded.

"This is your captain speaking..."

Because he was giving them instructions about how to disembark, Fidelity did listen but only with one ear, for she had to keep her own set of instructions clearly in her head. She, of course, had to see her children, too.

Acknowledgements

I'd like to thank my writers, who stuck by this project during its long and winding road to publication, especially Cecilia Tan, who believed in it enough to become its publisher.

I'd like to thank some of the bi activists and writers who inspired and encouraged me over the years: Lani Kaahumanu, Loraine Hutchins, Mike Szymanski, Fritz Klein, Robyn Ochs, Brenda Howard, Tamara Wyndham, Donna Redd, Jim Rado, and Paul Nocera. Also every bi boyfriend, girlfriend and friend I've ever had.

I'd like to thank my family, who were all supportive of this project and of me: my brother, Dan Kempner; my son, Ravi Lambert; my new sister-in-law, Truc Kempner; and also my late father, Colin Kempner, who wrote short stories, believed in me and loved me unconditionally. My mother, Fran Kempner, died before this project began, but I know she would have been my most enthusiastic supporter.

I'd like to thank the bi community, who inspired me to create this book because it is something we didn't have, but wanted.

CONTRIBUTORS

Sheela Lambert is a veteran bi/LGBT activist and writer living in New York City. She is the founder of the Bisexual Book Awards and the Bi Lines reading series. Her national bisexual column on Examiner.com has been informing readers since 2009 and she is also published by *LGBTQ America Today Encyclopedia, Huffington Post, Advocate.com, Curve Magazine, Lambda Literary Review, Journal of Bisexuality, Gay & Lesbian Review, AfterEllen, AfterElton, GO Magazine, Bisexual.com*, and *Hakomi Forum*. She spearheaded the successful campaign to add a bisexual award category to the Lambda Literary Awards in 2006 and served as a "Lammy" judge for six years. Her one-act play, *Lavender Heights*, was performed as a staged reading at the 1994 International Bisexual Conference in NYC. She produced and hosted the first weekly bi TV series on the planet, Bisexual Network, on NYC public access cable in 1993 and was a correspondent and producer on *Out in the 90's*, a GLBT public access cable show, from 1992-93. She was the lead activist who, together with transgender activist Pauline Park, spearheaded the successful inclusion campaigns convincing several important New York City organizations to change their names from "Lesbian and Gay" to "Lesbian, Gay, Bisexual and Transgender" including The Lesbian, Gay, Bisexual, and Transgender Community Center, Heritage of Pride's Annual New York City Pride March, Pride Rally, and Pride Festival, and The NewFest LGBT Film Festival. She has organized bi and LGBT readings, film programs, concerts, conferences, forums, workshops (including the Safer Sex Series for Bi Women and Lesbians, *Community, Inclusion, Unity*: The 4th Tri-State Bisexual Conference, and The National Summit on Putting the 'B' in LGBT) and other cultural programs in NYC for over 20 years.

Ammy Achenbach is a novelist of children's and young adult books. *A Few of the Many Adventures of Oliver Toliver* is her first novel, which she co-wrote with her father, Don Achenbach. She has an MA in English Literature and an MFA in Creative Writing, and she is currently working on a PhD in Literature and Criticism at Indiana University of Pennsylvania. She is a professor of English at three colleges. When she is not writing, she can be found reading or watching movies and playing with her three dogs.

Jacqueline Applebee is a black, British, bisexual writer who breaks down barriers with smut. Jacqueline's stories have appeared in various anthologies including *Best Women's Erotica*, *Ultimate Lesbian Erotica*, *Twice the Pleasure: Bisexual Women's Erotica* and *Best Bondage Erotica*. Jacqueline has also penned *An Expanded Love*, a romance about multiple loving.

Geer Austin's poetry and fiction has appeared in *Big Bridge*, *MiPOesias*, *Ganymede Unfinished*, *This Literary Magazine* and *Potomac Review*, among others. He is the former editor of NYB, a New York/Berlin arts magazine. He led creative writing workshops for many years independently and through the New York Writers Coalition, most recently at New Alternatives for LGBT Homeless Youth. He lives in New York City.

Rob Barton lives with two of his sons in Massachusetts where he owns and directs Barton School of Music. Rob is also a member of an international black belt hall of fame and is long time martial arts instructor with a Masters Degree in Martial Arts Philosophy. Rob has been a long time activist concerning human rights and freedoms. While most of his writing has been academic and in the areas of martial arts and religion, Rob is also a prolific songwriter, enjoys writing fiction and is always developing new stories and characters.

Award winning author **Kathleen Bradean**'s stories can be found in

Carnal Machines, The Harder She Comes, Best of Best Women's Erotica I and II, *Haunted Hearths and Sapphic Shades, The Sweetest Kiss: Vampire Tales*, and many other anthologies. She blogs weekly for *Oh Get A Grip*, and reviews erotica at EroticaRevealed.Com.

Chuck Bright has a Masters and a PhD in social work, which was his original professional background. He has been writing fiction for the past 10 years. He tries to tell stories from a humorous perspective, even if he is the only one laughing. He likes to entertain readers by creating humorous stories about death, dying, the afterlife and the types of people we might encounter along the way. As morbid a subject as death and dying is, adding humor takes away some of the sting.

Jenny Corvette is a freelance writer living in southwestern lower Michigan with her boyfriend, two dogs, and three cats. She enjoys writing horror, satire, and anything edgy enough to raise eyebrows. Her writing has led her to be threatened with arrest and lawsuit. When not writing, she enjoys painting and playing pool.

Kate Evans is the author of two novels (*For the May Queen* and *Complementary Colors*), a collection of poetry (*Like All We Love*), and a book about teaching and sexuality (*Negotiating the Self*). She lives near the beach in Santa Cruz, California and teaches at San Jose State University. Her blog is: www.beingandwriting.blogspot.com.

Katherine V. Forrest's fifteen works of fiction include the lesbian classics *Curious Wine* and *Daughters of a Coral Dawn*, and eight novels in the legendary Kate Delafield mystery series. Awards and honors include four Lambda Literary Awards, the Publishing Triangle's Bill Whitehead Lifetime Achievement Award and the Lambda Literary Foundation's Pioneer Award. She was supervising editor at Naiad Press for a decade, and is currently supervising editor at Spinsters Ink and editor at large at Bella Books.

Storm Grant is a writer of short and long tales, her work spanning both genders and genres. Storm's stories offer good guys and bad puns. Her alter ego, Gina X. Grant writes funny urban fantasy. Look for Gina's Reluctant Reaper series debuting from Pocket Star Books (Simon & Schuster) in early 2013. Check out her works at http://www.stormgrant.com or www.ginaXgrant.com.

Ann Herendeen writes from the "third perspective," the woman who prefers a bisexual husband and an m/m/f ménage. She is the author of two Harper Paperbacks: *Phyllida and the Brotherhood of Philander* (2008); and *Pride/Prejudice* (2010), which was a finalist for the 2011 Lambda Literary Award for Bisexual Fiction. Her short story, "A Charming Ménage," appeared in the 4th Gay City anthology: *At Second Glance* (Dec. 2011). Ann's current projects include a series of e-books, "Lady Amalie's memoirs;" two academic conference papers; and a third novel.

Ours M. Hugh is a storyteller, techgeek, occultist, bookworm, and an all-round oddball (though not in a bad way). He is from and lives in New York City with his wife, his son, and more books than someone who lives in Manhattan should make a habit of keeping. Ours is currently writing freelance for a games company in Iowa, and trying to shop his three novels to someone foolish enough to want to publish them.

Florence Ivy is a native of Long Island, NY, and a first year graduate of the Lily Lieb Port Creative Writing Program at Purchase College. Her main focus is in writing micro, or flash fiction, and she is currently working on a novel. She has been writing for over twenty-five years. In addition to her writing, Florence is an avid photographer, seamstress and gardener, usually found with a camera around her neck and dirt under her nails. She resides in Suffolk County, NY, in a house by the ocean, with her partner and two poorly coordinated cats. Currently, Florence works as a freelance staff writer, photographer, and videographer for Generations Beyond.

Deborah A. Miranda is the author of *Bad Indians: A Tribal Memoir* (Hey-Day 2013), as well as two poetry collections, *Indian Cartography* (Greenfield Review Press, 1999) and *The Zen of La Llorona* (Salt, 2004). She is co-editor of *Sovereign Erotics: An Anthology of Two-Spirit Literature* (U of Arizona Press, 2012), and her collection of essays, *The Hidden Stories of Isabel Meadows and Other California Indian Lacunae* is under contract with U of Nebraska Press. Miranda is an enrolled member of the Ohlone-Costanoan Esselen Nation of California, and is of Chumash and Jewish ancestry as well. As Associate Professor of English at Washington and Lee University, Deborah teaches Creative Writing, Composition, and Literature.

Jane Rule was born in Plainfield, New Jersey in 1931. She grew up in the Midwest and in California, where she graduated from Mills College. Rule moved to Vancouver in 1956, where she worked at the University of British Columbia, as did her partner Helen Sonthoff. Jane Rule's novels include *Desert of the Heart* (which inspired the film *Desert Hearts*), *Against the Season, The Young in One Another's Arms*, and *Memory Board*.

Jan Steckel is an award-winning author, a retired pediatrician, and a bisexual and disability rights activist. Her first full-length poetry book, *The Horizontal Poet* (Zeitgeist Press, 2011), won a 2012 Lambda Literary Award. Her *Mixing Tracks* (Gertrude Press, 2009) won the Gertrude Press Fiction Chapbook Award. Her chapbook, *The Underwater Hospital* (Zeitgeist Press, 2006), won a Rainbow Award for Lesbian and Bisexual Poetry. Her writing has been widely published and has been nominated twice for a Pushcart Prize. She lives in Oakland, California with her husband Hew Wolff.

Kate Durré is still discovering who she is. For now she lives in New York City trying to follow her dreams, encouraged by her loved ones (and dogs). This is her first published work.

Cecilia Tan is "simply one of the most important writers, editors, and innovators in contemporary American erotic literature," according to Susie Bright. A bisexuality activist since the 1980s, Tan is founder of Circlet Press, a category-busting independent press that mixes science fiction/fantasy with erotica, gays with lesbians, and bisexuality with everything. She was inducted into the Saints & Sinners "Hall of Fame" for GLBT writers in 2010 and in 2013 was nominated for a Lifetime Achievement Award in Erotica by *RT Book Reviews*. Her books include *Daron's Guitar Chronicles, Slow Surrender, The Prince's Boy, Black Feathers, The Siren and the Sword, White Flames,* and many others.

Sam Thomas has been a fan of both fiction and flowers since childhood. Her stories invite readers on a treasure hunt to find the spot marked X—whatever may lie beneath. She fuels her creativity with German coffee and Swedish chocolate. When not writing, she loves experimenting in the kitchen and testing the results on family and friends.

Gretchen Turner is constantly risking absurdity and is generally successful. She is an ambisextrous, gen(der)flex(ible), transcendental surrealist love poet, Family Guy sycophant, identical twin, athlete, and drummer. She jigs, doesn't jog and always runs late—rather, takes-her-sweet-time late. She's a multi-tasker (texts while driving/downloading iTunes songs, yerba mate and prayer beads between hands, knee on wheel). Gretchen has an MA in Literature from Columbia, the best family a human being could dream of, a fiancé over whom she's whipped and, coming soon, a bulldog named Vincenzo or Cher. www.godsagoodkisser.wordpress.com

James Williams's first book, *... But I Know What You Want: Sex Tales for the Different* (Greenery Press, 2003), was re-released in 2012 as an ebook by Renaissance titled *Red Nails In the Sunset*. "Angels Dance" can be found in his new ebook, *Liberation: And Other Tales of Sex and Sensibility*, also published by Renaissance. He prefers to keep a low profile but, at least for the time being, his out-of-date website is at www.jaswilliams.com

J.R. Yussuf is a New York-based actor, photographer, and writer. Since the ripe age of 16 years old he has studied the craft of writing and has gone as far as Florence, Italy, to study different forms of writing, acting, and classical music. He has been published in *Instigatorzine*, *FOCUS Magazine*, *The CultureLP* and the upcoming anthology *Double Consciousness: An Autoethnographic Guide to My Black American Existence*. He has written short stories, poetry, monologues, fictional letters, fictional journal entries, answering dear abi letters, journalism, pop culture, sexual health and political-cultural studies pieces. Yussuf graduated from Stony Brook University with his B.A. in Theater Arts.

More Books You Might Enjoy from Circlet Press

The Stars Change by Mary Anne Mohanraj

Nominated for a Bisexual Book Award!

On the brink of interstellar war, life (and sex) continues. Humans, aliens, and modified humans gather at the University of All Worlds in search of knowledge... and self-knowledge... but the first bomb has fallen and the fate of this multicultural, multispecies mecca is in question. A thought-provoking work on sexuality and the connections between people—whether male or female, human or alien—*The Stars Change* is part space opera, part literary mosaic of story, poem, and art.

Up For Grabs: Exploring the Worlds of Gender

ed. Lauren P. Burka

An anthology of erotic stories where gender is up for grabs. Thousands of people spend time on the Internet identified with a gender other than the one they were born with, for erotic gratification or to stretch their imaginations. But what if you got a tax break for changing your gender? What if you could choose to be no gender at all until you went on a date?

Up For Grabs 2: Exploring More Worlds of Gender

ed. Lauren P. Burka

As editor Lauren P. Burka says in her introduction, "All erotica is the story of sex breaking free from biological need to become the co-conspirator of pleasure." Never is that more apparent than in the sharp-eyed, sharp-minded stories she has selected here by asking the question "What happens to sex if we let go of every assumption we have about gender and start from scratch?"

CPSIA information can be obtained at www.ICGtesting.com
Printed in the USA
BVOW03s2053120614

356215BV00015B/35/P

9 781613 900888